Driving along in South Texas I saw an old man walking up the median strip pulling a wooden cross behind him. It was mounted on something like a golf cart with two spoked wheels. I slowed down to read the hand-lettered sign on his chest.

JACKSONVILLE FLA
OR BUST

It seemed an odd destination for a religious pilgrim. Penance maybe for some terrible sin. I waved and called out to him, wishing him luck, but he was intent on his marching and had no time for idle greetings. His step was brisk and I was convinced he wouldn't bust . . .

THE DOG OF THE SOUTH

"Darned funny."　　　　　　　　　*—The Washington Post Book World*

"An endearing and comic shaggy dog story of the human heart face-to-face with futility."　　　　　　　　*—The Chicago Sun-Times*

"Wildly funny . . . A fine novel."　　　　　　　*—Library Journal*

"A delightful, engrossing romp."　　　　　　*—Publishers Weekly*

"To borrow a sentence from this fine comic adventure novel, 'I was rocking back and forth like one of those toy birds that drinks water from a glass.'"　　　　　　*—The Cleveland Plain-Dealer*

"A gallery of bizarre personalities in absurd situations . . . Rich in funny one-liners, observant with original angles of satirical vision, it's a thoroughly diverting chase."　　　　*—Wall Street Journal*

"Even funnier and more perceptive than *True Grit* . . . His new novel also has more than a touch of Mark Twain in it."
　　　　　　　　　　　　　—The New York Daily News

Bantam Windstone Books
Ask your bookseller for the books you have missed

The Dog of the South

by

CHARLES PORTIS

BANTAM BOOKS
TORONTO · NEW YORK · LONDON · SYDNEY · AUCKLAND

THE DOG OF THE SOUTH
A Bantam Book / published by arrangement with
Alfred A. Knopf Inc.

PRINTING HISTORY
Alfred A. Knopf edition published June 1979
A Book-of-the-Month Club Selection, Summer 1979
Serialized in Arkansas magazine
Windstone Trade edition / August 1985

Windstone and accompanying logo of a stylized W are trademarks of
Bantam Books, Inc.

Library of Congress Cataloging in Publication Data

Portis, Charles.
    The dog of the South.

    Reprint. Originally published: New York:
Knopf, 1979.
    I. Title.
PS3566.0663D6   1985   813'.54   85-6003
              ISBN 0-553-34169-3 (pbk.)

Published simultaneously in the United States and Canada

PRINTED IN THE UNITED STATES OF AMERICA
S   0 9 8 7 6 5 4 3 2 1

. . . Even Animals near the Classis of plants seem to have the most restlesse motions. The Summer-worm of Ponds and plashes makes a long waving motion; the hair-worm seldome lies still. He that would behold a very anomalous motion, may observe it in the Tortile and tiring stroaks of Gnat-worms.

—SIR THOMAS BROWNE

The Dog of the South

One

My wife Norma had run off with Guy Dupree and I was waiting around for the credit card billings to come in so I could see where they had gone. I was biding my time. This was October. They had taken my car and my Texaco card and my American Express card. Dupree had also taken from the bedroom closet my good raincoat and a shotgun and perhaps some other articles. It was just like him to pick the .410—a boy's first gun. I suppose he thought it wouldn't kick much, that it would kill or at least rip up the flesh in a satisfying way without making a lot of noise or giving much of a jolt to his sloping monkey shoulder.

When the receipts arrived, they were in lumpy envelopes and the sums owed were such that American Express gave way to panic and urged me to call B. Tucker in New York at once and work out terms of payment. It was my guess that this "Tucker" was only a house name, or maybe a hard woman who sat by a telephone all day with a Kool in her mouth. I got out my road maps and plotted the journey by following the sequence of dates and locations on the receipts. I love nothing better than a job like that and I had to laugh a little as the route took shape.

What a trip. What a pair of lovebirds! Pure Dupree! The line started in Little Rock and showed purpose as it plunged straight down into Texas. Then it became wobbly and disorderly. There was one grand loop that went as far west as Moffit's Texaco station in San Angelo, where sheep graze, and there were tiny epicycles along the way that made no sense at all.

I was reminded of the dotted line in history books that represents the aimless trek of Hernando De Soto, a brave soldier who found no gold but only hardship and a wide muddy river to which his body was at last committed—at night, they say. What a man! I was at that time fascinated by the great captains of history and I sometimes became so excited when reading about such men as Lee or Hannibal (both defeated, it occurs to me) that I would have to get up and walk around the room to catch my breath.

Not that there was space for any real strolling in our apartment on Gum Street. Norma wanted to move to a bigger place and so did I—to a bigger and *quieter* place—but I resisted going to the houses and apartments she had scouted out because I knew from experience that they would not be suitable.

The last one had been a little chocolate-brown cottage, with a shed of the same rich color in the back yard. The real-estate fellow showed us around and he talked about the rent-like payments. In the shed we came across an old man lying on a cot. He was eating nuts from a can and watching a daytime television show. His pearly shins were exposed above his socks. A piece of cotton covered one eye.

"That's Mr. Proctor," said the real-estate bird. "He pays fifty a month for the shed and you can apply that, see, on your note." I didn't want an old man living in my back yard and the real-estate bird said, "Well, tell him to hit the road then," but I didn't want to do that either, to Mr. Proctor. The truth was, we couldn't afford a house, not even this cottage, living on my father's charity as we were, and Norma either could not or would not find an apartment with thick walls made of honest plaster. I had specified this as against the modern dry-wall material, which not only conducts sound readily but in many cases seems to amplify it.

I should have paid more attention to Norma. I should have talked to her and listened to her but I didn't do it. A timely word here and there might have worked wonders. I knew she was restless, and anxious to play a more active part in life. She spoke in just those terms, and there were other signals as well.

She announced one day that she wanted to give a party in our apartment with the theme of "Around the World in 80 Days." I couldn't believe my ears. A party! She talked about applying for a job as stewardess with Braniff Airlines. She bought a bicycle, an expensive multi-geared model, and joined a cycling club against my wishes. The idea was that she and her chums would pedal along leafy country lanes, shouting and singing like a bunch of Germans, but from all I could see they just had meetings in the damp basement of a church.

I could go on and on. She wanted to dye her hair. She wanted to change her name to Staci or Pam or April. She wanted to open a shop selling Indian jewelry. It wouldn't have hurt me to discuss this shop idea with her—big profits are made every day in that silver and turquoise stuff—but I couldn't be bothered. I had to get on with my reading!

Now she was gone. She had gone to Mexico with Guy Dupree, for that was where my dotted line led. The last position was the Hotel Mogador in San Miguel de Allende, where I drew a terminal cross on the map with my drafts-man's pencil and shaded it to give an effect of depth.

The last receipt was just twelve days old. Our Mexican friends have a reputation for putting things off until another day and for taking long naps but there had been no snoozing over this bill. I looked at Dupree's contemptuous approximation of my signature on the receipt. On some of the others he had signed "Mr. Smart Shopper" and "Wallace Fard."

Here he was then, cruising the deserts of Mexico in my Ford Torino with my wife and my credit cards and his black-tongued dog. He had a chow dog that went everywhere with him, to the post office and ball games, and now that red beast was making free with his lion feet on my Torino seats.

In exchange for my car he had left me his 1963 Buick Special. I had found it in my slot at the Rhino Apartments parking lot, standing astride a red puddle of transmission fluid. It was a compact car, a rusty little piece of basic transportation with a V-6 engine. The thing ran well enough and it seemed eager to please but I couldn't believe the Buick engineers ever had their hearts in a people's car. Dupree had shamefully neglected it. There was about a quarter-turn of slack in the steering wheel and I had to swing it wildly back and forth in a childlike burlesque of motoring. After a day or two I got the hang of it but the violent arm movements made me look like a lunatic. I had to stay alert every second, every instant, to make small corrections. That car had 74,000 miles on it and the speedometer cable was broken. There was a hole in the floor on the driver's side and when I drove over something white the flash between my feet made me jump. That's enough on the car for now.

This business came at a bad time. Just a month earlier— right after my twenty-sixth birthday—I had quit my job on the copy desk at the newspaper to return to school. My father had agreed to support me again until I had received a degree of some sort or at least a teaching certificate. He had also presented me with the American Express card, he having had a good business year sprucing up old houses with Midgestone. As I say, the birthday was my twenty-sixth, but for some reason I had been thinking throughout the previous year that I was already twenty-six. A free year! The question was: would I piddle it away like the others?

My new plan was to become a high-school teacher. I had accumulated enough college hours over the years for at least two bachelor's degrees but I had never actually taken one. I had never stayed long enough in any one course of study. I had no education hours at all but I did have some pre-law at Southwestern and some engineering at Arkansas. I had been at Ole Miss too, where I studied the Western campaigns of the Civil War under Dr. Buddy Casey. Don't talk about Virginia to Dr. Bud; talk about Forrest!

For a long time I had a tape recording of his famous lecture on the Siege of Vicksburg and I liked to play it in the morning while I was shaving. I also played it sometimes in the car when Norma and I went for drives. It was one of those performances—"bravura" is the word for it—that never become stale. Dr. Bud made the thing come alive. With nothing more than his knuckles and the resonating sideboards of his desk he could give you caissons crossing a plank bridge, and with his dentures and inflated cheeks and moist thick lips he could give you a mortar barrage in the distance and rattling anchor chains and lapping water and hissing fuses and neighing horses. I had heard the tape hundreds of times and yet each time I would be surprised and delighted anew by some bit of Casey genius, some description or insight or narrative passage or sound effect. The bird peals, for instance. Dr. Bud gives a couple of unexpected bird calls in the tense scene where Grant and Pemberton are discussing surrender terms under the oak tree. The call is a stylized one—*tu-whit, tu-whee*—and is not meant to represent that of any particular bird. It has never failed to catch me by surprise. But no one could hope to keep the whole of that lecture in his head at once, such are its riches.

I say I "had" the tape. It disappeared suddenly and Norma denied that she had thrown it away. After making a few inquiries and turning the apartment upside down I let the matter drop. That was my way. I once read about a man who would not let his wife know how he liked for things to be done, so that she could offend him. That was never my way. Norma and I had our squabbles, certainly, but never any scenes of rage like those on television with actors and actresses screaming at one another. It was give and take in our house. Two of my rules did cause a certain amount of continuing friction—my rule against smoking at the table and my rule against record-playing after 9 p.m., by which time I had settled in for a night of reading—but I didn't see how I could compromise in either of those areas.

Norma was married to Dupree when I met her. She had golden down on her forearms and a little blue vein or artery that ran across her forehead and became distended and pulsed noticeably when she was upset or expressing some strong opinion. You hardly ever see the wives of people who work for newspapers and I'm embarrassed to say I can't remember the occasion of our first meeting. I had sat next to Dupree on the rim of the copy desk. In fact, I had gotten him the job. He was not well liked in the newsroom. He radiated dense waves of hatred and he never joined in the friendly banter around the desk, he who had once been so lively. He hardly spoke at all except to mutter "Crap" or "What crap" as he processed news matter, affecting a contempt for all events on earth and for the written accounts of those events.

As for his height, I would put it at no more than five feet nine inches—he being fully erect, out of his monkey crouch —and yet he brazenly put down five eleven on all forms and applications. His dress was sloppy even by newspaper standards—thousands of wrinkles! It was a studied effect rather than carelessness. I know he had to work at it, because his clothes were of the permanent-press type and you can't make that stuff wrinkle unless you bake it in a dryer and then crumple it up. He had a nervous habit of rubbing his hands back and forth on his trousers when he was seated and this made for an unsightly condition called "pilling," where the surface fibers form hard little balls or pills from being scuffed about. Pilling is more often seen on cheap blankets than on clothing but all of Dupree's trousers were badly pilled in front. His shirts were downright dirty. He wore glasses, the lenses thick and greasy, which distorted the things of the world into unnatural shapes. I myself have never needed glasses. I can read road signs a half-mile away and I can see individual stars and planets down to the seventh magnitude with no optical aids whatever. I can see Uranus.

For eleven miserable months Norma was married to Dupree and after some of the things she told me I was amazed that she could go back to him. His kissing frenzies! His carbide cannon! Still, there it was. I had no idea that anything was going on. How had he made his new approaches? What were his disgusting courtship techniques? Had the cycling club been a ruse? There had been some night meetings. But Dupree already had a sweetheart! A friend at the paper told me that Dupree had been seeing this person for several months—a mystery woman who lived upstairs in a gray house behind the Game and Fish Building. What about her?

Norma and I were getting along well enough, or so I thought. I have mentioned her restlessness. The only other thing I could put my finger on was a slight change in her manner. She had begun to treat me with a hearty but impersonal courtesy, something like a nurse dealing with an old-timer. "I'll be right with you," she would say, or, when presenting me with something, "Here we are, Midge." She had always called me by my last name.

I think now this coolness must have started with our algebra course. She had agreed to let me practice my teaching methods on her and so I had worked out a lecture plan in elementary algebra. I had a little blackboard, green actually, that I set up in the kitchen every Thursday at 7 p.m. for my demonstrations. It was not the kind of thing you like to ask a person to do but Norma was a good sport about it and I thought if I could teach her ninth-grade algebra I could teach just about anything to anybody. A good sport, I say, but that was only at the beginning of the course. Later on she began to fake the answers on her weekly tests. That is, she would look up the answers to the problems in the back of the textbook and copy them without showing me her step-by-step proofs. But wasn't this a part of teaching too? Wouldn't I have to deal with widespread cheating in the raucous classrooms of our public schools? I handled it this way with Norma. I said nothing about her dishonesty and simply gave her a score of zero on each test. Still she continued to look up the answers, whether I was watching her or not. She would complete the test in two or three minutes and sign her name to it and hand it to me, saying, "There you go, Midge. Will there be anything else?"

Of course I knew she felt sorry for Dupree in his recent troubles and I suppose she must have come to see him as a romantic outlaw. I didn't feel sorry for him at all. The troubles were entirely of his own making. You can't go around bothering people and not expect some inconvenience yourself. The trouble was politics. He had lately become interested in politics and this had brought his nastiness into bloom.

That is, it was "lately" to me. I didn't see Dupree much for seven or eight years, when he was away at all those different schools, and the change was probably more gradual than it appeared to me. He had once been a funny fellow. I don't often laugh out loud, even when I can recognize a joke as being a good one, but Dupree could always make me laugh when he did a thing called The Electric Man. As The Electric Man or The Mud Man he could make anyone laugh. And sometimes he would go out one door and come in at another one, as though he had just arrived, having moved very quickly in concealment between the two points. It wasn't so funny the first time—but he would keep doing it!

To the best of my knowledge he had never even voted, and then someone must have told him something about politics, some convincing lie, or he read something—it's usually one or the other—and he stopped being funny and turned mean and silent. That wasn't so bad, but then he stopped being silent.

He wrote abusive letters to the President, calling him a coward and a mangy rat with scabs on his ears, and he even challenged him to a fistfight on Pennsylvania Avenue. This was pretty good coming from a person who had been kayoed in every beer joint in Little Rock, often within the first ten minutes of his arrival. I don't believe we've ever had a President, unless it was tiny James Madison with his short arms, who couldn't have handled Dupree in a fair fight. Any provocation at all would do. One of his favorite ploys was to take a seat at a bar and repeat overheard fatuous remarks in a quacking voice like Donald Duck. Or he would spit BB's at people. He could fire BB's from between his teeth at high velocity and he would sit there and sting the tender chins and noses of the drinkers with these little bullets until he was discovered and, as was usually the consequence, knocked cold as a wedge.

I will have to admit that Dupree took his medicine without whining, unlike so many troublemakers. I will have to admit that he was not afraid of physical blows. On the other hand he did whine when the law came down on him. He couldn't see the legal distinction between verbal abuse and death threats, and he thought the government was persecuting him. The threats were not real, in the sense that they were likely to be carried out, but the Secret Service had no way of knowing that.

And he had certainly made the threats. I saw the letters myself. He had written such things to the President of the United States as "This time it's curtains for you and your rat family. I know your movements and I have access to your pets too."

A man from the Secret Service came by to talk to me and he showed me some of the letters. Dupree had signed them "Night Rider" and "Jo Jo the Dog-Faced Boy" and "Hoecake Scarfer" and "Old Nigger Man" and "Don Winslow of the Navy" and "Think Again" and "Home Room Teacher" and "Smirking Punk" and "Dirt Bike Punk" and "Yard Man."

He was arrested and he called me. I called his father— they didn't speak—and Mr. Dupree said, "Leavenworth will be a good place for him." The U.S. Commissioner had set bond at three thousand dollars—not a great deal, it seemed to me, for such a charge—but Mr. Dupree refused to post it.

"Well, I didn't know whether you could afford it or not," I said, knowing he would be stung by any suggestion that he might not be rich. He didn't say anything for a long moment and then he said, "Don't call me again about this." Dupree's mother might have done something but I didn't like to talk to her because she was usually in an alcoholic fog. She had a sharp tongue too, drunk or sober.

It certainly wasn't a question of the money, because Mr. Dupree was a prosperous soybean farmer who had operations not only in Arkansas but in Louisiana and Central

America as well. The newspaper was already embarrassed and didn't want to get further involved. Norma put it to me that I ought to lend Dupree a hand since he was so absolutely friendless. Against my better judgment I got three hundred dollars together and arranged for a bondsman named Jack Wilkie to bail him out.

Not a word of thanks did I get. As soon as he was released from the county jail, Dupree complained to me that he had been fed only twice a day, oatmeal and pancakes and other such bloodless fare. A cellmate embezzler had told him that federal prisoners were entitled to three meals. Then he asked me to get him a lawyer. He didn't want Jack Wilkie to represent him.

I said, "The court will appoint you a lawyer."

He said, "They already have but he's no good. He doesn't even know the federal procedure. He'll start talking to this guy when he's supposed to be talking to that other guy. He waives everything. He's going to stipulate my ass right into a federal pen. A first offender."

"You'll have to get your own lawyer, Dupree."

"Where am I supposed to get him? I've called every son of a bitch in the yellow pages."

A good lawyer, he thought, would be able to forestall the psychiatric examination at the prison hospital in Springfield, Missouri. That examination was what he feared most, and with good reason, even though the finding would no doubt have provided a solid defense. In any case, he didn't really need a lawyer, good or bad, because on the following Friday night he jumped bail and ran off with my wife in my Ford Torino.

Since that night I had been biding my time but now that I knew where they were, more or less, I was ready to make my move. I had very little cash money for the trip and no credit cards. My father was floating somewhere on a lake near Eufaula, Alabama, in his green plastic boat, taking part in a bass tournament. Of course I had had many opportunities to explain the thing to him but I had been ashamed to do so. I was no longer an employee of the paper and I couldn't go to the credit union. My friend Burke never had any money. I could have sold some of my guns but I was reluctant to do so, saving that as a last resort. Gun fanciers are quick to sniff out a distress sale and I would have taken a beating from those heartless traders.

Then on the very day of my departure I remembered the savings bonds. My mother had left them to me when she died. I kept them hidden behind the encyclopedias where Norma never tarried and I had all but forgotten about them. Norma was a great one to nose around in my things. I never bothered her stuff. I had a drawer full of pistols in my desk and I kept that drawer locked but she got it open somehow and handled those pistols. Little rust spots from her moist fingertips told the story. Not even my food was safe. She ate very little, in fact, but if some attractive morsel on my plate happened to catch her eye she would spear it and eat it in a flash without acknowledging that she had done anything out of the way. She knew I didn't like that. I didn't tamper with her plate and she knew I didn't like her tampering with my plate. If the individual place setting means no more than that, then it is all a poor joke and you might as well have a trough and be done with it. She wouldn't keep her hands off my telescope either. But the Hope Diamond would have been safe behind those *Britannicas*.

I retrieved the bonds and sat down at the kitchen table to count them. I hadn't seen them in a long time and I decided to line them up shoulder to shoulder and see if I could cover every square inch of table surface with bonds. When I had done this, I stood back and looked at them. These were twenty-five-dollar E bonds.

Just then I heard someone at the door and I thought it was the children. Some sort of youth congress had been in session at the capitol for two or three days and children were milling about all over town. A few had even wandered into Gum Street where they had no conceivable business. I had been packing my clothes and watching these youngsters off and on all day through the curtain and now—the very thing I feared—they were at my door. What could they want? A glass of water? The phone? My signature on a petition? I made no sound and no move.

"Ray!"

It was Jack Wilkie and not the kids. What a pest! Day and night! I went to the door and unchained it and let him in but I kept him standing in the living room because I didn't want him to see my savings-bond table.

He said, "Why don't you turn on some lights in here or raise a shade or something?"

"I like it this way."

"What do you do, just stay in here all the time?"

He went through this same business at the beginning of each visit, the implication being that my way of life was strange and unwholesome. Jack was not only a bondsman and a lawyer of sorts but a businessman too. He owned a doughnut shop and some taxicabs. When I said he was a lawyer, I didn't mean he wore a soft gray suit and stayed home at night in his study reading Blackstone's *Commentaries*. If you had hired him unseen and were expecting that kind of lawyer, you would be knocked for a loop when you got to court and saw Jack standing there in his orange leisure suit, inspecting the green stuff under his fingernails. You would say, Well, there are a thousand lawyers in Pulaski County and it looks like I've got this one!

But Jack was a good-natured fellow and I admired him for being a man of action. I was uneasy when I first met him.

He struck me as one of these country birds who, one second after meeting you, will start telling of some bestial escapade involving violence or sex or both, or who might in the same chatty way want to talk about Christ's Kingdom on Earth. It can go either way with those fellows and you need to be ready.

He had some big news for me this time, or so he thought. It was a postcard that Norma had sent to her mother from Wormington, Texas. "Gateway to the Hill Country," it said under the photograph of a low, dim structure that was the Wormington Motel. Gateway claims have always struck me as thin stuff because they can only mean that you're not there yet, that you're still in transit, that you're not in any very well defined place. I knew about the card already because Mrs. Edge, Norma's mother, had called me about it the day before. I had met her in front of the Federal Building and looked it over. Norma said she was all right and would be in touch later. That was all, but Jack wanted to stand there and talk about the card.

I studied the motel picture again. Next to the office door of the place there was another door opening into what must have been a utility room. I knew that Norma with her instinct for the wrong turn had opened it and stood there a long time looking at the pipes and buckets and tools, trying to figure out how the office had changed so much. I would have seen in a split second that I was in the wrong room.

I said, "They're not in Wormington now, Jack. It was just a stopover. Those lovebirds didn't run off to Wormington, Texas."

"I know that but it's a place to start."

"They'll turn up here in a few days."

"Let me tell you something. That old boy is long gone. He got a taste of jail and didn't like it."

"They'll turn up."

"You should have told me he was a nut. I don't appreciate the way you brought me into this thing."

"You knew what the charge was. You saw those letters."

"I thought his daddy would be good for it. A slow-pay
rich guy maybe. I thought he just meant to let the boy stew
for a while."

"Guy has given Mr. Dupree a lot of headaches."

"I'm going to report your car stolen. It's the only way."

"No, I can't go along with that."

"Let the police do our work for us. It's the only way to
get a quick line on those lovebirds."

"I don't want to embarrass Norma."

"You don't want to embarrass yourself. You're afraid it'll
get in the paper. Let me tell you something. The minute that
bail is forfeited, it'll be in the paper anyway and by that
time you may not even get your car back."

There was something to this. Jack was no dope. The
paper didn't run cuckold stories as such but I thought it best
to keep my name out of any public record. That way I could
not be tied into Dupree's flight. Tongues were already wag-
ging, to be sure. Everyone at the paper knew what had happened but what they knew and what they could print—
without the protection of public records—were two different
things. All I wanted to do now was to get my car back. I was
already cuckolded but I wouldn't appear so foolish, I
thought, if I could just get my car back without any help.

Jack stood there and reviewed the whole case again. He
did this every time, as though I might be confused on certain points. When his eyes became adjusted to the murky
light, he saw my suitcase on the couch and I saw him taking
this in, a suitcase fact. He said, "I don't forfeit many bonds,
Ray." I had heard him say that before too.

He left and I quickly gathered my E bonds and stowed
them in the suitcase. I selected a .38 Colt Cobra from the

pistol drawer and sprayed it with a silicone lubricant and sealed it in a plastic bag and packed it next to the bonds. What else now? The lower-back capsules! Norma never went anywhere without her lower-back medicine and yet she had forgotten it this time, such was her haste in dusting out of town, away from my weekly embraces. I got it from the bathroom and packed it too. She would thank me for that. Those capsules cost four dollars apiece.

I made sure all the windows were locked and I found a country-music station on my big Hallicrafters radio and left it playing at high volume against the kitchen wall. There was a rock-and-roll twerp with a stereo set in the next apartment and his jungle rhythms penetrated my wall. Noise was his joy. He had a motorcycle too. The Rhino management had a rule prohibiting the repair of motorcycles in the parking lot but the twerp paid no attention to it. One night I called him. I was reading a biography of Raphael Semmes and I put it down and rang up the twerp and asked him if he knew who Admiral Semmes was. He said, "What!" and I said, "He was captain of the *Alabama*, twerp!" and hung up.

Everything was in readiness. My checklist was complete. I called a cab and typed a note and tacked it to the door.

> *I will be out of town for a few days.*
> *Raymond E. Midge*

The cabdriver honked and picked his way slowly down Broadway through the little delegates to that endless convention of Junior Bankers or Young Teamsters. Their numbers seemed to be growing. I had left the Buick Special with a mechanic on Asher Avenue to get the solenoid switch replaced on the starter. The cabdriver let me out in front of a filthy café called Nub's or Dub's that was next door to the

garage. Nub—or anyway some man in an apron—was standing behind the screen door and he looked at me. I was wearing a coat and tie and carrying a suitcase and I suppose he
thought I had just flown in from some distant city and then
dashed across town in a cab to get one of his plate lunches.
A meal wasn't a bad idea at that but it was getting late and I
wanted to be off.

The mechanic told me I needed a new motor mount and
he wanted to sell me a manifold gasket too, for an oil leak. I
wasn't having any of that. I wasn't repairing anything on
that car that wasn't absolutely necessary. This was a strange
attitude for me because I hate to see a car abused. Maintenance! I never went along with that new policy of the six-
thousand-mile oil change. It was always fifteen hundred for
me and a new filter every time.

And yet here I was starting off for Mexico in this junker
without so much as a new fan belt. There were Heath bar
wrappers, at least forty of them, all over the floor and seats
and I hadn't even bothered to clean them out. It wasn't my
car and I despised it. I had done some thinking too. The
shock of clean oil or the stiffer tension of a new belt might
have been just enough to upset the fragile equilibrium of the
system. And I had worked it out that the high mileage was
not really a disadvantage, reasoning in this specious way:
that a man who has made it to the age of seventy-four has a
very good chance of making it to seventy-six—a better
chance, in fact, than a young man would have.

Before I could get out of town, I remembered the silver
service that Mrs. Edge had passed along to Norma. What if
it were stolen? I wasn't worried much about my guns or my
books or my telescope or my stamps but if some burglar
nabbed the Edge forks I knew I would never hear the end of
it. My note would invite a break-in! I returned to the apartment and got the silver chest. On my note saying that I

would be out of town for a few days a smart-ass had written, "Who cares?" I ripped it off the door and drove downtown to the Federal Building where Mrs. Edge worked. She wore a chain on her glasses and she had a good job with a lot of seniority at the Cotton Compliance Board.

She wasn't in the office and no one could tell me where she was. What a sweet job! Just drift out for the afternoon! I called her house and there was no answer. I wondered if she might have found a place where she could dance in the afternoon. She was crazy about dancing and she went out almost every night with big red-faced men who could stay on the floor with her for three or four hours. I mean smoking soles! She called me a "pill" because I would never take Norma dancing. I say "never" and yet we had scuttled stiffly across the floor on certain special occasions, although our total dancing time could be readily computed in seconds, the way pilots measure their flying time in hours. I believe Mrs. Edge did prefer me over Dupree, for my civil manner and my neat attire if nothing else, but that's not to say she liked me. She had also called me "furtive" and "a selfish little fox."

I decided that she was probably out for an afternoon of city obstruction and I went to the west side of town and cruised the parking lots of the big shopping centers looking for her car. On certain days of the week she and several hundred other biddies would meet at these places and get their assignments, first having taken care to park their Larks and Volvos and Cadillacs across the painted lines and thus taking up two parking spaces, sometimes three. Then they would spread out over town. Some would go to super-markets and stall the checkout lines with purse-fumbling and check-writing. Others would wait for the noon rush at cafeterias and there bring the serving lines to a crawl with long deliberative stops at the pie station. The rest were on motor patrol and they would poke along on the inside lanes of busy streets and stop cold for left turns whenever they saw a good chance to stack up traffic. Another trick was to stick the nose of a car about halfway into a thoroughfare from a side street, thereby blocking all traffic in that lane. Mrs. Edge was a leader of this gang. Turn her loose and she would have a dancing academy in the post office!

It was dark when I gave up the search. This silver wasn't old or rare or particularly valuable and I was furious with myself at having wasted so much time over it. I didn't feel like going all the way back to the apartment, so I just left the chest in the car trunk.

I was off at last and I was excited about the trip. The radio didn't work and I hummed a little. When I reached Benton, I was already tired of driving that car. Twenty-five miles! I couldn't believe it. I had a thousand miles to go and I was sleepy and my arms were tired and I didn't see how I was going to make it to Texarkana.

I pulled in at a rest stop and lay down on the seat, which had a strong dog odor. My nose was right against the plastic weave. This rest stop was a bad place to rest. Big diesel rigs roared in and the drivers left their engines running and made everybody miserable, and then some turd from Ohio parked a horse trailer next to me. The horses made the trailer springs squeak when they shifted their weight. That squeaking went on all night and it nearly drove me crazy. I slept for about four hours. It was a hard sleep and my eyes were swollen. A lot of people, the same ones who lie about their gas mileage, would have said they got no sleep at all.

It was breaking day when I reached Texarkana. I stopped and added some transmission fluid and put through a call to Little Rock from a pay station and woke up Mrs. Edge. I asked her to call my father on his return and tell him that I had gone to San Miguel de Allende in Mexico and would be back in a few days. The silverware was safe. What? Mexico? Silver? She was usually pretty quick but I had given it to her in a jumble and she couldn't take it in. It was just as well, because I didn't want to discuss my private business with her.

The drive to Laredo took all day. Gasoline was cheap—22.9 cents a gallon at some Shamrock stations—and the Texas police didn't care how fast you drove, but I had to keep the Buick speed below what I took to be about sixty because at that point the wind came up through the floor hole in such a way that the Heath wrappers were suspended behind my head in a noisy brown vortex. It was late October. The weather was fine but the leaves weren't pretty; they had just gone suddenly from green to dead.

I bought a quart of transmission fluid in Dallas and I stopped twice to cash bonds. The girl teller in the bank at Waco stared at me and I thought I must be giving off a dog smell. I got a roll of quarters from her and hefted it in my fist as I drove along.

Just south of Waco I looked about for some sign of the big gas line, the Scott-Eastern Line, but I could never determine where it crossed under the highway. My father and Mr. Dupree had helped build it, first as swabbers and then as boy welders. The Sons of the Pioneers! They had once been fairly close friends but had drifted apart over the years, Mr. Dupree having made a lot more money. My father resented his great success, although he tried not to, always giving Mr. Dupree credit for his energy. The hammer and the cutting torch, he said, were Mr. Dupree's favorite tools. My father's touch was much finer, his welding bead smoother and stronger and more pleasing to the eye, or so I am told. Of course he no longer made his living at it but people still called him on occasion when there was a tricky job to be done, such as welding airtight pressure seams on thin metal, or welding aluminum. Thin metal? Give him two beer cans and he'll weld them together for you!

In South Texas I saw three interesting things. The first was a tiny girl, maybe ten years old, driving a 1965 Cadillac. She wasn't going very fast, because I passed her, but still she was cruising right along, with her head tilted back and her mouth open and her little hands gripping the wheel.

Then I saw an old man walking up the median strip pulling a wooden cross behind him. It was mounted on something like a golf cart with two spoked wheels. I slowed down to read the hand-lettered sign on his chest.

JACKSONVILLE

FLA OR BUST

I had never been to Jacksonville but I knew it was the home of the Gator Bowl and I had heard it was a boom town, taking in an entire county or some such thing. It seemed an odd destination for a religious pilgrim. Penance maybe for some terrible sin, or some bargain he had worked out with God, or maybe just a crazed hiker. I waved and called out to him, wishing him luck, but he was intent on his marching and had no time for idle greetings. His step was brisk and I was convinced he wouldn't bust.

The third interesting thing was a convoy of stake-bed trucks all piled high with loose watermelons and canta-loupes. I was amazed. I couldn't believe that the bottom ones weren't being crushed under all that weight, exploding and spraying hazardous melon juice onto the highway. One of nature's tricks with curved surfaces. Topology! I had never made it that far in my mathematics and engineering studies, and I knew now that I never would, just as I knew that I would never be a navy pilot or a Treasury agent. I made a B in Statics but I was failing in Dynamics when

I withdrew from the field. The course I liked best was one
called Strength of Materials. Everybody else hated it because of all the tables we had to memorize but I loved it, the
sheared beam. I had once tried to explain to Dupree how
things fell apart from being pulled and compressed and
twisted and bent and sheared but he wouldn't listen. Whenever that kind of thing came up, he would always say—*boast*,
the way those people do—that he had no head for figures
and couldn't do things with his hands, slyly suggesting the
presence of finer qualities.

Two

In Laredo I got a six-dollar motel room that had a lot of posted rules on the door and one rubber pillow on the bed and an oil-burning heater in the wall that had left many a salesman groggy. It was the kind of place I knew well. I always try to get a room in a cheap motel with no restaurant that is near a better motel where I can eat and drink. Norma never liked this practice. She was afraid we would be caught out in the better place and humiliated before some socialites we might have just met. The socialites would spot our room key, with a chunk of wood dangling from it like a carrot, or catch us in some gaffe, and stop talking to us. This Laredo room also had a tin shower stall and one paper bath mat.

I went to a discount store and bought three quarts of transmission fluid and some food for the road and a Styrofoam ice chest and a frozen pie. I didn't want the pie but I did want the carton it came in. Back in the shadows of my room I replaced the pie with the Colt Cobra and sealed the box with tape. The cylinder of the revolver made a bulge in the carton and I regretted that I had not brought a flat automatic. Then I put the innocent-looking carton at the bottom of the ice chest and covered it with little crescents of ice from the motel dispenser. This was against motel policy, the crescents being intended for solitary drinks in the room instead of bulk use.

But I filled the chest anyway and on top of the ice I arranged cans of beer and packets of baloney and cheese in a festive display. The pie itself, lemon, I carried about in the room for a while, putting it down here and there. I couldn't find a good place for it. Finally I took it outside and left it by the dumpster for a passing rat, who would squeak with delight when he saw those white billows of meringue.

The better motel was across the wide street. I went over and scouted the place out, the magazine rack and the lounge and the restaurant. No salad bar but that was all right. I noted too that a person would have to pass through the steaming nastiness of the kitchen in order to reach the toilet. The people who were running the motel seemed to be from some place like North Dakota instead of Texas, and they all seemed to be worried about something, distracted. I could hear carpentry work going on in the kitchen and occasional shouts.

You can usually count on a pretty good chicken-fried steak in Texas, if not a chicken-fried chicken, but I didn't like this setup. All afternoon I had been thinking about one of those steaks, with white gravy and a lot of black pepper, and now I was afraid these people from Fargo would bring me a prefabricated vealette pattie instead of fresh meat. I ordered roast beef and I told the waitress I wanted plenty of gristle and would like for the meat to be gray with an iridescent rainbow sheen. She was not in the mood for teasing, being preoccupied with some private distress like the others. She brought me a plate of fish sticks and the smallest portion of coleslaw I've ever seen. It was in a paper nut cup. I didn't say anything because they have a rough job. Those waitresses are on their feet all day and they never get a raise and they never get a vacation until they quit. The menu was complete fiction. She was serving the fish sticks to everybody, and not a uniform count either.

After supper I went into the darkened lounge. It was still "happy hour" and the place was packed with local people. I saw no socialites. I had trouble getting a stool at the bar because when one fell vacant I would wait for a minute or two to let it cool off, to let the body heat dissipate from the plastic cushion, and then someone else would get it. The crowd cleared out when the prices went up and then I had the bar pretty much to myself. I could see a man standing at the far end writing a letter with a pencil. He was laughing at his work, a lone bandit writing cruel taunts to the chief of police.

I ordered a glass of beer and arranged my coins before me on the bar in columns according to value. When the beer came, I dipped a finger in it and wet down each corner of the paper napkin to anchor it, so it would not come up with the mug each time and make me appear ridiculous. I drank from the side of the mug that a left-handed person would use, in the belief that fewer mouths had been on that side. That is also my policy with cups, any vessel with a handle, although you can usually count on cups getting a more thorough washing than bar glasses. A quick slosh here and there and those babies are right back on the shelf!

Across from me there was a dark mirror and above that a mounted deer's head with a cigarette in his mouth. Back in the table area a woman was playing an electric organ. No one was shouting requests to her. I was the only person in the place who applauded her music—a piece of traveler's bravado. And after a while I didn't clap either. I had no character at all. If the other customers had suddenly decided to club the poor woman with bottles, with those square gin bottles, I suppose I would have joined in. Here was something new. We all know about the gentry going to seed but here was something Jefferson had not foreseen: an effete yeoman.

An old man wearing clown shoes came through the door and began to play a kind of tune on a toy trombone. He hummed into the tiny instrument, as with a comb and tissue paper. The Mexican bartender chased him out. Then another man came in and sat down beside me. I was annoyed, because there were plenty of empty stools. I stiffened and waited for him to start talking. I avoided eye contact. Any minute now, I said to myself, this fellow is going to order an Old Charter and 7-Up and tell me he had gone to boot camp with Tyrone Power. I couldn't see his face but I watched his hairy paw as it reached across me and grabbed a handful of matchbooks from the courtesy bowl. Greenish fingernails and a heavy silver ring with a black stone.

He punched me on the shoulder and laughed. It was Jack Wilkie. I couldn't believe it.

He said, "How's the little car holding up?"

"It's doing all right."

"Little car drives out good, does it?"

"What are you doing here, Jack?"

"It's all in the day's work." He was windblown and his knit shirt was sagging and damp with sweat but he was pleased with the effect he had achieved and he kept punching me and laughing.

Mrs. Edge had told him about the Texarkana call and he had immediately divined my plan. He had made up the lost time easily enough in his Chrysler Imperial. Tomorrow morning he would drive to San Miguel and pick up Dupree and take him back to Little Rock. It was as simple as that. He seemed to think San Miguel was right across the border.

"You should have told me where he was, Ray."

"I was going to tell you as soon as I got my car back. I wanted to get my car without your help."

"You should have told me about this Mexico thing. We could have worked something out. This is business to me."

"I know that."

"What difference does it make as long as you get your car?"

"It's not the same thing."

I gave him what information I had and he wrote down "Hotel Mogador" on a paper napkin. He said I might as well ride along with him to San Miguel in the comfort of the big Chrysler. I halfway agreed. It seemed the only thing to do, except maybe forget the whole business and go back to Little Rock like a whipped dog. There was no way I could beat him to San Miguel in the little Buick.

I said, "How are you going to get Dupree out of Mexico? Your warrant won't be any good down there."

Jack was scornful. "*Warrant*. That's a good one. Warrant's ass. I don't need a warrant. All I need is a certified copy of the bond. I'm a party to the action. That's better than a warrant any day. I can take custody anywhere. The dumbest person in this motel knows that."

The woman at the organ was singing. She had been singing for some time but this was no background stuff; this song was a showstopper and we had to take notice: "And then they nursed it, rehearsed it, . . . And gave out the news . . ."

The old man with the big shoes came back and this time he was wearing a bellboy's cap with a strap under his chin. He ran through the place waving a scrap of paper and shouting, "Phone call! Phone call for the Sheriff of Cochise! Emergency phone call! Code ten!" The bartender ducked under the bar flap and popped a rag at him and chased him out again and I could hear the old man's shoes flopping down the hall.

Jack said, "Who was that old guy?"

I said, "I don't know."

"They ought to lock that son of a bitch up."

"I think it's Halloween."

"No, it's not. A guy like that wouldn't know what day it was anyway. This place smells like a kennel. Did you eat here?"

"Yes."

"Can you recommend anything?"

"I can't recommend what I had."

"Some hot-tamale crap?"

"I had fish."

"That's a mistake. A place like this. Let's go to some nice steakhouse. I'm hungry."

"I've already eaten."

"How about the track? Why don't we take a run out to the dog track and make some quick money? Let them dogs pay for our trip."

"They don't have dog races here, Jack."

"I think they do."

"They don't have legal gambling in Texas."

"I think they have dog races."

"I don't think so. Out in the streets maybe. Among themselves."

"Across the border then. I know they have some kind of racing in Juárez."

"That's way up there at El Paso."

I still didn't see how Jack could take Dupree out of Mexico without going through some sort of legal formality. He kept telling me he was "the surety" and "a party to the action" and that such a person could go anywhere in the world and do just as he pleased. He said, "I don't care where they are. I've taken these old boys out of Venezuela and the Dominican Republic."

We sat there and drank for a long time. Jack showed me his handcuffs, which he carried in a leather pouch on his belt. He also had a blackjack, or rather a "Big John" flat sap. He didn't carry a gun. He said he loved the bail-bond business. His wife thought it was sleazy and she wanted him to give it up and devote all his time to the practice of law, which he found dull.

"I was in the army and nobody wanted to see me," he said. "Then I was a salesman and nobody wanted to see me. Now they're glad to see me. Let me tell you something. You're doing that old boy a real service when you get him out of jail. Sure, everybody has to go to jail sometime, but that don't mean you have to stay there."

I asked Jack if he could help me get a job as an insurance adjuster. I had often thought of becoming an investigator of some kind and I asked him if he could put me on to something, perhaps a small shadowing job. The paper had once given me a trial as a police reporter, although hardly a fair one. Two days! Jack wasn't interested in this subject and he wouldn't discuss it with me.

He wanted to talk about his family. He had a jug-eared stepson named Gary who smoked marijuana and made D's in school and spent his money on trashy phonograph records. The boy also spent a lot of his time and money at an amusement arcade downtown and Jack said he had ugly sores in his right eyebrow from many hours of pressing his eye against the periscope of the submarine game. The thought of this boy and his smart mouth and his teen mustache made Jack angry. But he didn't hold it against his wife that she had given birth to the unsatisfactory kid and brought him to live in the Wilkie home.

He poked me with a finger and said, "My wife is just as sweet as pie. Get that straight." And a little later he said, "I'm glad my wife is not a porker." He told me she had "firm muscles" and he told me about all the birthday presents and Christmas presents he had given her in recent years. He said she had never locked him out of the house.

I didn't see how Jack Wilkie could have a very nice wife and I was tired of hearing about her. He left to get a cheeseburger and I thought about his remarks. The insinuation seemed to be that Norma was not as sweet as pie. When he got back, I asked him if that was his meaning and he said it wasn't.

He had spilled food on his knit shirt. I told him that I thought an investigator going on a trip should wear a coat and tie. He didn't hear me. He was looking at the mounted deer head. He jumped up on the bar and straddled the walkway behind the bar and took the cigarette from the deer's mouth and flung it down on the duckboards. Then he turned on the bartender. "That's not right and you know it's not right," he said. "That's not the thing to do. Don't put another cigarette in that deer's mouth."

The Mexican bartender was slicing limes. With his hooded eyes and his little mustache he looked like a hard customer to me. He was fed up with these antics in his bar, I could tell, and I thought he was going to do something. But he just said, "I didn't put that one in there."

Jack climbed down and started telling me about all the different people who had attacked him while he was just doing his job. Everybody who attacked him was crazy. He pulled up a trouser leg and showed me a pitted place on his calf where a crazy woman in Mississippi had stabbed him with a Phillips screwdriver. Then he raised his knit shirt and showed me a purple scar on his broad white back where he had been shot by a crazy man in Memphis. One of his lungs had filled up with blood and when he came around in the emergency room of Methodist Hospital he heard the doctor ask a nurse if she had the key to the morgue. A close call for Jack! Not everybody was glad to see him!

Nothing more was said about our business. I left him there drunk on the stool. He said he would see me at breakfast.

I returned to my room across the street and went to bed and lay with my head under the rubber pillow to keep out highway noise. I couldn't sleep. After a time I could hear knocking and bumping and voices outside. Someone seemed to be going from door to door. Maybe trick or treat, or the Lions Club selling brooms. Or the dumbest person in the motel looking for his room. My turn came and I went to the door. It was the old man in the big shoes. He was also wearing a white cotton jacket or smock. With his purple face up close to mine, I saw his bad eye and I had the momentary impression that I was looking at Mr. Proctor. But how could that be? Mr. Proctor was snug in his brown shed in Little Rock, eating canned peanuts and watching some hard-hitting documentary on television. The man gave me a card. Scriptural quotations, I thought, or the deaf-and-dumb signs.

"What is this? What are you doing?"

"I'm just fooling around," he said.

It was my guess that he had been a veteran handyman here on motel row, known all up and down the street as Dad or Pete. Then one day he was falsely accused of something, stealing sheets maybe, and fired summarily with no pension. He was now getting back at people. This was his way of getting back at the motel bosses. But when I asked about this, he said, "No, I'm just fooling around. It's something to do. My wife is an old shopping-cart lady. That's Mrs. Meigs I'm speaking of. She picks up bottles all day and I do this all night."

"You weren't wearing that jacket thing before."

"This is my traffic coat. Mrs. Meigs made it for me so the cars and trucks could see me at night and not run over me. It's just got this one button in the middle and these two pockets here at the bottom. How do you like it?"

"I like it all right. It looks like a pharmacist's coat."

"It don't have near enough pockets to suit me but you can't have everything."

"What else do you do? What else are you going to do tonight?"

"First let me tell you what I'm not going to do. I'm not going to stand here any longer and talk to you. If I gave this much time to everybody, I'd never get through my rounds, would I?"

He produced a harmonica, not a trombone this time, and rapped it against his palm in a professional way to dislodge any spittle or crumbs. He stuck it in his mouth and inhaled and exhaled, making those two different sounds, in and out, and then he rapped it again to clear the passages and put it away. I had nothing to say to that, to those two chords, and he bolted and was gone.

I took the card to bed and studied it. Tiny things take on significance when I'm away from home. I'm on the alert for omens. Odd things happen when you get out of town. At the top of the card there were two crossed American flags printed in color. Under that was the ever-popular "Kwitcherbellyachin" and at the bottom was "Mr. and Mrs. Meigs/ Laredo, Texas." On the back of the card Meigs or his wife had added a penciled postscript: "adios AMIGO and watch out for the FLORR."

I couldn't make anything out of this and I turned off the light. I could hear a Mexican shouting angrily at Meigs down the way. I still couldn't sleep. I got up again and drank one of the beers from the ice chest. I looked at the card again. "Kwitcherbellyachin"! I thought, Well, all right, I will. I decided to leave at once. I would get the jump on Jack. It was worth a try. I dressed quickly and loaded the suitcase and the ice chest in the trunk of the car.

Nothing at all was stirring in downtown Laredo. I didn't bother with the Mexican car insurance. I drove across the Rio Grande and on the other side of the bridge a Mexican officer flagged me into a parking compound that was enclosed by a high wire fence.

I was the only person entering Nuevo Laredo at that dead hour but it still took a long time to get my tourist card and car papers. The Mexican officer at the typewriter didn't believe that my Arkansas driver's license was really a driver's license. At that time it was just a flimsy piece of paper torn from a pad and it looked like a fishing license. I gave him the registration slip for my Torino and he didn't bother to look outside to see if that was in fact what I was driving. The big problem was the typing. When you run up against a policeman at a typewriter, you might as well get a Coke and relax.

While I was waiting, an idea drifted into my head that made me laugh a little. The idea was to get this Mexican fellow and Nub or Dub on a television show for a type-off. You would have them on a stage glaring at each other from behind their big Underwoods and Nub would try to peck out "Choice of 3 Veg." on his menu while this Mexican was trying to get "Raymond Earl Midge" down on his form. People would be howling from coast to coast at those two slowpokes. I slipped the man a dollar bill folded to the size of a stick of gum. I did the same with the porters and customs men outside.

This was the thing to do, I had been told, but it bothered me a little. You could look on a dollar as a tip and you could also look on it as a small bribe. I was afraid one of these fellows might turn out to be a zealot like Bruce Wayne, whose parents were murdered by crooks and who had dedicated his entire life to the fight against crime. An attempted bribe, followed by the discovery of a pistol concealed in a pie carton, and I would really be in the soup. But nothing happened. They palmed those dollars like carnival guys and nobody looked into anything. The customs man marked my suitcase with a piece of chalk and a porter stuck the decals on my windows and I was gone. I was free and clear in Mexico with my Colt Cobra.

Those boys were sleepy and not much interested in their work, it's true enough, but I was still pleased at the way I had brought it off. I couldn't get over how composed I had been, looking prison right in the face. Now I was surprised and light-headed, like a domestic fowl that finds itself able to fly over a low fence in a moment of terror. Vestigial Midge powers were rising in the blood. I was pleased too that I was in Mexico and not at home, but that works both ways because after sunrise I met Americans driving out of Mexico and they all appeared to be singing happy songs.

I waved at children carrying buckets of water and at old women with shawls on their heads. It was a chilly morning. *I'm a gringo of good will in a small Buick! I'll try to observe your customs!* That was what I put into my waves.

The poor people of Mexico were the ones without sunglasses. I could see that right off the bat. The others, descendants of the great Cortez, he who had burned his ships at Veracruz, were stealing small advantages in traffic. They would speed up and hog the center line when you tried to pass them. They hated to be passed. I say Cortez "burned" his ships because everyone else does, but I know perfectly well that he only had them dismantled there on the beach—not that it takes away from his courage.

A few miles from the border there was a checkpoint and an officer there examined my papers. Nothing matched! I was driving a completely different car from the one described on the form. He couldn't deal with such a big lie so early in the morning and he gave the papers back to me and waved me on.

The desert road was straight and the guidebook said it

was boring but I didn't find it so. I was interested in every-thing, the gray-green bushes, the cactus, a low brown hill, a spider crossing the road. Later in the morning a dark cloud came up that had a green rim and then rain fell in such torrents that cars and buses pulled over to wait it out. A desert rainstorm! You couldn't see three feet! I turned on the headlights and slowed down but I kept going until the brake linings got wet and wouldn't hold.

I don't like to piddle around when I'm on the road and this stop made me impatient. If you stop for ten minutes, you lose more than ten minutes' driving time. I don't know why, but I do know why slow ships can cross the Atlantic Ocean in just a few days. Because they never stop! My ankles and my new cordovan shoes were soaked from water sloshing up through the hole in the floor. I sat out the storm there on the shoulder of the road reading *The Life and Glorious Times of Zach Taylor,* by Binder. It was not the kind of title I liked but it was a pretty good book.

After the sun came out, I drove slow and rode the brakes for a while until they were dry. I was still on the straight part of the highway north of Monterrey when a big yellow car came racing up behind me and stayed right on my bumper. More Mexican stuff, I thought, and then I saw that it was Jack Wilkie in his Chrysler Imperial. I could see him in my mirror, laughing and tapping a finger on the steering wheel, in time, I supposed, to some radio music. I could see his big silver ring and some frosty flecks of doughnut sugar around his mouth. That was how close he was.

I tapped the brake pedal just enough to flash the brake light but I kept the accelerator depressed. Jack thought I was going to stop suddenly and he braked and skidded. His right-hand wheels dropped off the ledge of the pavement onto the dirt shoulder and dust was boiling up behind him. Then he recovered and got on my bumper again, still laughing. I didn't like that laughing. The brake-light trick was the only one I knew so I just started going faster and faster. Jack stayed right with me, inches away. He was playing with me. He could have passed me easily enough but he was going to run the Buick into the ground or make me give up, one or the other. I drove the little car as fast as it would go, which I guessed to be around ninety or so. That was nothing at all for the Imperial but I had a six-cylinder engine and a little air-cooled, two-speed transmission that was squealing like a pig.

We went roaring along like this for four or five miles, bumper to bumper, two hell drivers, and I was beginning to lose my stomach for it. I didn't even know what the point of it was. The sheet metal was vibrating and resonating and it appeared fuzzy to the eye. Particles of rust and dirt were dancing on the floor. Candy wrappers were flying everywhere.

I've had enough of this, I said to myself, and I was just about ready to quit when the exhaust system or the drive shaft dropped to the highway beneath the Chrysler and began to kick up sparks. Jack was done for the day. I shot over a rise and left him with a couple of honks. *Harvest yellow Imperial. Like new. Loaded. One owner. See to appreciate. Extra sharp. Good rubber. A real nice car. Needs some work. Call Cherokee Bail Bonds and ask for Jack. Work odd hours. Keep calling.*

Three

I lost some more time in and about the adobe city of Saltillo looking for the Buena Vista battlefield. I couldn't find it. Binder's maps were useless and the Mexicans pretended they had never heard of Zachary Taylor and Archibald Yell. At the height of the battle, when it might have gone either way, the cool Taylor turned to his artillery officer and said, "A little more grape, Captain Bragg." Remarks like that were embedded in my head and took up precious space that should have been occupied with other things but wasn't.

I gave up the search and pressed on south atop a desolate plateau. It was cool up there and the landscape was not like the friendly earth I knew. This was the cool dry place that we hear so much about, the place where we are supposed to store things. The car ran well and I glowed in the joy of solitary flight. It was almost a blessed state. Was I now a ramblin' man, like in the country songs? *Sorry, lady, but I got to be ramblin' on!* Or was this just a trip? Whenever I saw a person or a domestic animal, I would shout some greeting, or perhaps a question—"How do you like living here in Mexico?"—just the first thing that came into my head. I stopped for the night at a camper park in Matehuala. A young Canadian couple in a van shared their supper with me.

I slept in the car again, although I didn't much like it, being exposed that way to people walking by and peering in the windows, watching me sleep. It was like lying supine on the beach with your eyes closed and fearing that some terrible person in heavy shoes will come along and be seized by an impulse to stomp on your vulnerable belly. I rose early and shaved with cold water in the washhouse. The Canadians were up too, and they gave me a slice of pound cake and a cup of coffee. I was in San Miguel de Allende by noon.

The Hotel Mogador was only a block or so from the main square, or *jardín*, as they called it, which is to say "garden." There wasn't one guest in the place. Dupree and Norma had been gone for a little over three weeks. I was not greatly surprised at this, and not much concerned. From this point, I thought, tracing two foreigners and a chow dog in a blue Ford Torino could be no very hard task. I had not realized there were so many other Americans in Mexico.

The owner of the hotel was an accommodating man and he showed me their room, the blocky wooden bed, the short bathtub faced with little blue tiles. I had no particular feeling about the room but I certainly didn't want to stay in it, as the man suggested. I questioned him closely. Did they say where they were going? No. Had they perhaps moved to another hotel here? Possibly, but he had not seen them around town. Was there a trailer park in San Miguel? Yes, behind the Siesta Motel on the edge of town.

It had been in my mind all along that I would find them in a trailer park. I suppose I thought it would be a suitable place for their meretricious relationship. I had a plan for that trailer. I would jerk open the flimsy door with such force that the stop-chain would snap. Dupree would be sitting down eating a bowl of cereal, holding a big spoon in his monkey hand. I would throw an armlock on his neck from behind. While he sputtered and milk drops flew from his mouth, I would remove my car keys and my credit cards from his pockets. Norma would say, "Let him have some air!" and I would shove him away and leave them there in their sty without a word.

I drove out to the place on the edge of town but it wasn't a mobile-home community of the kind I had visualized. It was literally a trailer park, a dusty field where Mom and Dad could park their Airstream for a day or two and let their big Olds 98 cool off. The place was all but deserted. At one end of the field there was a square lump of a motor home and at the other end was an old school bus that had been painted white and rigged as a camper. The bus had been given a name, "The Dog of the South," which was painted in black on one side, but not by a sign painter with a straight-edge and a steady hand. The big childish letters sprawled at different angles and dribbled at the bottom. The white paint had also been applied in a slapdash manner, and it had drawn up in places, presenting a crinkled finish like that seen on old adding machines and cash registers. This thing was a hippie wagon.

I went to the Mogador and had lunch in the courtyard with the owner. I had to take two meals there with my room. There were flowers and cats all around us. I could see the pale blue sky above. We had onion soup and then some veal cutlets and rice. The hotel man fed table scraps to the cats and so I did the same. What a life!

He said he had been a bit mixed up before and had shown me the wrong room. The Norma-Dupree room was actually one floor above the first room he had shown me, and was in fact the very room he had given me. Did I wish to be moved? I said no, it made no difference. Then there was a disturbance in the kitchen and he went to investigate. When he came back, he said, "It was nothing, the mop caught fire. All my employees are fools."

This Mexican lunch was a long affair and before it was over we were joined by a tall bird wearing metallic-silver coveralls. He was a Canadian artist who made paper rabbits. He showed me one and it was a pretty well done bunny except for the big eyelashes. The price was ten dollars. I remarked that there seemed to be quite a few Canadians in Mexico.

He bristled. "Why shouldn't there be?"

"Out of proportion to your numbers, I mean. It was just a neutral observation."

"We're quite free to travel, you know. We can even go to Cuba if we wish."

"I'm not making myself clear."

"Do please make yourself clear."

"Well, there are two hundred million Americans and twenty million Canadians, and my country is closer to Mexico than yours, but I get the impression that there are just about as many Canadians here as Americans. At this table, for instance."

"You're not the only Americans. You people just stole that name."

"Look here, why don't you kiss my ass?"

"So bright of you. So typical."

It was my guess that this queer was having big trouble selling his overpriced rabbits. That was the only way I could account for his manner. The hotel man became jolly and tried to patch things up. But this too annoyed the artist and he got up and flounced out, stopping for a moment under the archway as he thought of something pretty good to call me, which was "rat face."

He thought it was pretty good but it was old stuff to me, being compared to a rat. In fact, I look more like a predatory bird than a rat but any person with small sharp features that are bunched in the center of his face can expect to be called a rat about three times a year.

We finished our meal in peace and then I went downtown to trade bonds for pesos. The bank was closed for lunch until 4 p.m. Some lunch! I wandered about town on foot looking for my Torino.

There was a bandstand in the central square, and some wrought-iron benches and some noisy flocking birds with long tail feathers. I took them to be members of the grackle family. There were elegant trees too, of the kind that architects like to sketch in front of their buildings. A few gringos were scattered around on the benches, dozing and reading newspapers and working crossword puzzles. I approached them one by one and made inquiries. I got nowhere until I mentioned the dog. They remembered the dog. Still, they could give nothing more than bare sighting reports. I could get no leads and no firm dates.

Hippies interfered with my work by stopping me and asking me the time. Why did they care? And if so, why didn't they have watches? The watch factories were humming day and night in Tokyo and Geneva and Little Rock so that everyone might have a cheap watch, but not one of these hippies had a watch. Maybe the winding put them off. Or maybe it was all mockery of me and my coat and tie. The same hippies seemed to be stopping me again and again, though I couldn't be sure.

A retired army sergeant told me that he had chatted for a bit with Dupree. He said they had discussed the curious drinking laws of the different states, and the curious alcoholic beverages of the world, such as ouzo and pulque, and he made me glad I wasn't there. In all his travels over the world, he said, he had found only one thing he couldn't drink and that was some first-run brandy in Parral, Chihuahua.

"Where did you talk to him?"

"That Southern boy?"

"Yes."

"Right here. I don't sit in the same place every day. It's not like I have my own bench but I *was* here that day. The boy sat over there and bought a Popsicle for his dog."

I wondered if the man might be confused. The Popsicle business sounded all right but I couldn't see Dupree sitting here being civil and swapping yarns with Sarge.

"Did he say where he was going from here?"

"I don't believe he did. He didn't have a whole lot to say."

"And the girl wasn't with him?"

"I didn't see any girl, just the dog. A big shaggy chow. The boy said he was going to trim his coat. He was worried about the tropical heat and humidity and he said he was going to give him a close trim with some scissors. He wanted to know where he could buy some flea powder and some heavy scissors."

"When was this?"

"It's been a while. I don't know. They come and go. Did he steal your dog?"

"No. Did you see him after that?"

"I saw him once in a car with some other people."

"Was it a Ford Torino?"

"No, it was a small foreign car. All beat up. It was some odd little car like a Simca. They were just cruising around the *jardín* here. I didn't pay much attention."

Other people? Foreign car? Dupree was not one to take up with strangers. What was this all about? But Sarge could tell me nothing more, except that the people were "scruffy" and appeared to be Americans. He pointed out the drugstore on the corner where he had sent Dupree for the flea powder. Then he took a ball-point pen and some glasses from his shirt pocket and I jumped up from the bench in alarm, fearing he was about to diagram something for me, but he was only rearranging his pocket stuff.

I thanked him and went to the drugstore and learned that an American wearing glasses had indeed bought some flea powder in the place. The woman pharmacist could tell me nothing else. I was tired. All this chasing around to prove something that I already knew, that Dupree had been in San Miguel. I couldn't get beyond that point. What I needed was a new investigative approach, a new plan, and I couldn't think of one. I looked over the aspirin display.

"¿Dolor?" said the woman, and I said Sí, and pointed to my head. Aspirins were too weak, she said, and she sold me some orange pills wrapped in a piece of brown paper. I took the pills to a café and crushed one on the table and tasted a bit of it. For all I knew, they were dangerous Mexican drugs, but I took a couple of them anyway. They were bitter.

On the way to the bank for a second try I got sidetracked into a small museum. The man who ran the place was standing on the sidewalk and he coaxed me inside. The admission fee was only two pesos. He had some good stuff to show. There were rough chunks of silver ore and clay figurines and two rotting mummies and colonial artifacts and delicate bird skulls and utensils of hammered copper. The man let me handle the silver. I wrote my name in the guest book and I saw that Norma and Dupree had been there. In the space for remarks Dupree had written, "A big gyp. Most boring exhibition in North America." Norma had written, "I like the opals best. They are very striking." She had signed herself Norma Midge. She was still using my name. I stood there and looked at her signature, at the little teacup handles on her capital N and capital M.

The book was on a high table like a lectern and behind it, tacked to the wall, was a map of Mexico. I drew closer to admire the map. It dated from around 1880 and it was a fine piece of English cartography. Your newer map is not always your better map! The relief was shown by hachuring, with every tiny line perfectly spaced. The engraver was a master and the printer had done wonders with only two shades of ink, black and brown. It was hand-lettered. I located myself at about 21 degrees north and 101 degrees west. This was as far south as I had ever been, about two degrees below the Tropic of Cancer.

Then after a few minutes it came to me. I knew where Dupree had gone and I should have known all along. He had gone to his father's farm in Central America. San Miguel was technically within the tropics but at an elevation of over six thousand feet the heat here would not be such as to cause dog suffering. And there was no humidity to speak of. They were on that farm in British Honduras. That monkey had taken my wife to British Honduras and he had planned it all in the Wormington Motel!

I was excited, my *dolor* suddenly gone, and I wanted to share the good news with someone. *¡Misión cumplida!* That is, it was not exactly accomplished, but the rest would be easy. I looked about for a place to gloat and soon hit on a bar called the Cucaracha.

It was a dark square room with a high ceiling. Some padded wooden benches were arranged in a maze-like pattern. They faced this way and that way and they were so close together that it was hard to move about. I drank bourbon until I figured out what it cost and then I switched to gin and tonic, which was much cheaper.

The customers were mostly gringos and they were a curious mix of retired veterans and hippies and alimony dodgers and artists. They were friendly people and I liked the place immediately. *We've all run off to Mexico*—that was the thing that hung in the air, and it made for a kind of sad bonhomie. I was suprised to find myself speaking so freely of my private affairs. The Cucaracha people offered tips on the drive south to British Honduras. I basked in their attention as a figure of international drama. My headache returned and I took some more pills.

One of the hippies turned out to be from Little Rock. I never thought I would be glad to see a hippie but I was glad to see this fellow. He had a hippie sweetheart with him who was wearing white nurse stockings. She was a pretty little thing but I didn't realize it for a while because her electrified hair was so ugly. It was dark in there too. I asked the hippie what he did and he said he drank a liter of Madero brandy every day and took six Benzedrine tablets. He asked me what I did and I had to say I did nothing much at all. Then we talked about Little Rock, or at least I did. I thought we might have some mutual friends, or if not, we could always talk about the different streets and their names. The hippie wasn't interested in this. He said, "Little Rock is a pain in the ass," and his sweetheart said, "North Little Rock too."

But it didn't matter, I was having a good time. Everything was funny. An American woman wearing a white tennis hat stuck her head in the doorway and then withdrew it in one second when she saw what kind of place it was. The Cucaracha gang got a good laugh out of this, each one accusing the other of being the frightful person who had scared her away. I talked to a crippled man, a gringo with gray hair, who was being shunned by the other drinkers. He said he had shot down two Nip planes when he was in the Flying Tigers. He now owned a Chiclets factory in Guadalajara. People hated him, he said, because his principles didn't permit him to lend money, or to buy drinks for anyone but himself. He described for me the first six plays of an important Stanford football game of 1935, or I should say the first six plays from scrimmage, since he didn't count the kickoff as a play.

There were two Australian girls across the room and the

Flying Tiger said they wanted to see me. He told me they had been trying to get my attention for quite a while. I went over at once and sat with them. These girls were slender cuties who were hitchhiking around the world with their shoulder bags. But it was all a hoax, the invitation, and they didn't want to see me at all. I sat down by another girl, this one a teacher from Chicago, and then I had to get up again because the seat was saved, or so she said. I watched that empty seat for a long time and it wasn't really saved for anyone. A hippie wearing striped bib overalls came in from the bar and sat beside her. She advised him that the seat was saved but that bird didn't get up. "You can't save seats," he said. What a statement! You can't save seats! I would never have thought of that in a thousand years!

I forgot about the bank business and I sat there and drank gin and tonic until the quinine in the tonic water made my ears hum. Someone that night told me about having seen Dupree with a fellow wearing a neck brace but I was too drunk to pursue it and the thing went completely out of my mind. I began to babble. I told everybody about my father's Midgestone business, how the stone veneer was cut with special band saws, and how it was shaped and sanded. I told them about my great-grandfather building the first greenhouse in Arkansas and how he had developed a hard little peach called the Lydia that was bird-resistant and well suited for shipping, although tasteless. I couldn't stop talking. I was a raving bore and I knew it too, but I couldn't stop. It was important to me that they know these things and who would tell them if I didn't?

They fled my presence, the hippies and vets and cuties alike, and left me sitting alone in the corner. I kept drinking, I refused to leave. They had all turned on me but I wasn't going to let them run me off. There was a lot of old stuff on the jukebox and I who had never played a jukebox in my life had the waiter take my change after each drink and play "It's Magic" by Doris Day. She was singing that song, a new one to me, when I first entered the place. I had heard of Doris Day but no one had ever told me what a good singer she was.

Sometime around midnight the hippie couple from Little Rock got into a squabble. I couldn't hear what he was saying because his voice was low but I heard her say, "My *daddy* don't even talk to me like that and you *damn* sure ain't!" The little girl was blazing. He put his hand out to touch her or to make some new point and she pushed it away and got up and left, stepping smartly in her white stockings and brushing past an old man who had appeared in the doorway.

He was a fat man, older than the Flying Tiger, and he was looking from left to right like an animal questing for food. He wore a white hat and a white shirt and white trousers and a black bow tie. This old-timer, I said to myself, looks very much like a boxing referee, except for the big floppy hat and the army flashlight clipped to his belt.

He looked around and said, "Where's the boy who's going to British Honduras?"

I said nothing.

He raised his voice. "I'm looking for the boy who's going to British Honduras! Is he here?"

If I had kept my mouth shut for five more seconds, he would have gone his way and I would have gone mine. I said, "Here I am! In the corner! I'm not supposed to talk!" I hadn't spoken for a long time and my voice croaked and had no authority in it.

"Where?"

"Over here!"

"I can't see you!"

"In the corner!"

He bumped his way across the room and took off his hat

and joined me on the bench. His white pants were too long and even when he was seated there was excess cloth piled up on top of his shoes. "I couldn't see you over all those heads," he said.

I was still fuming, a resentful drunk, and I took my anger out on him. "You couldn't see any normal human being over here from where you were standing. I'm not a giraffe. For your information, sir, a lot of navy pilots are five seven. Why don't you try calling Audie Murphy a runt? You do and you'll wake up in St. Vincent's Infirmary."

He paid no attention to this rant. "My bus broke down and I need to get back on the road," he said. "When are you leaving?"

"They won't let me talk in here."

"Who won't?"

"All these juiceheads. You'd think they owned the place. I have just as much right to be here as they do and if they don't want to hear about the greenhouse they can all kiss my ass! These juiceheads never grew anything in their lives!"

Neither had I for that matter but it wasn't the same thing. The old man introduced himself as Dr. Reo Symes. He looked to be in bad health. His belt was about eight inches too long, with the end curling out limp from the buckle. There were dark bags under his eyes and he had long meaty ears. One eye was badly inflamed and this was the thing that made me feel I was talking to Mr. Proctor or Mr. Meigs.

He said he was from Louisiana and had been making his way to British Honduras when his school-bus camper broke down. He was the owner of The Dog of the South. He asked if he might ride along with me and share the expenses. Overdoing everything like the disgusting drunk that I was, I told him that he would be more than welcome and that there would be absolutely no charge. His company would be payment enough. He questioned me about my driving skills and I assured him that I was a good driver. He said he was afraid to take a Mexican bus because the drivers here had a reputation for trying to beat out locomotives at grade crossings. He offered me some money in advance and I waved it aside. I told him I would pick him up in the morning.

I had planned on searching the sky that night for the Southern Cross and the Coalsack but when I left the bar it was overcast and drizzling rain. I bought two hot dogs from a man pushing a cart around the square. One block away the town was totally dark. I staggered down the middle of the cobbled street and tried to make it appear that I was sauntering. In the darkened doorways there were people smoking cigarettes and thinking their Mexican thoughts.

A hotel cat, a white one, followed me up the stairs to my room and I gave him one of the hot dogs. I didn't let him in the room. That would be a misplaced kindness. He would take up with me and then I would have to leave. Just inside the door there was a full-length mirror and the image it gave back was wavy and yellowish. I knew that Norma must have stood before it and adjusted her clothes. What would she be wearing? I liked her best in her winter clothes and I couldn't remember much about her summer things. What a knockout she was in her white coat and her red knit cap! With Jack Frost nipping her cheeks and her wavy nose!

Four

Rain was still falling when I got up in the morning. After I had paid the hotel bill, I had seven or eight dollars and around sixty pesos left. There was a terrible metallic clatter when I tried to start the car. A bad water pump or a bad universal joint will give you notice before it goes but this was some sudden and major failure, or so I thought. A broken connecting rod or a broken timing chain. Strength of materials! Well, I said to myself, the little Buick is done.

I got out and opened the hood. There was the white cat, decapitated by the fan blades. I couldn't believe it. He had crawled up into the engine compartment of this car, not another car, and there was my bloody handiwork. I couldn't handle anything. I couldn't even manage the minor decencies of life. I could hardly get my breath and I walked around and around the car.

A boy with some schoolbooks stopped to watch me and I gave him ten pesos to remove the carcass. I tried to get a grip on myself. Idleness and solitude led to these dramatics: an ordinary turd indulging himself as the chief of sinners. I drove down to the square and waited for the bank to open. My hands were shaking. I had read somewhere that white cats were very often deaf, like Dalmatian dogs. I had dry mouth and tunnel vision.

The bank manager said he could not cash the bonds but he could accept them as a deposit if I wished to open a checking account. They should clear in about a month. A month! Why had I not cashed them all in the States? What a piddler! Norma would have enjoyed this and I couldn't have blamed her for it. I was always impatient with this kind of childish improvidence in other people.

The Siesta trailer park was now a field of mud. Dr. Symes was having coffee in his white Ford bus. The passenger seats had been removed from the thing and replaced by a clutter of household furnishings that had not been anchored or scaled down or customized in any way. There was a dirty mattress on the floor and a jumble of boxes and chairs and tables. It was an old man's mess on top of a hippie mess. I accepted a roll and passed up the coffee. I loved those Mexican rolls but I didn't like the looks of the doctor's cup and I've never cared for instant coffee because it has no smell.

I was frank with him. I explained the bonds problem and I showed him exactly how much money I had. It was a bad moment. I was already embarrassed by my behavior in the bar and now, after all the expansive talk of a free ride, I was making myself look like a cheap liar. I made him a proposition. I would drive him to British Honduras if he would pay for the gasoline and other expenses. When we reached Belize, I would wire home for money and repay him half of his outlay. In the meantime I would give him five of my savings bonds to hold.

He was suspicious and I could understand that, although the deal seemed fair enough to me. The bonds were not negotiable, he said, and they were of no use to him. I pointed out that they did have a certain hostage value. It would be in my interest to redeem them. He looked at me and he looked outside at the car. It sat funny because the tires were of different sizes. He said, "All right then, let's go," and he flung his coffee through a window.

There was a staple-and-hasp affair on the bus door and he locked it with a brass padlock. He brought along his grip and a gallon of drinking water in a plastic jug and a sack of marshmallows. We left The Dog of the South parked there in the mud.

He was wary. He had little to say. He tried the radio, longer than I would have, and then gave it up. He said, "If a man wanted to get the news in this car, he would be out of luck, wouldn't he?"

"This is not my car. Everything works in my car."

The skies were clearing and the morning sun was blinding. He reached up for the right-hand sun visor that had never been there. His hand fell away and he grunted.

"It runs okay," I said.

"What's all that vibration?"

"The motor mounts are shot."

"The what?"

"The motor mounts. They look like black jelly down there. A V-6 shakes a lot anyway. It'll be all right after we get up some speed."

"Do you think it'll make it?"

"Yes, I do. It's a good car." I had said that just to be saying something but I thought it over and decided it was true.

"I hope a wheel doesn't fly off this thing," he said.

"I do too."

He worried a lot about that, a wheel flying off, and I gathered it had happened to him once and made an impression on him.

When we reached Celaya, which was only thirty miles or so from San Miguel, I left the highway and went downtown. I drove slowly up one street and down another. I thought I might see some shell-pocked buildings or at least a statue or a plaque of some kind.

Dr. Symes said, "What are you doing now?"

"This is Celaya."

"What about it?"

"There was a big battle here in 1915."

"I never heard of this place."

"I figure it was the third bloodiest battle ever fought in this hemisphere."

"So what?"

"Some sources say the fourth bloodiest. Obregón lost his arm here. Pancho Villa's army was routed. Do you know what he said?"

"No."

"He said, 'I would rather have been beaten by a Chinaman than by that *perfumado*, Obregón.'"

"Who were they fighting?"

"It was a civil war. They were fighting each other."

"I never heard of it."

"Well, it wasn't that long ago, and it was all right here, in this very town. I'll bet there are plenty of old-timers walking around here who were in that fight. If my Spanish was better, I would try to find one and talk to him."

"Let's don't do that."

The doctor made a show of counting his money. He said he had only about fifty dollars. His scuffed leather wallet was about a foot long and it was chained to his clothing in some way. It was like the big wallets carried by route men, by milkmen and potato-chip men.

There were three grades of gasoline in Mexico at that time and I had been buying the top grade, the Pemex 100. Now, to save money, the doctor's money, I began using the middle grade, which was supposed to be around 90 octane. I don't believe it was that high, because on the long mountain pulls the pistons rattled like empty bottles in a sack.

This noise bothered the doctor. He said, "The old Model

A had a spark advance you could manipulate. I don't know why they got rid of it. Well, that's your Detroit smarties. The hand choke too. That's gone. *Been* gone."

"What's wrong with your bus?"

"I think it's a burnt wheel bearing. My right front wheel. The wheel was shaking and there was a grinding racket coming out of that hub. I had a man look at it in a garage in Ciudad Victoria."

"What did he say?"

"I don't know what he said. He greased it. I went on and it did all right for a while. Then that wheel commenced shaking again and I was afraid that booger might fly off on me."

But the doctor didn't talk much, except to make complaints, and I thought it was going to be a long silent trip. I made some travel observations. I said that Mexican parents seemed to be kinder and more affectionate to their children than American parents. He said nothing. I remarked on the new buildings, on the flamboyant Mexican architecture. He said, "There's not much going on inside those buildings."

My abrupt steering movements bothered him too. He sat rigid in the seat and watched and listened. He complained about the dog smell on the seat and the dust that came up from the floor. He drank from a bottle of B and B liqueur. He said he had the chronic bronchitis of a singer and had used this liqueur for his throat ever since the government had barred the use of codeine in cough syrup.

"Pure baloney," he said. "I've seen every kind of addict there is and I've never known one person who was addicted to codeine. I've taken fifty gallons of the stuff myself. Wine will drive you crazy faster than anything I know and you can buy all the wine you want. Well, that's your Washington smarties. They know everything."

"Are you a medical doctor?"

"I'm not in active practice at this time."

"I once looked into medicine myself. I sent off for some university catalogues."

"I'm retired from active practice."

"These doctors make plenty of money."

"That's generally true, yes. I would be well fixed today if I had paid more attention to my screening methods. Screening is your big worry. I was always more concerned with healing. That was a serious mistake on my part. My entire life was ruined by a man named Brimlett. I didn't screen him."

After a time he seemed to realize that I wasn't going to rob him and I wasn't going to wreck the car. He relaxed and took off his big hat. There was a pointed crest of hair at the back of his head like that of a jaybird. He couldn't remember my name and he kept calling me "Speed."

I learned that he had been dwelling in the shadows for several years. He had sold hi-lo shag carpet remnants and velvet paintings from the back of a truck in California. He had sold wide shoes by mail, shoes that must have been almost round, at widths up to EEEEEE. He had sold gladiola bulbs and vitamins for men and fat-melting pills and all-purpose hooks and hail-damaged pears. He had picked up small fees counseling veterans on how to fake chest pains so as to gain immediate admission to V.A. hospitals and a free week in bed. He had sold ranchettes in Colorado and unregistered securities in Arkansas.

He said he had had very little trouble with the law in recent years, although he had been arrested twice in California: once for disturbing divine service, and again for impersonating a naval officer. They were trifling matters. He was collared in San Diego on the last charge; the uniform was a poor fit and he was too old for the modest rank he had assumed. He said he was only trying to establish a short line of credit at a bank. A friend from Tijuana named Rod Garza bailed him out and the thing never even came to trial. The church arrest had grown out of a squabble with some choir members who had pinched him and bitten him and goosed him. They were trying to force him out of the choir, he said, because they claimed he sang at an odd tempo and threw them off the beat. One Sunday he turned on them and whipped at them with a short piece of grass rope. Some of the women cried.

I asked him if he had ever visited Yosemite National Park when he was in California.

"No, I never did."

"What about Muir Woods?"

"What?"

"Muir Woods. Near San Francisco."

"I never heard of it."

"I'd like to see some of that country. I've been to New Mexico and Arizona but I never made it all the way to California. I'd like to go out there sometime."

"You'll love it if you like to see big buck niggers strutting around town kissing white women on the mouth and fondling their titties in public. They're running wild out there, Speed. They're water-skiing out there now. If I was a nigger, that's where I would go. It was a nigger policeman that arrested me outside that little church in Riverside. Can you beat it? He put the cuffs on me too, like I was Billy Cook. You don't expect a California nigger to defer to a white man but I thought he might have shown some consideration for my age."

"Did you go to jail?"

"Just overnight, till Monday morning. The municipal judge fined me thirty-five dollars and told me to find myself another church to sing in."

I asked him if he was going to British Honduras on vacation and he said, "Vacation! Do you think I'm the kind of man who takes vacations?"

"What are you going down there for?"

"My mother's there. I need to see her."

His mother! I couldn't believe it. "Is she sick?" I said.

"I don't know. I need to see her on some business."

"How old is she?"

"She's so old she's walking sideways. I hate to see it too. That's a bad sign. When these old folks start creeping around and shuffling their feet, church is about out."

He wanted to see her about some land she owned in Louisiana near the town of Ferriday. It was an island in the Mississippi River called Jean's Island.

"It's not doing her any good," he said. "She's just turned it over to the birds and snakes. She pays taxes on it every year and there's not one penny of income. There's no gain at all except for the appreciated value. She won't give it to me and she won't let me use it. She's my mother and I think the world of her but she's hard to do business with."

"It's not cultivated land?"

"No, it's just rough timber. The potential is enormous. The black-walnut trees alone are worth fifty thousand dollars for furniture veneer. The stumps could then be cut up and made into pistol grips. How does fifty thousand dollars sound to you?"

"It sounds pretty good."

"Some of those trees are whoppers. Double trunks."

"Maybe you could get a timber lease."

"I'd take a lease if I could get it. What I want is a deed. I don't mean a quitclaim either, I mean a warranty deed with a seal on it. So you understand what I'm telling you?"

"Yes."

"Did you say *timber* lease?"

"Yes."

"That's what I thought you said. Why would you want to cut the timber?"

"That was your idea. The walnut trees."

"I was only trying to suggest to you the value of the place. I'm not going to cut those trees. Are you crazy? Cut the trees and the whole thing would wash away and then where would you be? Do you want my opinion? I say leave the trees and make a private hunting preserve out of the place. I'm not talking about squirrels and ducks either. I mean stock the place with some real brutes. Wart hogs and Cape buffalo. I don't say it would be cheap but these hunters have plenty of money and they don't mind spending it."

"That's not a bad idea."

"I've got a hundred ideas better than that but Mama won't answer my letters. What about a Christian boys' ranch? It's an ideal setting. You'd think that would appeal to her, wouldn't you? Well, you'd be wrong. How about a theme park? Jefferson Davis Land. It's not far from the old Davis plantation. Listen to this. I would dress up like Davis in a frock coat and greet the tourists as they stepped off the ferry. I would glower at them like old Davis with his cloudy eye and the children would cry and clutch their mothers' hands and then—here's the payoff—they would see the twinkle in my clear eye. I'd have Lee too, and Jackson and Albert Sidney Johnston, walking around the midway. Hire some people with beards, you know, to do that. I wouldn't have Braxton Bragg or Joseph E. Johnston. Every afternoon at three Lee would take off his gray coat and wrestle an alligator in a mud hole. Prize drawings. A lot of T-shirts and maybe a few black-and-white portables. If you don't like that, how about a stock-car track? Year-round racing with hardly any rules. Deadly curves right on the water. The Symes 500 on Christmas Day. Get a promotional tie-in with

the Sugar Bowl. How about an industrial park? How about
a high-rise condominium with a roof garden? How about a
baseball clinic? How about a monkey island? I don't say it
would be cheap. Nobody's going to pay to see one or two
monkeys these days. People want to see a lot of monkeys.
I've got plenty of ideas but first I have to get my hands on
the island. Can you see what I'm driving at? It's the hottest
piece of real estate in Louisiana, bar none."

"Are you a student of the Civil War, Dr. Symes?"

"No, but my father was."

"What was that about Bragg? You said you wouldn't
have Bragg walking around in your park."

"My father had no time for Bragg or Joseph E. Johnston.
He always said Bragg lost the war. What do you know about
these revolving restaurants, Speed?"

"I don't know anything about them but I can tell you
that Braxton Bragg didn't lose the war by himself."

"I'm talking about these restaurants up on top of buildings that turn around and around while the people are in
there eating."

"I know what you're talking about but I've never been in
one. Look here, you can't just go around saying Braxton
Bragg lost the war."

"My father said he lost it at Chickamauga."

"I know what Bragg did at Chickamauga, or rather what
he didn't do. I can't accept Joseph E. Johnston's excuses
either for not going to help Pemberton but I don't go around
saying he lost the war."

"Well, my father believed it. Pollard was his man. A fellow named Pollard, he said, wrote the only fair account of
the thing."

"I've read Pollard. He calls Lincoln the Illinois ape."

"Pollard was his man. I don't read that old-timey stuff

myself. That's water over the dam. I've never wasted my time with that trash. What's your personal opinion of these revolving restaurants?"

"I think they're all right."

"Leon Vurro's wife said I should have a fifty-story tower right in the middle of the park with a revolving restaurant on top. What do you think?"

"I think it would be all right."

"That's your opinion. I happen to have my own. Let's cost it out. Let's look a little closer. All right, your sap tourists and honeymooners are up there eating and they say, 'Let's see, are we looking into Louisiana now or Mississippi, which?' I say what the hell difference would it make? One side of the river looks just like the other. You think it would be cheap? All that machinery? Gears and chains breaking every day? You'd have to hire two or three union bastards full time just to keep it working. What about your light bill? A thousand dollars a month? Two thousand? You'd have to charge eighteen dollars for a steak to come out on a deal like that. And just so some sap and his family can see three hundred and sixty degrees of the same damned cotton fields. I don't like it myself. Do you have the faintest notion of what it would cost to erect a fifty-story tower? No, you don't, and neither does Bella Vurro. And you probably don't care. I'm the poor son of a bitch who will have to shoulder the debt."

"Look here. Dr. Symes, I know that Bragg should have been relieved earlier. Everybody knows that today. Joe Johnston too, but that's a long way from saying they lost the war."

"What line of work are you in, Speed?"

"I'm back in college now. I'm trying to pick up some education hours so I can get a teaching certificate."

"What you are then is a thirty-year-old schoolboy."

"I'm twenty-six."

"Well, I don't guess you're bothering anybody."

"The Civil War used to be my field."

"A big waste of time."

"I didn't think so. I studied for two years at Ole Miss under Dr. Buddy Casey. He's a fine man and a fine scholar."

"You might as well loiter for two years. You might as well play Parcheesi for two years."

"That's a foolish remark."

"You think so?"

"It's dumb."

"All right, listen to me. Are you a reader? Do you read a lot of books?"

"I read quite a bit."

"And you come from a family of readers, right?"

"No, that's not right. That's completely wrong. My father doesn't own six books. He reads the paper about twice a week. He reads fishing magazines and he reads the construction bids. He works. He doesn't have time to read."

"But you're a big reader yourself."

"I have more than four hundred volumes of military history in my apartment. All told, I have sixty-six lineal feet of books."

"All right, now listen to me. Throw that trash out the window. Every bit of it."

He reached into his grip and brought out a little book with yellow paper covers. The cellophane that had once been bonded to the covers was cracked and peeling. He flourished the book. "Throw all that dead stuff out the window and put this on your shelf. Put it by your bed."

What a statement! Books, heavy ones, flying out the windows of the Rhino apartment! I couldn't take my eyes from the road for very long but I glanced at the cover. The title was *With Wings as Eagles* and the author was John Selmer Dix, M.A.

Dr. Symes turned through the pages. "Dix wrote this book forty years ago and it's still just as fresh as the morning dew. Well, why shouldn't it be? The truth never dies. Now this is a first edition. That's important. This is the one you want. Remember the yellow cover. They've changed up things in these later editions. Just a word here and there but it adds up. I don't know who's behind it. They'll have Marvin watching television instead of listening to dance music on the radio. Stuff like that. This is the one you want. This is straight Dix. This is the book you want on your night table right beside your glass of water, *With Wings as Eagles* in the yellow cover. Dix was the greatest man of our time. He was truly a master of the arts, and of some of the sciences too. He was the greatest writer who ever lived."

"They say Shakespeare was the greatest writer who ever lived."

"Dix puts William Shakespeare in the shithouse."

"I've never heard of him. Where is he from?"

"He was from all over. He's dead now. He's buried in Ardmore, Oklahoma. He got his mail in Fort Worth, Texas."

"Did he live in Fort Worth?"

"He lived all over. Do you know the old Elks Club in Shreveport?"

"No."

"Not the new one. I'm not talking about the new lodge."

"I don't know anything about Shreveport."

"Well, it doesn't matter. It's one of my great regrets that I never got to meet Dix. He died broke in a railroad hotel in Tulsa. The last thing he saw from his window is anyone's guess. They never found his trunk, you know. He had a big tin trunk that was all tied up with wire and ropes and belts and straps, and he took it with him everywhere. They never found it. Nobody knows what happened to it. Nobody even knows what was in the trunk."

"Well, his clothes, don't you think?"

"No, he didn't have any clothes to speak of. No *change* of clothes. His famous slippers of course."

"His correspondence maybe."

"He burned all letters unread. I don't want to hear any more of your guesses. Do you think you're going to hit on the answer right off? Smarter people than you have been studying this problem for years."

"Books then."

"No, no, no. Dix never read anything but the daily papers. He *wrote* books, he didn't have to read them. No, he traveled light except for the trunk. He did his clearest thinking while moving. He did all his best work on a bus. Do you know that express bus that leaves Dallas every day at noon for Los Angeles? That's the one he liked. He rode back and forth on it for an entire year when he was working on *Wings.* He saw the seasons change on that bus. He knew all the drivers. He had a board that he put on his lap so he could spread his stuff out, you see, and work right there in his seat by the window."

"I don't see how you could ride a bus for a year."

"He was completely exhausted at the end of that year and he never fully recovered his health. His tin trunk had a thousand dents in it by that time and the hinges and latches were little better than a joke. That's when he began tying it up with ropes and belts. His mouth was bleeding from scurvy, from mucosal lesions and suppurating ulcers, his gums gone all spongy. He was a broken man all right but by God the work got done. He wrecked his health so that we might have *Wings as Eagles.*"

The doctor went on and on. He said that all other writing, compared to Dix's work, was just "foul grunting." I could understand how a man might say such things about the Bible or the Koran, some holy book, but this Dix book, from what I could see of it, was nothing more than an inspirational work for salesmen. Still, I didn't want to judge it too quickly. There might be some useful tips in those pages, some Dix thoughts that would throw a new light on things. I was still on the alert for chance messages.

I asked the doctor what his mother was doing in British Honduras.

"Preaching," he said. "Teaching hygiene to pickaninnies."

"She's not retired?"

"She'll never retire."

"How does she happen to be in British Honduras?"

"She first went down there with some church folks to take clothes to hurricane victims. After my father died in 1950, she went back to help run a mission. Then she just stayed on. The church bosses tried to run her off two or three times but they couldn't get her out because she owned the building. She just started her own church. She says God told her to stay on the job down there. She's deathly afraid of hurricanes but she stays on anyway."

"Do you think God really told her to do that?"

"Well, I don't know. That's the only thing that would keep me down there. Mama claims she likes it. She and Melba both. She lives in the church with her pal Melba. There's a pair for you."

"Have you ever been down there?"

"Just once."

"What's it like?"

"Hot. A bunch of niggers."

"It seems a long way off from everything."

"After you get there it doesn't. It's the same old stuff."

"What does your mother do, go back and forth to Louisiana?"

"No, she doesn't go back at all."

"And you haven't seen her but once since she's been there?"

"It's a hard trip. You see the trouble I'm having. This is my last shot."

"You could fly down in a few hours."

"I've never been interested in aviation."

"I'm going down there after a stolen car."

"Say you are."

He kept twisting about in the seat to look at the cars approaching us from behind. He examined them all as they passed us and once he said to me, "Can you see that man's arms?"

"What man?"

"Driving that station wagon."

"I can see his hands."

"No, his arms. Ski has tattoos on his forearms. Flowers and stars and spiders."

"I can't see his arms. Who is Ski?"

He wouldn't answer me and he had no curiosity at all about my business. I told him about Norma and Dupree. He said nothing, but I could sense his contempt. I was not only a schoolboy but a cuckold too. And broke to boot.

He nodded and dozed whenever I was doing the talking. His heavy crested head would droop over and topple him forward and the angle-head flashlight on his belt would poke him in the belly and wake him. Then he would sit up and do it over again. I could see a tangle of gray hair in his long left ear. I wondered at what age that business started, the hair-in-the-ear business. I was getting on myself. The doctor had taken me for thirty. I felt in my ears and found nothing, but I knew the stuff would be sprouting there soon, perhaps in a matter of hours. I was gaining weight too. In the last few months I had begun to see my own cheeks, little pink horizons.

I was hypnotized by the road. I was leaning forward and I let the speed gradually creep up and I bypassed Mexico City with hardly a thought for Winfield Scott and the heights of Chapultepec. To pass it like that! Mexico City! On the long empty stretches I tried to imagine that I was stationary and that the brown earth was being rolled beneath me by the Buick tires. It was a shaky illusion at best and it broke down entirely when I met another car.

A front tire went flat in a suburb of Puebla and I drove on it for about half a mile. The spare was flat too, and it took the rest of the afternoon to get everything fixed. The casing I had driven on had two breaks in the sidewall. I didn't see how it could be repaired but the Mexican tire man put two boots and an inner tube in the thing and it stood up fine. He was quite a man, doing all this filthy work in the street in front of his mud house without a mechanical tire breaker or an impact wrench or any other kind of special tool.

We found a bakery and bought some rolls and left Puebla in the night. Dr. Symes took a blood-pressure cuff from his grip. He put it on his arm and pumped it up and I had to drive with one hand and hold the flashlight with the other so he could take the reading. He grunted but he didn't say whether it pleased him or not. He crawled over into the back seat and cleared things out of his way and said he was going to take a nap. He threw something out the window and I realized later it must have been my Zachary Taylor book.

"You might keep your eye peeled for a tan station wagon," he said. "I don't know what kind it is but it's a nice car. Texas plates. Dealer plates. Ski will be driving. He's a pale man with no chin. Tattoos on his forearms. He wears a little straw hat with one of those things in the hatband. I can't think of the word."

"Feather."

"No, I can think of feather. This is harder to think of. A brass thing."

"Who is this Ski?"

"Ted Brunowski. He's an old friend of mine. They call him Ski. You know how they call people Ski and Chief and Tex in the army."

"I've never been in the service."

"Did you have asthma?"

"No."

"What are you taking for it?"

"I don't have asthma."

"Have you tried the Chihuahua dogs in your bedroom at night? They say it works. I'm an orthodox physician but I'm also for whatever works. You might try it anyway."

"I have never had asthma."

"The slacker's friend. That's what they called it during the war. I certified many a one at a hundred and fifty bucks a throw."

"What do you want to see this fellow for?"

"It's a tan station wagon. He's a pale man in a straw hat and he has no more chin than a bird. Look for dealer plates. Ski has never been a car dealer but he always has dealer plates. He's not a Mason either but when he shakes your hand he does something with his thumb. He knows how to give the Masonic sign of distress too. He would never show me how to do it. Do you understand what I'm telling you?"

"I understand what you've said so far. Do you want to talk to him or what?"

"Just let me know if you see him."

"Is there some possibility of trouble?"

"There's every possibility."

"You didn't say anything about this."

"Get Ski out of sorts and he'll crack your bones. He'll smack you right in the snout, the foremost part of the body.

He'll knock you white-eyed on the least provocation. He'll teach you a lesson you won't soon forget."

"You should have said something about this."

"He kicked a merchant seaman to death down on the ship channel. He was trying to get a line on the Blackie Steadman mob, just trying to do his job, you see, and the chap didn't want to help him."

"You should have told me about all this."

"Blackie was hiring these merchant seamen to do his killings for him. He would hire one of those boys to do the job on the night before he shipped out and by the time the body was found the killer would be in some place like Poland. But Ski got wise to their game."

"What does he want you for?"

"He made short work of that sailor. Ski's all business. He's tough. He's stout. I'm not talking about these puffy muscles from the gymnasium either, I'm talking about hard thick arms like bodark posts. You'd do better to leave him alone."

All this time the doctor was squirming around in the back trying to arrange himself comfortably on the seat. He made the car rock. I was afraid he would bump the door latch and fall out of the car. He hummed and snuffled. He sang one verse of "My Happiness" over and over again, and then, with a church quaver, "He's the Lily of the Valley, the bright and morning star."

I tuned him out. After a while he slept. I roared through the dark mountains, descending mostly, and I thought I would never reach the bottom. I checked the mirror over and over again and I examined every vehicle that passed us. There weren't many. The doctor had given me a tough job and now he was sleeping.

The guidebook advised against driving at night in Mexico but I figured that stuff was written for fools. I was leaning forward again and going at a headlong pace like an ant running home with something. The guidebook was right. It was a nightmare. Trucks with no taillights! Cows and donkeys and bicyclists in the middle of the road! A stalled bus on the crest of a hill! A pile of rocks coming up fast! An overturned truck and ten thousand oranges rolling down the road! I was trying to deal with all this and watch for Ski at the same time and I was furious at Dr. Symes for sleeping through it. I no longer cared whether he fell out or not.

Finally I woke him, although the worst was over by that time.

"What is it?" he said.

"I'm not looking for that station wagon anymore. I've got my hands full up here."

"What?"

"It's driving me crazy. I can't tell what color these cars are."

"What are you talking about?"

"I'm talking about Ski!"

"I wouldn't worry about Ski. Leon Vurro is the man he's looking for. Where did you know Ski?"

"I don't know Ski."

"Do you want me to drive for a while?"

"No, I don't."

"Where are we?"

"I don't know exactly. Out of the mountains anyway. We're near Veracruz somewhere."

I kept thinking I would pull over at some point and sleep until daylight but I couldn't find a place that looked just right. The Pemex stations were too noisy and busy. The doctor had me stop once on the highway so he could put some drops in his red eye. This was a slow and messy business. He flung his elbows out like a skeet shooter. I held the army flashlight for him. He said the drops were cold. While

I was at it, I checked the transmission fluid and there were a lot of little blue flashes playing around the engine where the spark-plug cables were cracked and arcing.

He napped again and then he started talking to me about Houston, which he pronounced "Yooston." I like to keep things straight and his movements had me confused. I had thought at first that he came to Mexico direct from Louisiana. Then it was California. Now it was Houston. Ski was from Houston and it was from that same city that the doctor had departed in haste for Mexico, or "Old Mexico" as he called it.

"Who is this Ski anyway?"

"He's an old friend of mine. I thought I told you that."

"Is he a crook?"

"He's a real-estate smarty. He makes money while he's sleeping. He used to be a policeman. He says he made more unassisted arrests than any other officer in the colorful history of Harris County. I can't vouch for that but I know he made plenty. I've known him for years. I used to play poker with him at the Rice Hotel. I gave distemper shots to his puppies. I removed a benign wart from his shoulder that was as big as a Stuart pecan. It looked like a little man's head, or a baby's head, like it might talk, or cry. I never charged him a dime. Ski has forgotten all that."

"Why did you tell me he was looking for you?"

"He almost caught me at Alvin. It was nip and tuck. Do you know the County Line Lounge between Arcadia and Alvin?"

"No."

"The Uncle Sam Muffler Shop?"

"No."

"Shoe City?"

"No."

"Well, it was right in there where I lost him. That traffic circle is where he tore his britches. I never saw him after that. He has no chin, you know."

"You told me that."

"Captain Hughes of the Rangers used to say that if they ever hanged old Ski they would have to put the rope under his nose."

"Why was he after you?"

"Leon Vurro is the man he really wants."

The highways of Mexico, I thought, must be teeming with American investigators. The doctor and I, neither of us very sinister, had met by chance and we were both being more or less pursued. What about all the others? I had seen some strange birds down here from the States. Creeps! Nuts! Crooks! Fruits! Liars! California dopers!

I tried not to show much interest in his story after the way he had dozed while I was telling mine. It didn't matter, because he paid no attention to other people anyway. He spoke conversational English to all the Mexicans along the way and never seemed to notice that they couldn't understand a word he said.

The story was hard to follow. He and a man named Leon Vurro had put out a tip sheet in Houston called the *Bayou Blue Sheet*. They booked a few bets too, and they handled a few layoff bets from smaller bookies, with Ski as a silent partner. They worked the national time zones to their advantage in some way that I couldn't understand. Ski had many other interests. He had political connections. No deal was too big or too small for him. He managed to get a contract to publish a directory called *Stouthearted Men*, which was to be a collection of photographs and capsule biographies of all the county supervisors in Texas. Or maybe it was the county clerks. Anyway, Ski and the county officers put up an initial sum of $6,500 for operating expenses. Dr. Symes and Leon Vurro gathered the materials for the book and did some work on the dummy makeup. They also sold advertisements for it. Then Leon Vurro disappeared with the money. That, at any rate, was the doctor's account.

"Leon's an ordinary son of a bitch," he said, "but I didn't think he was an out-and-out crook. He said he was tired. Tired! He was sleeping sixteen hours a day and going to the picture show every afternoon. I was the one who was tired, and hot too, but we could have finished that thing in another two weeks. Sooner than that if Leon had kept his wife out of it. She had to stick her nose into everything. She got the pictures all mixed up. She claimed she had been a trapeze artist with Sells-Floto. Told fortunes is more like it. Reader and Advisor is more like it. A bullwhip act is more like it. She looked like a gypsy to me. With that fat ass she would have broke the trapeze ropes. Gone through the net like a shot. We had to work fast, you see, because the pictures were turning green and curling up. I don't know how they got wet. There's a lot of mildew in Houston. You can bet I got tired of looking at those things. I wish you could have seen those faces, Speed. Prune Face and BB Eyes are not in it with those boys."

"You must think I'm a dope," I said. "You never intended to publish that book."

"No, it was a straight deal. Do you know the Moon Publishing Company?"

"No."

"They have offices in Palestine, Texas, and Muldrow, Oklahoma."

"I've never heard of it."

"It's a well-known outfit. They do job printing and they put out calendars and cookbooks and flying-saucer books and children's books, books on boating safety, all kinds of stuff. *A Boy's Life of Lyndon B. Johnson.* That's a Moon book. It was a straight enough deal."

"How much money did Leon Vurro get?"

"I don't know. Whatever was there, he cleaned it out. It's a shame too. We could have finished that thing in two weeks. We were already through the M's and that was half-way. More, really, because there wouldn't be many X's and Z's. You never know. Maybe Leon was right. You have to know when to lay 'em down. It was a weekend deal, you see. There's a lot of mischief on weekends and not just check-kiting either. Leon cleared out the account on Friday after-noon. I was in San Antonio trying to sell ads for that fool book. The word got out fast on Leon but it didn't get to me. It didn't reach the Alamo City. I got back in my room in Houston on Sunday night. I was staying at Jim's Modern Cabins out on Galveston Road. My cabin was dark and the window was open. You had to leave your windows open. Jim doesn't have air conditioning except in his own office. He's got a big window unit in his office that will rattle the walls. I walked by my front window and I could smell Ski's fruity breath. He has diabetes, you see. These young doctors tell everybody they have diabetes but Ski really has it. I knew he was waiting inside that cabin in the dark and I didn't know why. I left with hardly any delay and then it was nip and tuck in south Houston. I made it on down to Corpus and traded my car for that hippie bus at the first car lot that opened up. I knew I didn't have any business driving a car forty feet long but that was the only unit on the lot the fellow would trade even for. I thought it might make a nice little home on the road. Your top gospel singers all have private buses."

"Why would Ski be after you if Leon Vurro got the money?"

"Leon's wife was behind all that. Bella set that up. I never said she was dumb."

"How do you know all that stuff if you left town so fast? That part is not clear to me."

"You get a feel for these things."

"I don't see how you could get a feel for all the circumstances."

"I should never have tied up with Leon. People like that can do nothing but drag you down. He didn't know the first thing about meeting the public and he was never dressed properly. They'll bury that son of a bitch in his zipper jacket."

"How did you know, for instance, that Leon had cleaned out the bank account?"

"I always tried to help Leon and you see the thanks I got. I hired him to drive for me right after his rat died. He was with Murrell Brothers Shows at that time, exhibiting a fifty-pound rat from the sewers of Paris, France. Of course it didn't really weigh fifty pounds and it wasn't your true rat and it wasn't from Paris, France, either. It was some kind of animal from South America. Anyway, the thing died and I hired Leon to drive for me. I was selling birthstone rings and vibrating jowl straps from door to door and he would let me out at one end of the block and wait on me at the other end. He could handle that all right. That was just about his speed. I made a serious mistake when I promoted Leon to a higher level of responsibility."

I pressed the doctor with searching questions about the Houston blowout but I couldn't get any straight answers and so I gave it up.

Five

The sun came up out of the sea, or I should say the Bay of Campeche. The warm air seemed heavy and I had the fanciful notion that it was pressing against us and holding us back. I say "seemed" because I know as well as any professional pilot that warm air is less dense than cool air. I had forgotten about the baloney and cheese in the ice chest. We ate the marshmallows and rolls, and after the rolls got hard I threw them out to goats along the way.

In the town of Coatzacoalcos I double-parked on a narrow street in front of an auto supply store and bought two quarts of transmission fluid and a small can of solvent. This solvent was a patent medicine from the States that was supposed to cure sticking valves and noisy valve lifters. Dr. Symes was worried about the clicking noise. He wouldn't shut up about it.

Down the way I found a shady grove of palm trees just off the road. I got out my plastic funnel and red fluid and topped up the transmission. Then I read all the print on the solvent can. There were warnings about breathing the stuff and lengthy instructions as to its use. At the very bottom there was a hedging note in red that had caught my eye too late: "May take two cans." I poured half of it through the carburetor at a fast idle and emptied the rest into the crankcase. The clicking went on as before.

Dr. Symes said, "I can still hear it. I think you've made it worse. I think it's louder than it was."

"It hasn't had time to work yet."

"How long does it take?"

"It says about five minutes. It says it may take two cans."

"How many cans did you get?"

"One."

"Why didn't you get two?"

"I didn't know that at the time."

He took the empty can from me and studied it. He found the red note and pointed it out to me. "It says, 'May take two cans.' "

"I know what it says now."

"You should have known a car like this would need two cans."

"How was I to know that? I didn't have time to read all that stuff."

"We'll never get there!"

"Yes, we will."

"Never! We'll never make it! Look how little it is!" The size of the can was funny to him. He went into a laughing fit and then a coughing fit, which in turn triggered a sneezing fit.

"Half of the cars on the road are making this noise," I said. "It's not serious. The engine's not going to stop."

"One can! One can of this shit wouldn't fix a lawn mower and you expect it to fix a Buick! Fifty cans would be more like it! You chump! You said you'd take me to Mama and you don't even know where we are! You don't know your ass from first base! I never can get where I want to go because I'm always stuck with chumps like you! Rolling along! Oh, yes! Rolling along! Rolling on home to Mama!"

He sang these last words to a little tune.

I knew where we were all right. It was the doctor himself who had funny notions about geography. He thought we were driving along the Pacific Ocean, and he had the idea that a momentary lapse at the wheel, one wrong turn, would always lead to monstrous circular error, taking us back where we started. Maybe it had happened to him a lot.

We drove straight through without stopping anywhere to sleep. The road was closed on the direct route across southern Campeche and so we had to take the longer coastal road, which meant waiting for ferries and crossing on them in the night. It also meant that we had to go north up into Yucatán and then south again through Quintana Roo to the border town of Chetumal.

What these ferries crossed were the mouths of rivers along the Gulf, two rivers and a lagoon, I believe, or maybe the other way around, a long stretch of delta at any rate. Dr. Symes remained in the car and I strode the decks and took the air, although there was nothing to see in the darkness, nothing but the bow waves, curling and glassy. There was fog too, and once again I was denied the spectacle of the southern heavens.

I had told the doctor that the engine wasn't going to stop and then in the midday heat of Yucatán it did stop. He might have thrown one of his fits if we had not been in a village with people standing around watching us. He sulked instead. I thought the fuel filter was clogged, the little sintered bronze device in the side of the carburetor. I borrowed two pairs of pliers and got it out and rapped it and blew through it. That didn't help. A Mexican truck driver diagnosed the trouble as vapor lock. He draped a wet rag over the fuel pump to cool it down, to condense the vapor in the gas line. I had never seen that trick before but it worked and we were soon off again.

The road was flat and straight in this country and there was very little traffic. Visibility was good too. I decided to let the doctor drive for a bit while I took a short nap. We swapped seats. He was a better driver than I had any reason to expect. I've seen many worse. The steering slack didn't throw him at all. Still he had his own style and there was to be no sleeping with him at the wheel. He would hold the accelerator down for about four seconds and then let up on it. Then he would press it down again and let up on it again. That was the way he drove. I was rocking back and forth like one of those toy birds that drinks water from a glass.

I tried to read the Dix book. I couldn't seem to penetrate the man's message. The pages were brittle and the type was heavy and black and hard to read. There were tips on how to turn disadvantages into advantages and how to take insults and rebuffs in stride. The good salesman must make *one more call*, Dix said, before stopping for the day. That might be the big one! He said you must save your money but you must not be afraid to spend it either, and at the same time you must give no thought to money. A lot of his stuff was formulated in this way. You must do this and that, two contrary things, and you must also be careful to do neither. Dynamic tension! Avoid excessive blinking and wild eye movement, Dix said, when talking to prospects. Restrain your hands. Watch for openings, for the tiniest breaches. These were good enough tips in their way but I had been led to expect balls of fire. I became impatient with the thing. The doctor had deposited bits of gray snot on every page and these boogers were dried and crystallized.

"This car seems to be going sideways," he said to me.

The car wasn't going sideways and I didn't bother to answer him.

A little later he said, "This engine seems to be sucking air."

I let that go too. He began to talk about his youth, about his days as a medical student at Wooten Institute in New Orleans. I couldn't follow all that stuff and I tuned him out as best I could. He ended the long account by saying that Dr. Wooten "invented clamps."

"Medical clamps?" I idly inquired.

"No, just clamps. He invented the clamp."

"I don't understand that. What kind of clamp are you talking about?"

"Clamps! Clamps! That you hold two things together with! Can't you understand plain English?"

"Are you saying this man made the first clamp?"

"He got a patent on it. He invented the clamp."

"No, he didn't."

"Then who did?"

"I don't know."

"You don't know. And you don't know Smitty Wooten either but you want to tell me he didn't invent the clamp."

"He may have invented some special kind of clamp but he didn't invent *the clamp*. The principle of the clamp was probably known to the Sumerians. You can't go around saying this fellow from Louisiana invented the clamp."

"He was the finest diagnostician of our time. I suppose you deny that too."

"That's something else."

"No, go ahead. Attack him all you please. He's dead now and can't defend himself. Call him a liar and a bum. It's great sport for people who sit on the sidelines of life. They do the same thing with Dix. People who aren't fit to utter his name."

I didn't want to provoke another frenzy while he was driving, so I let the matter drop. There was very little traffic, as I say, in that desolate green scrubland, and no rivers and creeks at all, but he managed to find a narrow bridge and meet a cattle truck on it. As soon as the truck hove into view, a good half-mile away, the doctor began to make delicate speed adjustments so as to assure an encounter in the exact center of the bridge. We clipped a mirror off the truck and when we were well clear of the scene I took the wheel again.

Then one of the motor mounts snapped. The decayed rubber finally gave way. Strength of materials! With this support gone the least acceleration would throw the engine over to the right from the torque, and the fan blades would clatter against the shroud. I straightened out two coat hangers and fastened one end of the stiff wires to the exhaust manifold on the left side, and anchored the other ends to the frame member. This steadied the engine somewhat and kept it from jumping over so far. I thought it was a clever piece of work, even though I had burned my fingers on the manifold.

For a little car it had a lot of secrets. Another tire went flat near Chetumal, the left rear, and I almost twisted the lug bolts off before I figured out that they had left-hand threads. Far from being clever, I was slow and stupid! Of all the odd-sized tires on the car this one was the smallest, and when I got it off I saw molded in the rubber these words: "Property of U-Haul Co. Not to be sold." A trailer tire!

Dr. Symes waited in the shade of some bushes. My blistered fingers hurt and I was angry at myself and I was hot and dirty and thirsty. I asked him to bring me the water jug. He didn't answer and I spoke to him again, sharply. He just stared at me with his mouth open. His face was gray and he was breathing hard. One eye was closed, the red one. The old man was sick! No laughing fits here!

I took the grip and the water jug to him. He drank some chalky-looking medicine and almost gagged on it. He said he was dizzy. He didn't want to move for a few minutes. I drank the last of the tepid water in the jug and lay back in the shade. The sand was coarse and warm. I said I would take him to a doctor in Chetumal. He said, "No, it's just a spell. It'll pass. I'll be all right in a minute. It's not far to Mama's place, is it?"

"No, it's not far now."

He took off his long belt and this seemed to give him some relief. Then he took off his bow tie. He unchained the giant wallet from his clothes and handed it to me, along with his flashlight, and told me to see that his mother got these things, a Mrs. Nell Symes. I didn't like the sound of that. We sat there for a long time and said nothing.

The booted tire thumped all the way in to Chetumal, and then to the border crossing, which was a river just outside of town. The officer there on the Mexican end of the bridge paid no attention to my faulty papers but he didn't like the doctor, didn't want to touch him or brush up against him, this hollow-eyed old gringo with his mouth open, and he was determined not to let him leave Mexico without his bus. Dr. Symes's tourist card was clearly stamped *"Entro con Automóvil,"* as was mine, and if one enters Mexico with an *automóvil* then one must also leave with it.

I explained that the doctor's bus had broken down through no fault of his own and that he intended to return for it after a brief visit with his ailing mother in Belize. The officer said that anyone might tell such a story, which was true enough. The law was the law. Produce the bus. Dr. Symes offered the man a hundred pesos and the man studied the brown note for an instant and then shook his head; this was a serious matter and money could not settle it, certainly not a hundred pesos.

I took the doctor aside and suggested that he give the man five hundred pesos. He said, "No, that's too much."

"What are you going to do then?"

"I don't know, but I'm not giving that son of a bitch forty dollars."

I saw a red bus cross the bridge with only a brief inspection at each end. I told the doctor I would take him back to Chetumal. He could wait there until dark and catch a red bus to Belize. Then, very likely, there would be a different officer here at this post. The doctor would probably not be noticed and the bus ride would not be a long one. It was only another eighty miles or so to Belize.

He was wobbly and vague. He had heat staggers. I couldn't get any sense out of him. He had diarrhea too, and he was drinking paregoric from a little bottle. We drove back to Chetumal, the tire bumping.

He said, "Are you going to dump me, Speed?"

"You won't let me take you to a doctor."

"I never thought you would just throw me out."

"I'm not throwing you out. Listen to what I'm saying. You can take a bus across the border tonight. I'll see that you get on it. I'll follow the bus."

"I thought we had a deal."

"I don't know what you expect me to do. I can't force these people to let you out of the country."

"You said you'd take me to Belize. I thought it was a straight deal."

"I'm doing the best I can. You forget I have my own business to see to."

"That's hard, Speed. That's strong. I don't know you but I know that's not worthy of you."

"What you need is a doctor."

"I'll be all right if I can just get something cool to drink."

I parked on the waterfront in Chetumal and got him out of the car and walked him over to a dockside refreshment stand. We sat on folding metal chairs under a palm-thatched cabaña rig. He looked like a dead man. When the waitress came over, he rallied a little and tried to smile. He said, "Little lady, I want the biggest Co'-Cola you are permitted to serve." She was a pretty Indian girl with sharp black eyes. He tried to wink, and said, "They're getting these little girls out of Hollywood now." A man at the next table was eating a whole fresh pineapple with a knife. I ordered a pineapple for myself and a Coca *grande* for the doctor.

There was a rising wind. Small boats were chugging about in the bay. Vultures walked boldly along the dock like domestic turkeys. The doctor drank three Cokes and asked for his wallet back. I gave it to him.

"What happened to my flashlight?"

"It's in the car."

He saw something shiny and leaned over and scratched at it, trying to pick it up.

I said, "That's a nailhead."

"I knew it wasn't a dime. I just wanted to see what it was."

"I've got to get the spare fixed and I need to see about the bus. I want you to wait right here and don't go wandering off."

"I'm not riding any bus."

"What are you going to do then?"

"I'm not going off a cliff in a Mexican bus."

His old carcass was very dear to him.

We sat in silence for a while. I went to the car and got my Esso map of British Honduras. It was a beautiful blue map with hardly any roads to clutter it up. Just down the bay from here was a coastal village in British Honduras called Corozal. Why couldn't the border be bypassed by water? There were plenty of boats available. It wouldn't be much of a trip—a matter of a few miles.

I proposed this plan to the doctor and showed him how things lay on the map. To keep it from blowing away, I had to anchor the corners with bottles. Over and over again I explained the scheme to him but he couldn't take it in. "Do what, Speed?" he would say. He was fading again.

Most of the boats were now coming in. I walked along the dock and talked to the owners, trying to explain and sell the plan to them in my feeble Spanish. I got nowhere. They wanted no part of it. There was too much wind and the water was too rough and it would soon be dark. Maybe tomorrow, they said, or the next day. I put the map back in the car and returned to the table. Dr. Symes was drinking yet another Coke. The girl wanted her money and he was trying to match her for it, double or nothing. He had a ready line of patter for all cashiers, the idea being to confuse them so that they might make an error in his favor.

"It's no use," I said. "The wind is too high. It's too dangerous. It was a bad plan anyway. You'll have to ride the red bus and that's all there is to it."

"The wind?" he said.

Newspapers were being whipped against our legs and the tablecloth was snapping and donkeys were leaning against buildings and the heavy traffic light that hung over the intersection was standing about thirty degrees off vertical, and into the teeth of this gale he asked me that question.

"A bus. I'm going to put you on a bus. It's the only way."

"Not a bus, no."

"Do you want to see your mother or do you want to stay here?"

"Mama?"

"She's waiting for you just down the road. You can be there in no time. The bus is safe, I tell you. This is flat country. There are no mountains between here and Belize, not one. It's a coastal plain. I'll see that you get there. I'll drive right along behind the bus."

"Send me over the mountains in a bus, is that it? That's your answer for everything. Did you make sure it has no brakes? I don't even know the name of this town. I wanted to go to Belize and you land us in this place instead. Why do we keep hanging around here anyway?"

"You can be in Belize in just a few hours if you'll listen to me and do what I say. Do you understand what I'm telling you?"

In my desperation I had fallen into the doctor's habits of speech. He must have spent half his life shouting that hopeless question. I thought of hiring an ambulance. Surely the border guards would not interfere with a mercy dash. But wouldn't it be very expensive?

Someone pinched me on the fleshy part of my upper arm and I jumped. An Indian boy about seventeen years old was standing behind me. "Corozal?" he said. He took me over to the slip where his wooden boat was tied up, a slender homemade craft with an old-fashioned four-cycle outboard engine on the stern. It was about a six-horse engine, with a high profile. I asked about life preservers. *No hay*, he said. I indicated that the water was rough and getting rougher all the time. He shrugged it off as inconsequential. We quickly reached an agreement.

The doctor was too weak and confused to resist. I took his wallet again for safekeeping and we loaded him into the boat. I gave the boy a ten-dollar bill and promised him a twenty—a balloon payment to encourage compliance—upon delivery of the old man in Corozal. The boy jerked the rope many times before the engine started. Then he pushed off and I, with great misgivings, watched them leave, the little boat battering sluggishly through the whitecaps. The sun was going down. The doctor had lied to me about his funds. That wallet was packed with twenties and fifties.

I drove back to the border crossing and had no trouble getting out of Mexico. At the other end of the bridge I had to deal with a British Honduras officer. He was a dapper

Negro in shorts and high stockings and Sam Browne belt. I had shed my coat long ago but I was still wearing my tie. I was filthy and I needed a shave.

He asked my occupation. I said I was a businessman. He pointed out that my spare tire was flat. I thanked him. Was I a doctor? What was I doing with a doctor's bag? What was the silverware for? I had no very good answers for him. He poked into everything, even the ice chest. The ice had melted days ago and the cheese and baloney were spoiled. The water was brown from the rusting rims of the beer cans. At the bottom of this mess my Colt Cobra was washing about in the plastic bag. I had forgotten all about it. The old man had made me neglect my business! The officer wiped the pistol dry with a handkerchief and stuck it in his hip pocket. He shook his finger at me but said nothing. He was keeping it for himself.

He asked if I planned to sell the Buick and I said no. He wrote his name and address for me on the back of a card advertising the Fair Play Hotel in Belize and said he would be happy to handle the sale. I took the card and told him I would keep it in mind. He said I didn't look like much of a businessman to him. I described my Torino and asked about Norma and Dupree and the dog—and was I knocked for a loop when this bird said he remembered them. He remembered the car and the pretty girl and yes, the red dog, and the fellow with the glasses who was driving; he remembered him very well.

"Played that 'Sweet Lorraine' on the mouth harp."

"No, that wouldn't be him. That wouldn't be Dupree."

"Yes, and 'Twilight Time' too."

I couldn't believe my ears. Was it possible that some identical people had passed through here with a chow dog in a blue Torino? An antimatter Dupree playing tunes on a mouth organ! A young Meigs! The doctor had told me that I could expect the same old stuff down here but this didn't sound like the same old stuff to me.

I asked about the road to Belize. Was it paved? Should I chance it with no spare tire? He said it was an excellent road, much better than anything I had seen in Mexico. And not only that, but I would now be able to get some good gasoline for a change. The Mexican petrol was inferior stuff, he said, and it smelled funny. Here it had the proper smell.

There was a T-head pier in Corozal and I stood at the end of it and waited anxiously in the dark. The wind had dropped off somewhat. Now it was cool. I supposed there was some colorful local name for it, for this particular kind of wind. I was just fifteen degrees or so above the equator and I was at sea level and yet I was chilly. A cool snap like this on the Louisiana island and the doctor would have a thousand coughing chimps on his hands. I could make out a few stars through the drifting clouds but not the Southern Cross.

I began to worry more and more about that little boat in open water at night. It wasn't the open sea but it was a big bay, big enough for trouble. Why had I suggested this? It would all be my fault, the sea disaster. Criminal folly! The boat would be swamped and the doctor, a nuisance to the end, would flail away in the water and take the Indian boy down with him.

A Spanish-looking man joined me at the edge of the pier. He was barefooted, his trouser legs rolled up, and he was pushing a bicycle. He parked the bike and looked out at the water, his hands in his pockets, a brooding figure. I didn't want to intrude on his thoughts but when the wind blew his bike over I thought it would then be all right to speak, the clatter having broken his reverie. I said, "*Mucho viento.*"

He nodded and picked up his bike and left. Much wind. What a remark! No wonder everybody took foreigners for dopes.

I heard the engine popping and then I saw the boat low in the water. Choppy waves were breaking against it. The boy was angry because the doctor had vomited marshmallows and Coke in his boat. The old man was wet and only semiconscious. We laid him out on the pier and let him drain for a minute. It was like trying to lug a wet mattress. I gave the boy an extra ten dollars for his trouble. He helped me get the doctor into the car and then he fearlessly took to the dark water again.

Part of the road to Belize was broken pavement and the rest was washboard gravel. Great flat slabs of concrete had been wrenched out of place as though from an earthquake. What a road! Time after time the Buick's weak coil springs bottomed out, and I mean dead bottom. When we came bounding back up on the return phase, I feared that something would tear loose, some suspension component. I worried about the tires too. The gravel part was only a little better. I tried to find a speed at which we could skim along on the crests of the corrugations but with no luck. We skittered all over the roadbed. The doctor groaned in the back seat. I too was beginning to fade. My head throbbed and I took some more of the bitter orange pills.

Six

It was late when we reached Belize and I didn't feel like asking directions and floundering around in a strange place. It wasn't a big town but the streets were narrow and dark and irregular. I found a taxicab at a Shell station and I asked the Negro driver if he knew a Mrs. Nell Symes, who had a church here. It took him a while to puzzle it out. Did I mean "Meemaw?" Well, I didn't know, but I hired him to go to Meemaw's anyway and I trailed along behind in the Buick.

The church was a converted dwelling house, a white frame structure of two stories. Some of the windows had fixed wooden louvers and some had shutters that folded back. The roof was galvanized sheet iron. It was just the kind of old house that needed the Midgestone treatment.

A wooden sign beside the door said:

Unity Tabernacle
" Whosoever will "

The house was dark and I rapped on the door for a long time before I roused anyone. I heard them coming down the stairs very slowly. The door opened and two old ladies looked out at me. One was in a flannel bathrobe and the other one was wearing a red sweater. The one in the sweater had wisps of pink hair on her scalp. It was a bright chemical pink like that of a dyed Easter chick. I could see at once that the other one was Dr. Symes's mother. She had the same raccoon eyes. She used an aluminum walking stick but she didn't appear to be much more decrepit than the doctor himself.

"Mrs. Symes?"

"Yes?"

"I have your son out here in the car."

"What's that you say?"

"Dr. Symes. He's out here in the car."

"Reo. My word."

"He's sick."

"Who are you?"

"My name is Ray Midge. He rode down from Mexico with me."

"Are you with the postal authorities?"

"No, ma'am."

"We weren't even thinking about Reo, were we, Melba?"

The other lady said, "*I* sure wasn't. I was thinking about a snack."

Mrs. Symes turned back to me. "Has he got some old floozie with him?"

"No, ma'am, he's by himself."

"You say he's in the car?"

"Yes."

"Why is he staying in the car? Why doesn't he get out of the car?"

"He's sick."

"Go see if it's really him, Melba."

Melba came out to the car. I opened a door so the dome light would come on. She studied the rumpled figure in the back seat. "It's Reo all right," she said. "He's asleep. He's lost weight. His clothes are smoking. He's wearing those same old white pants he had on last time. I didn't know pants lasted that long."

Mrs. Symes said, "He may have several pair, all identical. Some men do that with socks."

"I think these are the same pants."

"What about his flashlight?"

"I don't see it."

"It's in there somewhere," I said.

Neither of the ladies was able to help me unload the doctor. I couldn't carry him but I managed to drag him inside, where I laid him out on a church pew. He was limp and his flesh was cool and his clothes were indeed steaming. Then I went back and got his grip. Mrs. Symes was not much concerned about his condition. She seemed to think he was drunk.

"That poison has to be metabolized," she said. "You can't hurry it along."

I said, "He's not drunk, ma'am, he's sick. I believe he needs a doctor."

Melba said, "We don't use doctors."

"You're lucky to have good health."

"Our health is not particularly good. We just don't go to doctors."

The downstairs part was a chapel and they lived upstairs. Mrs. Symes asked if I would like some supper. I don't like to eat or sleep or go to the bathroom in other people's homes but this was an emergency. I needed food and I kept hanging about in hopes of just such an invitation. I followed them up the stairs.

The electric lights flickered on and off and then failed altogether. I sat at the kitchen table in the soft yellow glow of a kerosene lamp. Mrs. Symes gave me some cold chicken and some warmed-over rice and gravy and biscuits. There was a bowl of stewed tomatoes too. What a meal! I was so hungry I was trembling and I made a pig of myself. Melba joined me and fell to on a second supper. She ate heartily for a crone, sighing and cooing between bites and jiggling one leg up and down, making the floor shake. She ate fast and her eyes bulged from inner pressures and delight. This remarkable lady had psychic gifts and she had not slept for three years, or so they told me. She sat up in a chair every night in the dark drinking coffee.

Mrs. Symes asked me a lot of personal questions. She and Melba, unlike the doctor, found my mission romantic, and they pressed for details. I was dizzy and tired and not at all in the mood for a truth session but I didn't see how I could leave abruptly after eating their food. Melba asked to see a picture of Norma. I didn't have one. Some detective! Some husband! They could tell me nothing about Mr. Dupree's farm. They had never heard the name. Their church work was concerned entirely with Negro children, they said, and I gathered that they had little to do with the other white people in the country. They did know some Mennonite farmers, from whom they bought milk, and they seemed to have an uneasy professional acquaintance with an Episcopal missionary whom they called "Father Jackie." Mrs. Symes was suspicious of the doctor's unexpected arrival.

She said, "Do you know the purpose of his visit?"

"He said he was worried about your health."

"What else did he say?"

"He said you had a church here."

"What else?"

"That's about all."

"How would you characterize his mood? Generally speaking."

"I would say it varied according to circumstances. He was not in one mood the whole time."

"I mean his feeling about coming here. Was it one of apprehension? Resignation?"

"I can't say it was either one of those. I don't really know him well enough to answer your question, Mrs. Symes. To say whether his mood departed from normal in any way."

"Is that his automobile out there?"

"No, ma'am. He has a bus but it broke down on him in Mexico."

"A bus?"

"It's an old school bus. It's fixed up so you can sleep in it and cook in it."

"Did you hear that, Melba? Reo has been living in a school bus."

"A school bus?"

"That's what Mr. Midge here says."

"I didn't know you could do that."

"I didn't either. I wonder how he gets his mail."

"He doesn't live in the bus all the time," I said. "It's the kind of thing you take trips in, like a trailer."

"I'll bet Reo talked your head off."

"Well, he didn't talk so much tonight. He's been feeling bad."

"He didn't talk at all until he was six years old. He was a strange child. Otho thought he was simple. What did he tell you about Jean's Island?"

"He said he had some plans for developing it."

"Did he say he owned it?"

"No, he didn't say that. He said you owned it."

"That island was dedicated as a bird sanctuary years ago."

"I see."

"How can you *develop* a place, as you put it, if it's already been dedicated?"

"Well, I don't know. I guess you can't."

"If I turned it over to Reo, the bulldozers would be there tomorrow morning. It would be the biggest mess you ever saw. Some people just love to cut trees and the poor whites are the worst about it. I don't know where Reo gets that streak. Man is the most destructive creature there is, Mr. Midge."

Melba said, "Except for goats. Look at Greece."

"I wouldn't mind letting Reo have the place if he would live on it and farm it and behave himself, but he won't do that. I know him too well. The first thing you know, Marvel Clark or some other floozie would get her hands on it. I know Marvel too well and she's got enough of my stuff as it is. But she will never get her hands on that land as long as I have anything to say about it."

I said, "Do you think I should go downstairs and check on him?"

"He'll be all right. That poison has to be worked out through the breath. What did he tell you about his arthritis clinic in Ferriday?"

"I don't believe he mentioned that."

"Did he tell you about his Gifts for Grads?"

"Gifts for Dads?"

"Gifts for *Grads*. It was a mail-order scheme. He was advertising expensive watches at bargain prices in all kinds of sleazy magazines. People would send him money but he wouldn't send them any watches. A postal inspector came all the way down here from Washington, D.C., looking for him. He said Reo was going all over the country making fraudulent representations and calling himself Ralph Moore and Newton Wilcox."

"Dr. Symes didn't say anything about Gifts for Grads."

"Is that woman Sybil still living with him?"

"I just don't know about that. He was by himself when I met him in Mexico."

"Good riddance then. He brought an old hussy named Sybil with him the last time. She had great big bushy eyebrows like a man. She and Reo were trying to open up a restaurant somewhere in California and they wanted me to put up the money for it. As if I had any money. Reo tells everybody I have money."

Melba said, "No, it was a singing school. Reo wanted to open a singing school."

"The singing school was an entirely different thing, Melba. This was a restaurant they were talking about. Little Bit of Austria. Sybil was going to sing some kind of foreign songs to the customers while they were eating. She said she was a night-club singer, and a dancer too. She planned to dance all around people's tables while they were trying to eat. I thought these night clubs had beautiful young girls to do that kind of thing but Sybil was almost as old as Reo."

"Older," said Melba. "Don't you remember her arms?"

"They left in the middle of the night. I remember that. Just picked up and left without a word."

"Sybil didn't know one end of a piano keyboard from the other."

"She wore white shiny boots and backless dresses."

"But she didn't wear a girdle."

"She wore hardly anything when she was sunning herself back there in the yard."

"Her shameful parts were covered."

"That goes without saying, Melba. It wasn't necessary for you to say that and make us all think about it."

"Dr. Symes didn't say anything about Sybil to me."

"No, I don't suppose he did. Did he tell you about the hearing-aid frauds of 1949?"

"No, ma'am."

"No, I don't suppose he did. The shame and scandal killed Otho just as sure as we're sitting here. Reo lost his medical license and he's been a sharper and a tramp ever since. My own son, who took an oath to do no harm."

I didn't know who Otho was but it was hard to believe that any person in Louisiana had ever keeled over from fraud shock. I tried to think about that dramatic scene and then Melba put her face in mine and started talking to me. Both ladies were talking to me at the same time.

Melba said that her first husband had abandoned her in Ferriday and that her second husband, a handsome barber who didn't believe in life insurance, had dropped dead in New Orleans at the age of forty-four. After that, she made her own way, giving piano lessons and selling foundation garments. She now received a tiny green Social Security check and that was her entire income. Five dollars of it went each month to Gamma chapter of some music teachers' sorority. She didn't remember much about the first husband but she thought often of the opinionated barber husband, idle in his shop in the quiet 1940 New Orleans sunlight, watching the door for customers and searching through the *Times-Picayune* over and over again for unread morsels.

Mrs. Symes raised her voice. "I wish you would hush for a minute, Melba. I've heard all that stuff a thousand times. I'm trying to ask a question. It looks like I could ask one question in my own home."

Melba didn't stop talking but I turned my head a bit toward Mrs. Symes.

She said, "What I'm trying to find out is this. When you are at your home in Arkansas, Mr. Midge, do you get much mail?"

"I don't follow."

"Cards, letters. First-class matter."

"Not much, no, ma'am."

"Same here. I'm not counting all those absurd letters from Reo. Are you a witnessing Christian?"

"I attend church when I can."

"Do you pray every night for all the little babies in Little Rock?"

"No, ma'am, I don't."

"What kind of Christian do you call yourself?"

"I attend church when I can."

"Cards on the table, Mr. Midge."

"Well, I think I have a religious nature. I sometimes find it hard to determine God's will."

"Inconvenient, you mean."

"That too, yes."

"What does it take to keep you from attending church?"

"I go when I can."

"A light rain?"

"I go when I can."

"This 'religious nature' business reminds me of Reo, your man of science. He'll try to tell you that God is out there in the trees and grass somewhere. Some kind of *force*. That's pretty thin stuff if you ask me. And Father Jackie is not much better. He says God is a perfect sphere. A ball, if you will."

"There are many different opinions on the subject."

"Did you suppose I didn't know that?"

"No, ma'am."

"What about Heaven and Hell. Do you believe those places exist?"

"That's a hard one."

"Not for me. How about you, Melba?"

"I would call it an easy one."

"Well, I don't know. I wouldn't be surprised either way. I try not to think about it. It's just so odd to think that people are walking around in Heaven and Hell."

"Yes, but it's odd to find ourselves walking around here too, isn't it?"

"That's true, Mrs. Symes."

"All the children call me Meemaw. Why don't you do like they do and call me Meemaw?"

"Well. All right."

"Have you read the Bible?"

"I've read some of it."

"Do you go through your Bible looking for discrepancies?"

"No, ma'am."

"That's not the way to read it. I have a little test I like to give to people like you who claim to be Bible scholars. Do you mind taking a little test for me?"

"Is it a written test?"

"No, it's just one question."

"I don't mind taking your test, Meemaw, but there is a misunderstanding here. You asked me if I had read the Bible and I said I had read some of it. I did not say I was a Bible scholar."

"We'll soon know, one way or the other. All right, the wedding feast at Cana. John 2. Jesus turned six pots of water into six pots of so-called wine. His first miracle. His mother was there. Now do you believe that was alcoholic wine in those pots or unfermented grape juice?"

"What does the Bible say?"

Melba said, "The Bible just says wine. It says good wine."

"Then that's what I say. I say wine."

Mrs. Symes said, "It's your notion then that Jesus was a bootlegger?"

"No, it's not."

"He was no more a bootlegger than I am. That so-called wine was nothing more than fresh and wholesome grape juice. The word is translated wrong."

"I didn't know that."

"Do you claim to know the meaning of every word in the Greek language?"

"No, I don't. I don't know one word of the Greek language."

"Then why should your opinion be worth anything in a matter like this? Father Jackie is bad enough and you don't even know as much as he does."

Melba said, "Let's see what he knows about Swedenborg."

"He won't know anything about Swedenborg."

"It won't hurt to see, will it?"

"Go ahead and ask him then."

"What do you know about a man named Emanuel Swedenborg, Mr. Midge?"

"I don't know anything about him."

"He personally *visited* Heaven and Hell and returned to write an astonishing book about his experiences. Now what do you think of that?"

"I don't know what to think."

Mrs. Symes said, "Have you read Mrs. Eddy's books?"

"No, ma'am."

"What is your work in this world?"

"I don't know what it is yet. I'm back in school now."

"It's getting pretty late in the day for you to have so few interests and convictions. How old are you, Mr. Midge?"

"I'm twenty-six."

"Later than I thought. Think about this. All the little animals of your youth are long dead."

Melba said, "Except for turtles."

Something small and hard, possibly a nut, dropped on the tin roof and we waited in silence for another one but it didn't come. I asked directions to the Fair Play Hotel, and Meemaw, as I now addressed her, told me I would be more comfortable at the Fort George or the Bellevue. I was agreeable and didn't pursue the matter, but the man at the border had given me a card for the Fair Play and it was there I meant to stay. The lights came back on and in a very few minutes Melba's electric coffeepot began to bubble and make respiratory noises like some infernal hospital machine. Mrs. Symes looked me over closely in the light.

"I know you'll excuse a personal reference, Mr. Midge. Are you handicapped?"

"I don't follow."

She lifted one of my trouser legs an inch or so with the tip of her aluminum cane. "Your feet, I mean. They look odd the way you have them splayed out. They look like artificial feet."

"My feet are all right. These are new shoes. Perhaps that accounts for their unnatural fullness."

"No, it's not that, it's the way you have them turned out. Now there, that's better. You remind me a whole lot of Otho. He never could get the hang of things."

"I've heard you mention Otho two or three times but I don't know who he is."

"Otho Symes, of course. He was my husband. He never could get the hang of things but he was just as good as gold."

Melba said, "He was a nervous little man. I was afraid to say boo to him."

"He wasn't nervous until he had his operation."

"He was nervous before his operation and after his operation both."

"He wasn't nervous until they put that thing in his neck, Melba. I ought to know."

"You ought to but you don't. This boy doesn't want to hear any more about Otho and I don't either. I want to find out something about his wife and why she left him. He hasn't told us that."

"I don't know why she left."

"You must have some idea."

"No, I was very much surprised."

Mrs. Symes said, "Are you trying to tell us that you and your wife were on cordial terms?"

"We got along all right."

"Never a harsh word?"

"She called me a pill sometimes."

"A pill, eh."

"That was her mother's word but Norma took it up."

"They were both calling you a pill to your face?"

"Yes. Not, you know, day and night."

"Did she open your mail and read it?"

"No, ma'am. That is, I don't think she did."

Melba put her rouged face in mine again and said, "One moment, Mr. Midge. You told us just a while ago that you didn't get any mail. Now you're talking about people intercepting your mail. Which is it? Do you get any mail or not?"

"I said I didn't get much mail. I get some."

Mrs. Symes said, "I'll bet the little girl's kitchen was just filthy all the time."

"No, it wasn't either."

"Can she cook anything that's fit to eat?"

"She's a pretty good cook."

"Can she make her own little skirts and jumpers?"

"I don't think so. I've never seen her sewing anything."

"What about raisins? Does she like raisins?"

"I've never seen her eating any raisins."

"I'll bet she likes yellow cake with hot lemon sauce poured over it."

"I believe she does, yes. I do too."

"What about chocolate cake?"

"She likes all kinds of cake."

"All right then, tell me this. When she's eating chocolate cake late at night, does she also drink sweet milk from a quart bottle till it runs from the corners of her mouth?"

"I've never seen her do that."

"That's a picture I have of gluttony."

"I don't know how you got the idea that Norma is a glutton, Meemaw. The fact is, she eats very little. She's very particular about what she eats and how she eats it."

"A clean feeder then, according to you."

"Very clean."

"Melba used to do that very thing late at night. That cake thing with the milk."

"No, I didn't."

"Yes, you did."

"There never was a bigger lie. I don't know why you keep telling people that."

"I know what I know, Melba."

The lights went off again. I thanked them for the supper and the hospitality and got up to leave. Melba asked me to wait a minute. She had the burning lamp in her hand and she had turned the wick up a notch or two for a bright flame. Then she went to a dark corner and struck a pose there with the lamp, holding it above her head. She said, "Now I just wonder if you two can guess who I am."

Mrs. Symes said, "I know. The Statue of Liberty. That's easy."

"No."

"Florence Nightingale then."

"No."

"You're changing it every time I guess it."

"I'm the Light of the World."

"No, you're not, you're just silly. You're so silly, Melba, it's pitiful. It's downright embarrassing to me when we have guests."

This time I did leave but before I got all the way down the stairs Mrs. Symes called after me. She asked if I thought there was any chance that Reo was going about doing good by stealth. It wouldn't have hurt me to say yes, there was an excellent chance of that, but I said I just didn't know. She asked if I had any Lipton's dried soups in the car, or a fall and winter Sears catalogue. Of course I didn't and I felt bad because I had nothing like that to give them, even though they had roughed me up a little with their hard questions.

Seven

I left Dr. Symes steaming in the dark chapel and made my way back to the arched bridge over the little river that ran through Belize. I had guessed, correctly, that this bridge was the center of town. Two or three blocks upstream I found the Fair Play Hotel, which was a white frame house like the tabernacle. I parked the car in front and again went through the unpleasant business of waking people up.

A thin Negro woman was the manager of the place. She was surly, as anyone might have been in the circumstances, but I could sense too a general ill-feeling for me and my kind. She woke a small Negro boy named Webster Spooner, who slept in a box in the foyer. It was a pretty good wooden box with bedding in it. I knew his name because he had written it on a piece of paper and taped it to his box. At the foot of his makeshift bed there was a tomato plant growing in an old Texaco grease bucket.

I wrote and addressed a brief message to my father asking him to wire me $250. The woman said she would have Webster Spooner attend to it when the cable office opened in the morning. I gave her a five-dollar bill and a few ten-peso notes—all the money in my pocket—and she pinned it to the message and put it away in a shoe box.

Would my car be safe on the street? It might be or it might not be, she said, but in any case there was no enclosed parking. I thought of removing the cable from the coil to the distributor so as to foil thieves but I was too weary to fool with that car anymore. The woman, whose name was Ruth, went back to bed. Webster Spooner carried my bag upstairs and showed me to my room. He said he would keep an eye on the car. I didn't see how he was going to do that from his box. I knew he was a sound sleeper. The woman Ruth had almost had to kill him to get him awake.

My room overlooked the black water of the little river or creek. I opened a window and I could smell it. One drop of that stinking water would mean instant death! As soon as I arrive at any destination, my first thoughts are always of departure and how it may be most quickly arranged, but it was not so in this case. Fatigue perhaps. I settled in. I went to bed and stayed there for two days.

Twice a day Webster Spooner came by and took my order for a bowl of sliced bananas and a small can of Pet milk. I had the same thing each time and he carefully wrote it down each time in his notebook.

Webster said he had other jobs. He washed police cars and he sold newspapers and greeting cards. The tomato plant was one of his projects. He sometimes referred to the woman Ruth as his "ahntee," which is to say his aunt, but I got the impression that they were not actually related. He said she took half his earnings.

He always had a fresh question for me when he caught me awake. Could a Dodge Coronet outrun a Mercury Montego? How did you keep score in the game of bowling? They got very few American guests here at the Fair Play, he said, and the ones they did get drove sorry-looking cars like mine or else they were hippies with dirty feet and no cars at all. Ruth didn't like the Americans but he, Webster, rather liked them, even if they did keep him hopping with their endless demands for ice and light bulbs and towels and flyswatters. Even the wretched hippies expected service. It was in the blood.

I discovered later that Ruth called me "Turco" and "the Turk" because of my small pointed teeth and my small owl beak and my small gray eyes, mere slits but prodigies of light-gathering and resolving power. What put it into her head that these were distinctive Turkish features, I had no way of knowing, nor did I know why she should be down on the Turks too, but there it was. "See what the Turk wants now," she would say to Webster, and, "Is Turco still in bed?"

I had him get me some envelopes and an assortment of colorful stamps and I addressed some British Honduras covers to myself in Little Rock. I slept off and on and I had a recurring dream. I read the Dix book, or tried to. My mind wandered, even on the strong passages that the doctor had underlined. I read a guidebook. The writer said the people of this country were "proud," which usually means "barely human" in the special lingo of those things. But wasn't Ruth proud? The very word for her. I calculated the trip expenses. In the bathroom down the hall I found a paperback book with no covers and took it back to bed with me. I read almost two pages before I realized it was fiction, and worse, a story set in the future. Some bird was calling up for a "helicab." I dropped it on the floor, which is to say I didn't fling it across the room, although I could tell it had been flung many times. I listened to the radio that was always playing in the next room. That is, I listened to the English portions. There were alternate hours of broadcasting in English and Spanish.

I paid particular attention to a California evangelist who came on each morning at nine. I looked forward to this program. Was the man a fraud? He was very persuasive and yet there was a Satanic note in his cleverness. I couldn't work it out.

The headboard of the bed was covered with some cheap white synthetic material—in this land of mahogany—and

the name KARL was carved into it in block letters. Each time
I woke up, I was confused and then I would see that KARL
and get my bearings. I would think about Karl for a few
minutes. He had thought it a good thing to leave his name
here but, ever wary, not his full name. I wondered if he
might be in the next room. With his knife and radio he might
be on the move constantly, like J. S. Dix.

The recurring dream made me sweat and writhe in the
damp bedclothes. I couldn't trace it back to any event in my
waking life, so to speak. I relate this dream, knowing it is ill-
mannered to do so, because of its anomalous character. Most
of my dreams were paltry, lifeless things. They had to do
with geometric figures or levitation. My body would seem to
float up from the bed, but not far, a foot or so. There was no
question of flying. In this Belize dream there were other
people. I was sitting at a low coffee table across from an
intelligent, well-dressed woman who wanted to "have it
out." She had a fat son named Travis who was about seven
years old. This boy was encouraged by his mom to have
opinions and make pert remarks. The three of us were always seated around the coffee table on the stylish woman's
pneumatic furniture. She drove home telling points in some
dim quarrel while the boy Travis chirped out show-business
quips.

"Be my guest!" he would chirp, and, "Oh boy, that's the
story of my life!" and, "Yeah, but what do you do for an
encore!" and, "Hey, don't knock it if you ain't tried it!" and,
"How's that for openers?" and, "You bragging or complain-
ing!" and, "Welcome to the club, Ray! Ha ha ha ha ha ha ha
ha." I had to sit there and take it on the chin from both
the woman and Travis.

Ruth sent for me early on the third day. I took a bath and
shaved and put on some clean clothes. My legs were shaky
as I went down the stairs. Ruth wanted her room money and

her Pet milk money. I had heard nothing from Little Rock. Norma had abandoned me, and now, it seemed, my father as well. I tried to figure out how many days I had been gone. It was just possible that he had not yet returned from the Alabama bass rodeo. Flinging his plastic worm all over the lake! His Lucky 13! His long-tailed jigs! He caught fish that weighed three pounds and he talked about them "fighting." Killer bass! It was possible too that he was tired of fooling with me, as with Mr. Dupree and Guy. Weaned at twenty-six! Places like Idaho had governors my age. The great Humboldt was exploring the Orinoco at my age instead of sniveling about a money order.

Ruth was hard to deal with. Her Creole speech was hard to understand. She wouldn't look at me when I spoke to her and she wouldn't answer me or give any sign of acknowledgment. I was thus forced to repeat myself and then she would say, "I heard you the first time." But if I didn't repeat myself we would just stand there in a silent and uneasy impasse.

I offered to let her hold some bonds until my money arrived. She wanted cash and she wanted it at that moment. I didn't know what to say to her, how to keep talking in the assertive Dix manner. She glowered and looked past me. A crackpot like Karl had the run of the place but my E bonds were no good. That was her idea of fair play. Webster Spooner was listening to all this. He was reclining in his box and working in his notebook but he was listening too.

"He have money in that long notecase," he said. "Big money."

It was true. I still had the doctor's wallet and I had forgotten about it. I went back to the room and got it from the suitcase. I paid Ruth twenty American dollars and I thought this would put me on a new footing with her, but it seemed to make her even more disagreeable. I asked her where the government agriculture office was and she ignored me. I asked her where the police station was and she turned her back to me and went through the curtain to her living quarters. I rang the bell but she wouldn't come back.

I was annoyed with Webster for poking around my room while I was asleep but I didn't mention it. I asked if he could run an errand for me. He said nothing and kept working in his notebook. He and Ruth both had decided that I was the sort of person they didn't have to listen to. There were certain white people that they might have to listen to but I was not one of them. I spoke to him again.

"I'm busy," he said.

"What are you doing?"

"I'm drawing the car of tomorrow."

"Yes, I see now. It looks fast. That's nice work. Everything will have to wait until you're finished with it."

I went out into the soft tropic morning. Roosters were crowing all over Belize. My two-day torpor was gone and I was ready for business. Webster had put his tomato plant out on the sidewalk for the sunlight hours. There were two green tomatoes on it.

The little Buick was filthy but it appeared to be intact. There was a leaflet under the windshield wiper. The letters at the top of the sheet were so big and they were marching across the paper in such a way that I had to move my head back a little from normal reading range to make out the words.

LEET WANTS THIS CAR

Hullo, my name is Leet and I pay cash for select motor cars such as yours. I pay promptly in American ($) Dollars. I pay the duty too so as to spare you bother on that Score. Please see me at once on the Franklin Road just beyond the abandoned Ink factory and get an

immediate price quotation. Before you deal with a
nother person ask yourself these important questions.
Who is this Person? Where was he yesterday and
where will he be tomorrow? Leet has been in business
at the same location for Six Years and he is not going
any where. Here's hoping we may get together soon. I
am a White Man from Great Yarmouth, England, with
previous service in the Royal Navy. With every good
wish, I am, yours for Mutual Satisfaction,

> Wm. Leet
> Leet's Motor Ranch
> Franklin Road
> Belize, B.H.

I threw it away and got my Esso map from the glove
compartment and retrieved the doctor's flashlight from
under the seat.

Where were the government buildings? I set out toward
the arched bridge to find them. No one was about on the
streets. I stopped to read signs and posters. A band called
the Blues Busters was appearing at an all-night dance. The
movie house was featuring a film of a Muhammad Ali fight. I
made a plan for breakfast. I would stop at the second restaurant that I came to on my left.

It was a Chinese place and not a restaurant as such but
rather a grocery store with a coffee machine and an ice-
cream machine and a few tables. An old Chinese man was
wiping off the stainless-steel ice-cream machine. Maintenance! The firemen of Belize were gathered there at two
tables for coffee and rolls. A piece of luck, I thought, my
hitting on the very place that the firemen liked. They looked
at me and lowered their voices. I didn't want to interfere
with their morning chat so I bought a cone of soft ice cream
and left.

Across the way on the bank of the river there was a public market, a long open shed with a low tin roof, where bananas and pigs and melons were sold, though not this early in the morning. Outside the shed on the dock there were three men skinning a giant brown snake that hung from a hook. There, I said to myself, is something worth watching. I went over and took up a close viewing position and ate my ice cream. The job was soon done, but not with any great skill. The long belly cut was ragged and uncertain. It might have been their first snake. They kept the skin with its reticulated pattern and dropped the heavy carcass into the river where it hung for a moment just beneath the surface, white and sinuous, and then sank.

As I thought over what I had seen, very much puzzled as to how the specific gravity of snake flesh could be greater than that of water, someone came up behind me and pinched my upper arm and made me jump, as before, in Chetumal. I had come to fear this salute. It was Webster Spooner this time. He had his newspapers and greeting cards. He seemed to be embarrassed.

"Are you vexed with me, sor, for going through your things?"

"I am a little, yes."

"I was looking for a President Kennedy dollar."

"I don't have one."

"I know you don't."

"You missed the big snake. There was a monster snake hanging up there just a minute ago. Some sort of constrictor."

"I see him last night."

"How would you like to tangle with that big fellow?"

Webster twisted about and gasped as though in the clutches of the snake. "He be badder than any shark."

"I saw your tomatoes. They looked pretty good."

"A bug done eat one of 'em up."

One bug! A whole tomato! I asked again about the government offices and this time Webster was helpful and agreeable. But it was Sunday, I was surprised to learn, and the offices wouldn't be open. I unfolded the blue map and spread it out on one of the market tables.

"All right, Webster, look here. You will recognize this as a map of your country. An American named Dupree owns a farm here somewhere. I need to find that farm. I want you to go to your police connections and get them to mark the location of that farm on this map. I'm going to give you five dollars now and that's for the policeman. When you bring the map back to me, I'll have five dollars for you. How do you like that?"

He took pains to get Dupree spelled right in his notebook and he didn't whine or raise difficulties, as might have been expected from the corrupt Travis. I described my Torino and told him to be on the lookout for it. He asked me if I could get him a Kennedy dollar. He had that coin on the brain. Every time he got his hands on one, he said, Ruth took it away from him.

"I'll see if I can find you one," I said. "It's a half dollar and I should tell you that it probably won't be silver. All our coins now are cupronickel tokens of no real value. I want that Dupree information just as soon as you can get it. I'll be walking around town for a while and then I'll be at the Unity Tabernacle. I'll wait for you there. Do you know that church?"

Webster not only knew it, he was a sort of lapsed member. The tomato plant in the Texaco bucket had started as a church project. He didn't go much anymore, he said, because he had seen all the movies. He liked the singing and the Christmas program and the Easter egg hunt and he didn't mind seeing the Heckle and Jeckle cartoons over and over again. But the rest of it was too hard. And Mrs. Symes, no fool, had rearranged the schedule so that the Bible quiz was now held *before* the movie—and no one was admitted late.

He showed me his selection of greeting cards. I bought one, and a newspaper too, the first one I had ever seen that was actually called the *Daily Bugle*. It was made up entirely of political abuse, mean little paragraphs, and I threw it away.

For the next two hours or so I made figure-eight walking circuits of all the downtown blocks. I saw a good many Ford Galaxies, the big favorite here, but no sleek Torino of any model. Some of the dwelling houses had cozy English names . . . Rose Lodge, The Haven. I stopped at the Fort George Hotel for coffee. Some British soldiers were there, still a little drunk from the Blues Busters dance, and they were talking to an American woman who was at the next table with a small boy. They asked her why Americans said "budder" and "wadder" instead of "butter" and "water" and she said she didn't know. I asked them about their regiment and they said it was the Coldstream Guards. Were they lying? I couldn't tell. The Coldstream Guards! The hotel desk clerk was a woman and she said she vaguely remembered a Mr. Dupree, remembered his renting a car, and she thought his farm was south of town somewhere but she wasn't sure.

The door of Unity Tabernacle was bolted against quiz-dodgers. I hammered away on it until I was admitted by a boy monitor wearing a safety-patrol belt. The chapel was dark. Mrs. Symes was showing a George Sanders movie to a dozen or so Negro children who were scuffling on the pews. She herself was running the projector and I stood beside her and watched the show for a while. It was a Falcon picture. A wild-eyed man with a tiny mustache was trying desperately to buy a ticket in an enormous marble train station. Mrs.

Symes said to me, "He's not going anywhere. The Falcon is laying a trap for that joker." Then she gave me a pledge card, a card promising an annual gift of $5 ( ), $10 ( ), or $25 ( ) toward the support of the Unity mission. I filled it out under the hot inner light of the projector. The name and address spaces were much too short, unless you wrote a very fine hand or unless your name was Ed Poe and you lived at 1 Elm St., and I had to put this information on the back. I pledged ten dollars. It was just a pledge and I didn't have to pay the money at that moment.

The doctor had been removed to a bed upstairs. I found him awake but he was still gray in the face and his eye looked bad. He was sitting up, shapeless as a manatee in a woman's pink gown. He was going through a big pasteboard box that was filled with letters and photographs and other odds and ends. His hair had been cut, the jaybird crest was gone. He needed a shave. Melba gave me some coffee and a piece of cinnamon toast. She said that the three of us presented an interesting tableau, what with one person in bed, one in a chair, and one standing. Dr. Symes was fretful. He wouldn't talk until Melba had left us.

"What happened to your hair?" I said.

"Mama cut it with some shears."

"Do you need anything?"

"Yes, I do. They won't let me have any medication, Speed. They've put my bag away. They don't even keep a thermometer. I've lost my money and I've lost my book. I can't find my grooming aids. Some Mexican has got my flashlight."

I gave him his wallet and his flashlight and told him that the Dix book was safe in my room. This brought him around a little. He fingered through the money but he didn't count it.

"I appreciate this, Speed. You could have put the blocks to me but you didn't do it."

"I forgot all about it."

"Where in the world have you been?"

"Asleep."

"Is that asthma acting up on you?"

"No."

"Where are you staying?"

"At a hotel down there on the creek."

"A nice place?"

"It's all right."

"Do they have roof-garden dancing and a nice orchestra?"

"It's not that kind of hotel. How's your diarrhea?"

"I've got that gentleman turned all the way around. I'm excreting rocks now when I can do my job at all. Did you get your sweetie back?"

"I'm not trying to get her back. I'm trying to get my car back."

"Well, did you get it?"

"Not yet. I'm working on it."

"Taking to your bed won't get it. You need to get after it."

"I know that."

"You need to read Dix. You need to read Dix on how to close."

"I didn't get very far in that book."

"He tells you how to close a sale. Of course it has a wider application. The art of closing, of consummation. Master that and you have the key to the golden door of success. You need to let Dix take you by the hand."

"I read the part about not imposing on people but I never did that anyway."

"You read it wrong. It is *necessary* to impose on them. How else can you help a sap? Did you read the chapter on generating enthusiasm?"

"I read part of it."

"Read it all. Then read it again. It's pure nitro. The Three T's. The Five Don'ts. The Seven Elements. Stoking the fires of the U.S.S. *Reality*. Making the Pep Squad and staying on it."

"I read the part about the fellow named Floyd who wouldn't work."

"Marvin, not Floyd. Where do you get Floyd? There's no Floyd in any book Dix ever wrote. No, this was Marvin. It's a beautiful story and so true to life too. Old sorry Marvin! Pouting in his hotel room and listening to dance music on the radio and smoking one cigarette after the other and reading detective magazines and racing sheets. Sitting on the bed trying to dope out his six-dollar combinations. That guy! Wheeling his sap bets for the daily double! Dix knew Marv so well. Do you recall how he summed him up—'Hawking and spitting, we lay waste our powers.' I was once a Marvin myself if you can believe that. I had the blues so bad I was paralyzed. Then I read Dix and got off my ass."

"My money hasn't come in from Little Rock yet."

"What's the holdup?"

"I don't know."

"How long do you expect me to carry you?"

"It should come in today. I'm looking for it today. Anyway, you've still got my bonds."

"I don't want any more of your bonds. I'm caught up on bonds."

"It should come in today. I figure I owe you about thirty dollars."

"How do you figure that?"

"It's about fourteen hundred miles from San Miguel. I figure sixty dollars for the gas and oil and other stuff."

"How much for the motorized canoe ride?"

"Do you think I'm going to pay half of that?"

"People are careless when they're spending other people's money. That stuff is hard to come by."

"It wasn't a canoe. It was a boat."

"I have to work for my money. I'm not like you."

He had sorted the memorabilia from the box into three piles on the bed and took a long brown envelope from one of the piles and waved it at me. "Come here a minute, Speed. I want to show you something."

It was a new plan for Jean's Island. On the back of the envelope he had sketched an outline of the island, which was shaped like a tadpole. On the bulbous end he had drawn a dock and some rectangles that represented barracks. This was to be a nursing-home complex for old people called The City of Life. He and his mother would live on the island in a long yellow house, he at one end and she at the other, her bathtub fitted with a grab-bar. Together they would run the nursing home. He would supervise the medical care and she would minister to the spiritual needs. He anticipated a licensing problem because of his record but he thought he could get around that by registering the thing in his mother's name. And in Louisiana there was always some official you could pay to expedite such matters. He had also drawn in a nine-hole golf course. I didn't get the connection between the nursing home and the golf links and I asked him about this but he wasn't listening.

"A lot of bedpans and bitching, you think, but I'm talking about a seventeen-percent bottom-line profit," he said. "I don't mind fooling with these old people. Never have. Put a half-grain of phenobarbital in their soup every night and they won't give you much trouble. They've all got money these days. They all get regular checks from the government."

"You've got quite a few buildings there. What about your construction money?"

"No problem at all. Tap the Feds for some Hill-Burton funds. Maybe float some Act 9 industrial bonds. Hell, mortgage the island. Roll over some short notes. I figure about eight thousand five hundred square feet under roof for the long house, with about six thousand feet of that heated and cooled. The rest in storage rooms and breezeways. Put your cooling tower down at this end, with about forty-five tons of air conditioning. I don't say it's a sure thing. If it was a sure thing, everybody would be in it. But you have to go with the odds and you have two high cards right off in me and Mama."

"Your mother said that island was dedicated as a wildlife refuge."

"Have you been discussing my business with her?"

"She was the one who brought it up."

"Jean's Island has never been dedicated in any legal sense."

"I'm just telling you what she said."

"She meant it was posted, that's all. No hunters and no trespassers. She doesn't know the difference. Why would she be paying taxes on it if it was dedicated?"

"I don't know."

"You're mighty right you don't. Did you get the impression that she might be willing to come to terms on the island?"

"I didn't get that impression."

"Not favorably disposed then."

"She's afraid some woman will get her hands on the property."

"Some woman?"

"She talked about a woman named Sybil."

"What has Sybil got to do with it?"

"I don't know."

"Sybil's all right."

"Your mother doesn't approve of her."

"Sybil's all right but she came down here and showed her ass is what she did. She ran her mouth all the time. I was disappointed. It was a misplaced confidence on my part. I should never have brought her down here, but it was Sybil's car, you see."

"There was another woman. Your mother mentioned another woman named Marvel Clark."

"Marvel!"

"Marvel Clark. Do you know her?"

"Do I know Marvel. My old valentine. Mama must be losing her mind. What has Marvel got to do with anything?"

"Is she one of your sweethearts?"

"She's a rattlesnake. I didn't see it at first. Mama told me not to marry her. She knew those Clarks. I didn't see it until we were married and then I saw it with great clarity. Even so, I miss her sometimes. Some little thing will remind me of her. Can you imagine that? Missing a coiled rattler."

"I didn't realize you had a wife."

"I don't have a wife. Marvel gave me the gate thirty-five years ago, Speed. She said she'd had enough. She said she would shave her head and become a nun in the Catholic church before she would ever get married again. She cleaned me out good. She got my house and she got a lot of Mama's furniture and she even had my medical equipment attached."

"Well, there you are. Your mother is afraid she will get the island too."

"Get it how? Not through me."

He searched through the box and brought out an old photograph showing a thin girl in a dotted dress. She was sitting in a playground swing and she was holding a squinting child on her knees. This was the doctor's former wife, Marvel Clark Symes, and their infant son Ivo. Dr. Symes with a wife! I couldn't believe it. She was a pretty girl too, and not a floozie at all. And baby Ivo! Of course the boy was grown now; that picture must have been forty years old.

Ivo was a roofing contractor in Alexandria, Louisiana, the doctor told me, where Marvel Clark now made her home as well. He said he had not communicated in any way with her for more than twenty years. I gathered that he was also estranged from his son, calling him as he did, "a roofing thug," and saying that he hoped God would let him, the doctor, live long enough to see Ivo in the penitentiary at Angola.

"I don't know what Mama can be thinking about," he said. "There is no possible way Marvel could get the land through me. She has no more legal claim on me than does any strange woman passing by on the street."

"I'm just telling you what she said."

"The divorce was final. That bond has been severed and forever set at naught. Those are the very words on the decree. That's as final as you can get. How much more do you want?"

"I don't know anything about it."

"You're mighty right you don't. Go look it up at the courthouse in Vidalia and then you might know something about it."

I went to the window and watched the street below for Webster Spooner. I looked across the rusty tin roofs of Belize. I couldn't see the ocean but I knew it was out there where the roofs stopped. Dr. Symes asked if I would get him some medicine and some shaving gear. I said I would and he began to write prescriptions on scraps of paper. Downstairs I could hear some bouncy 1937 clarinet tootling.

"What is that?"

"What?"

"That music."

"That's Felix the Cat. Mama loves a picture show. I brought her some cartoons and shorts when I was down here with Sybil. Felix the Cat and Edgar Kennedy and Ted Fiorito with his dance band. I brought Melba a thousand-piece puzzle. Mama loves a picture show better than anybody I know except for Leon Vurro. Listen to this, Speed. Here's what I had to put up with. I would be in that hot cabin in south Houston trying to flatten out those photographs with brickbats and Leon would be off downtown in some cool picture show watching *Honky-Tonk Women* or *Women in Prison.* A grown man. Can you beat it? I've never wasted my time on shows. Don't you know they've got those stories all figured out before you even get to the show? Leon would sit there in the dark like a sap for two or three hours watching those stories and then he would come out on the street just as wild as a crib rat, blinking his eyes and looking around for women to squeeze. Not Bella but strange women. Oh, yes, I used to do it myself. There is very little folly I have missed out on in my life. I never wasted my time on shows but I was a bigger hog for women than Leon ever was. Talk about your prisoners of love. Talk about your boar minks. There was a time when I was out almost every night squeezing women but I stopped that foolishness years ago. A big waste of time and money if you want my opinion, not to mention the toll on your health."

Melba was sitting in her chair in the next room, the central room, and when the cartoon was over she went downstairs to play the piano. The children sang, their devotions passing up through this bedroom and on through the tin roof to the skies. Dr. Symes hummed along with them and sang bits of the hymn.

"This is not a feasible program," he said, indicating the business downstairs. "I think the world of Mama but this is just not a feasible setup. Fooling around with a handful of kids. Don't take my word for it. Check it out with your top educators and your top communicators. What you want is a broad base. This is a narrow base. What you want is a healing service under a tent, and then when things go slack you can knock the poles down and fold that booger up and move on. Or a radio ministry. A telephone ministry would beat this. You'll never prosper on a deal like this. It doesn't make any sense. This is like old man Becker in Ferriday. Let me tell you what he would do. He would be in the back of his hardware store weighing out turnip seed at eight cents a pound, just busting his ass with that little metal scoop, the sweat just rolling off him, while people were standing in line up front trying to buy five-thousand-dollar tractors."

He gave me some money and I left to get the medicine. There were amber nose deposits on the prescriptions. The old man left a mucous track behind him like a snail. I bought a razor at Mr. Wu's grocery but I couldn't find a drugstore that was open so I walked across town to the hospital, another white building. The nurse who ran the dispensary was an Englishwoman. She didn't believe those prescriptions for a minute but she sold me the stuff anyway, some heart medicine called Lanoxin, and some Demerol, which I knew to be dope, and some other things in evil little bottles that I suspected of being dope. It was all for a "Mr. Ralph Moore" and the doctor had signed his own name as the prescribing physician. I explained that he was the son of Mrs. Symes at the Unity church. He had also asked me to get him a dozen syringes but the woman wouldn't sell me any. I didn't press the matter. Babies were crying and I wanted to get out of that place.

Near the hospital there was a city park, a long green field with a statue at one end that looked new and not very important. There was a steel flagpole with no flag. The brass swivel snaps on the rope were jingling against the pole. A woman was sitting tailor-fashion on the grass with a sketch pad. I recognized her as the American girl who had been in the Fort George dining room. The small boy was asleep on a beach towel beside her. I waved. She didn't want to raise her busy hand from the pad but she did nod.

The service was over when I got back to the tabernacle. Mrs. Symes and Melba and a chubby Negro girl in a green dress were in the doctor's room drinking iced tea. The girl was helping Mrs. Symes stick paper stars in an attendance ledger. There was a Scrabble board on the bed and the doctor and Melba were playing this word game. He said, "The millionaires in Palm Beach, Florida, are not having any more fun than we are, Melba." I gave him the sack of drugs and shaving supplies and he left at once for the bathroom. Mrs. Symes asked where I had attended church.

"Actually I haven't been yet."

"Did you sleep late?"

"I've been pretty busy."

"Our lesson here today was on effectual calling."

"I see."

"Do you indeed? Do you even know what effectual calling is?"

"I can't say I do, no, ma'am. I suppose it must be some special religious term. I'm not familiar with it."

"Elizabeth, can you tell Mr. Midge about effectual calling?"

The plump girl said, "Effectual calling. Effectual calling

is the work of God's spirit, whereby, convincing us of our sin and misery, enlightening our minds in the knowledge of Christ, and renewing our wills, He doth persuade and enable us to embrace Jesus Christ freely offered to us in the gospel."

"That's very good, but what about the benefits? That's what we want to know. What benefits do they that are effectually called partake of in this life?"

The girl had a ready answer for that too. "They that are effectually called," she said, "do in this life partake of justification, adoption, sanctification, and the several benefits which, in this life, do either accompany or flow from them. We gain assurance of God's love, peace of conscience, joy in the Holy Ghost, increase of Grace, and perseverance therein to the end."

"That's very good, Elizabeth. There are not twenty-five Americans who could answer that question, and we call ourselves a Christian people. Or don't you agree, Mr. Midge?"

"It was a hard question."

"Mr. Midge here goes to college and he has a good opinion of himself but he may not be quite as clever as he thinks. It may even be, Elizabeth, that we can teach him a thing or two."

The girl was pleased with her performance. She had finished her tea and now had her hands arranged in a prim manner on her knees, her small pink fingernails glowing against the green dress.

There was no sign of Webster Spooner. Mrs. Symes had not seen him. She said Webster was a good reader and a good speller and a good singer but he wouldn't stay in his seat. The girl Elizabeth said he was a bad boy who always answered "*Yo*" instead of "Present" when the roll was called.

"I don't think we can call Webster a bad boy, can we?" said Mrs. Symes. "He's not a bad boy like Dwight."

The girl said, "No, but Dwight is a very bad boy."

Mrs. Symes asked me what the doctor had been talking about and I said very honestly that we had been discussing her missionary work. I felt like a spy or a talebearer, reporting back and forth on these conversations. She said she knew what Reo thought of her program but what did I think? I said I thought it was a good program.

She said one couldn't judge these things by the conventional standards of worldly success. Noah preached for six hundred years and converted no one outside his immediate household. And Jeremiah, the weeping prophet, he too was widely regarded as a failure. All you could do was your best, according to your lights. She told me that there was no one named Raymond in the Bible and that drunkenness was the big social problem in this country.

Then she talked to me at length about Father Jackie, the Episcopal missionary. He had the only Tarzan film in the country, she said, and he had finally agreed to let her have it for one showing. Father Jackie had a prankish nature that was very tiresome, and the negotiations for the film had been maddening and exhausting—but well worth the effort. The word on Tarzan would spread fast! Father Jackie was busy these days drafting a new catechism for the modern world, and he was composing some new Christmas carols too, and so he had decided to cut back on his movies and his preaching and teaching duties in order to complete these tasks. He was an odd bird, she said, but he had a good heart. His mother was now visiting him here in Belize.

Melba said, "His mother? I didn't know that. His mother is here?"

"I told you about meeting her in the swap shop."

"No, you didn't."

"Yes, I did."

"You didn't tell me any such thing."

"You never listen to me when I have some piece of news like that."

"What does she look like?"

"I don't know what she looks like, Melba. She just looks like all the rest of us."

"The reason I ask is that I had a vision of an older woman with a white parasol. She was holding it on her shoulder and buying something at the market. Eggs, I think. I saw her just as clearly as I see you now."

"This woman didn't have a parasol. She wasn't even wearing a hat."

"Was she a kind of yellowish woman?"

"She *was yellow*, yes."

"Yellow eyes?"

"I didn't notice her eyes so much but her face was certainly yellow."

"A yellow face."

"That's what I said."

"That's what I said too."

"You said yellow eyes."

"At first I just said yellow."

That ended that. I played Scrabble with Melba. Mrs. Symes hugged and kissed the girl Elizabeth, calling her "baby," or rather, "bebby," and the girl went away. I could hear Dr. Symes in the bathroom singing a song called "My Carolina Sunshine Girl." He was shaving too, among other things, and he looked much better when he came back. He stood beside his mother for a moment and put his arm around her shoulder.

"How are you feeling this morning, Mama?"

"I never felt better in my life, Reo. Stop asking me that."

A small framed picture on the wall caught his attention and he went over to examine it. It was a picture of something brown.

"What is this?" he said. "Is this the Mount of Olives?"

"I don't know what that is," she said. "It's been up there for years. We never use this room any more since Melba has been staying in her chair."

"Who painted this picture? Where did you get it, Mama? I'd like to know how I could get a copy of it."

"You can have that one if you want it."

He crawled back into bed and resumed the Scrabble game. "Where is your puzzle, Melba?" he said. "Where is that jumbo puzzle I brought you the last time? Did you ever finish it?"

"No, I never did start it, Reo. It looked so hard. I gave it to one of the children."

"It was a funny picture of dogs wearing suits."

"Yes, dogs of different breeds smoking pipes and playing some card game."

"Mama, why don't you show Speed here your hurricane poem. He's a college professor and he knows all about poetry."

"No, I don't want to get that stuff out right now. I've got it all locked up."

"What about your stories, Melba? Why don't you show Speed some of your stories?"

"He doesn't want to see those things."

"Yes, he does too. Don't you, Speed?"

I explained that I was very far from being a college professor and that I never read poems or fictional stories and knew nothing about them. But the doctor kept on with this and Melba brought me her stories. They were in airmail tablets, written in a round script on both sides of the thin paper.

One was about a red-haired beauty from New Orleans who went to New York and got a job as a secretary on the second floor of the Empire State Building. There were mysterious petty thefts in the office and the red-haired girl solved the mystery with her psychic powers. The thief turned out to be the boss himself and the girl lost her job and went back to New Orleans where she got another job that she liked better, although it didn't pay as well.

Melba had broken the transition problem wide open by starting almost every paragraph with "Moreover." She freely used "the former" and "the latter" and every time I ran into one of them I had to backtrack to see whom she was talking about. She was also fond of "inasmuch" and "crestfallen."

I read another story, an unfinished shocker about a father-and-son rape team who prowled the Laundromats of New Orleans. The leading character was a widow, a mature red-haired woman with nice skin. She had visions of the particular alleys and parts where the rapes were to occur but the police detectives wouldn't listen to her. "Bunk!" they said. She called them "the local gendarmes," and they in turn called all the girls "tomatoes."

A pretty good story, I thought, and I told Melba I would like to see the psychic widow show up the detectives and get them all fired or at least reduced in rank. The doctor was going back and forth to the bathroom, taking dope, I knew, and talking all the time. He wouldn't read the stories but he wanted to discuss them with us. He advised Melba to get them copyrighted at once.

"What if some sapsucker broke in here and snatched one of your stories, Melba, and then put his own name on it and sold it to some story magazine for ten thousand dollars? Where would you be then?"

Melba was upset. She asked me how one went about this copyright business and I couldn't tell her because I didn't know. Dr. Symes said she would be wiser to keep the stories locked in her drawer instead of showing them to every strange person who came in off the street. He gave no thought to the distress he had caused the old lady and he went on to something else, telling of the many red-haired people he had known in his life. Mrs. Symes had known some of the ruddy folk herself and she spoke of their hot tempers and their sensitive skin, but the doctor wasn't interested in her experiences.

"You'll never find a red-headed person in a nuthouse," he said to me. "Did you know that?"

"I've never heard that."

"Go to the biggest nuthouse you want to and if you can find a red-headed nut I'll give you fifty dollars. Wooten told me that years ago and he was right. Wooten was a doctor's doctor. He was the greatest diagnostician of our time, bar none. Surgery was only his hobby. Diagnosis, that's the high art of medicine. It's a genetic thing, you see, with these redheads. They never go crazy. You and I may go crazy tomorrow morning, Speed, but Melba here will never go crazy."

Melba had been stirring her iced tea violently for about four minutes. She put her face in mine and winked and said, "I'll bet I know what you like." From her leering expression I thought she was going to say, "Nooky," but she said, "I'll bet you like cowboy stories."

The morning wore on and still there was no Webster. I thought of calling the hotel and the cable office but Mrs. Symes had no telephone. I kept hanging around, thinking she would surely ask me to stay for lunch. I was weak from my dairy diet. The doctor said he would like some jello and I wondered at his craving for gelatinous food. Mrs. Symes said jello was a good idea. I could smell the sea and what I wanted was a plate of fried shrimp and fried potatoes.

But jello it was and by that time the doctor was so full of dope and so addled from the heat that I had to help him to the table. His eyelids were going up and down independently of one another and his red eye was glowing and pulsing. He talked about Louisiana, certain childhood scenes, and how he longed to go back. He said, "Mama, you're just going to fall in love all over again with Ferriday." Mrs. Symes didn't argue with him, this return to the homeland being clearly out of the question. Then he wanted to move the dining table over by the window where there was more light. She said, "This table is right where I want it to be, Reo."

Melba and I filled up on lime jello—transparent, no bits of fruit in suspension—and peanut-butter cookies with corrugations on top where a fork had been lightly pressed into them. That was our lunch. The doctor talked on and on. He held a spoonful of jello above his bowl but thoughts kept racing into his head and he could never quite get it to his mouth.

"Speed, I want you to do me a favor."

"All right."

"I want you to tell Mama and Melba about my bus. They'll get a big kick out of that. Can you describe it for them?"

"It's an old Ford school bus painted white."

"All white?"

"Totally white."

"Are you sure about that?"

"Everything was painted white. The windows and the bumpers and the wheels. The grille and all the brightwork too. The propane bottle. It looked like house paint and it was brushed on instead of sprayed."

"Wasn't there something painted in black on the sides?"

"I forgot about that. 'The Dog of the South.'"

"The Dog of the South? Do you mean to say that was the name of the bus?"

"Yes."

"All right then, ladies, there you are. Very fitting, wouldn't you say? No, I take that back. A dog, any dog with a responsible master, is well off compared to me."

Melba said, "You shouldn't call yourself a dog, Reo."

"It's time for plain speaking, Melba. Let's face it, I'm a beggar. I'm old and sick. I have no friends, not one. Rod Garza was the last friend I had on this earth. I have no home. I own no real property. That bus you have just heard described is my entire estate. I haven't been sued in four years—look it up: City of Los Angeles versus Symes, it's still pending for all I know—but if anyone was foolish enough to sue me today, that old bus would be the only thing he could levy against."

Mrs. Symes said, "Whose fault is it, Reo? Tell me that."

"It's all mine, Mama, and nobody knows it better than I do. Listen. If I did have a home and in that home one room was set aside as a trophy room—listen to this—the walls of that room would be completely barren of citations and awards and scrolls and citizenship plaques. Can you imagine that? Can you imagine the terrible reproach of those blank walls to a professional man like me? You could hardly blame me if I kept that shameful room closed off and locked. That's what a lifetime of cutting corners has done for me."

"You had some good friends in Ferriday," Mrs. Symes said. "Don't tell me you didn't."

"Not real friends."

"You went to their barbecues all the time."

"The kind of people I know now don't have barbecues, Mama. They stand up alone at nights in small rooms and eat cold weenies. My so-called friends are bums. Many of them are nothing but rats. They spread T.B. and use dirty language. Some of them can even move their ears. They're wife-beaters and window peepers and night crawlers and dope fiends. They have running sores on the backs of their hands that never heal. They peer up from cracks in the floor with their small red eyes and watch for chances."

Melba said, "That was the road of life you chose, Reo. It was you who sought out those low companions."

"You're absolutely right, Melba. You've done it again. You've put your finger on it. A fondness for low company. I wasn't born a rat or raised a rat. I don't even have that excuse. I wasn't raised a heathern. My mother and father gave me a loving home. They provided me with a fine medical education at Wooten Institute. I wore good clothes, clean clothes, nice suits from Benny's. I had a massive executive head and million-dollar personality. I was wide awake. I was just as keen as a brier. Mama can tell you how frisky I was."

She said, "I was always afraid you would be burned up in a night-club fire, baby."

The doctor turned on me. "Listen to me, Speed. A young man should start out in life trying to do the right thing. It's better for your health. It's better in every way. There'll be plenty of time later for you to cut these corners, and better occasions. I wish I had had some older man to grab my shoulder and talk turkey to me when I was your age. I needed a good shaking when my foot slipped that first time, and I didn't get it. Oh, yes. My face is now turned toward that better land, but much too late."

Mrs. Symes said, "You had a good friend in Natchez named Eddie Carlotti. He had such good manners. He never forgot himself in the presence of ladies like so many of your friends would do. He drove a Packard automobile. It was an open car."

"A human rat," said the doctor. "The world's largest rodent. He's four times the size of that rat Leon used to show. That wop is probably in the Black Hand Society now, shaking down grocery stores. I could tell you a few things about Mr. Eddie Carlotti but I won't. It would turn your stomach."

"What about the Estes boy who was so funny? He always had some new joke or some comical story to tell."

"Chemical story?" said Melba.

"*Comical* story! He and Reo were inseparable chums at one time."

"Another rat," said the doctor. "And I'm not talking now about brown *norvegicus*, your common rat, I'm talking about *Rattus rattus* himself, all black and spitting. Walker Estes would trip a blind man. The last time I saw him he was stealing Christmas presents out of people's cars and trucks. Working people too. I can tell you who didn't think he was funny. It was that sharecropper's little daughter who cried on Christmas morning because there was no baby doll for her, and no candy or sparklers either."

Melba said, "It's amazing what people will do."

"Listen, Melba. Listen to this. I'd like to share this with you. There used to be a wonderful singer on the radio called T. Texas Tyler. Did you ever hear him?"

"When was he on the radio?"

"He was on late at night and he was just a fine fellow, a tremendous entertainer. He had a wonderful way with a song. He sang some lovely Western ballads. They always introduced him as 'T. Texas Tyler, the man with a million friends.' I used to envy that man, and not just for his beautiful voice. I would think, Now how in the world would they introduce me if I had a singing program on the radio? They couldn't say, 'The singing doctor,' because I was no longer a licensed physician. They wouldn't want to say, 'The man with a few rat friends,' and yet anything else would have been a lie. They wouldn't know what to do. They would just have to point to me and let me start singing when that red light came on. Don't ask me what happened to Tyler, because I don't know. I don't have that information. He may be living in a single-wide trailer somewhere, a forgotten old man. Where are those million friends now? It's a shame how we neglect our poets. It's the shame of our nation. Tyler could sing like a bird and you see what it got him in the end. John Selmer Dix died broke in a railroad hotel in Tulsa. It wasn't a mattress fire either. I don't know who started that talk. Dix had his enemies like anybody else. The lies that have been told about that man! They said his eyes were real close together. A woman in Fort Worth claims she saw him flick cigarette ashes on a sleeping baby in a stroller cart. And Dix didn't even smoke! He published two thin books in forty years and they called him a chatterbox. He had the heart of a lion and yet there are people who believe, even to this day, that he was found cowering in the toilet when they had that big Christmas fight at the Legion hut in Del Rio. Anything to smear his memory! Well, it doesn't matter, his work was done. The New York jumping rats have already begun to tamper with it."

Mrs. Symes said, "Reo, you were speaking of rats and that made me think of the river rat named Cornell something who used to take you duck hunting. A famous duck-caller. Cornell something-or-other. His last name escapes me."

"Cornell Tubb, but it's no use going on with this, Mama."

"I remember his full name now. It was Cornell Tubb. Am I wrong, Melba, in thinking that you have some Tubb connections?"

"My mother was a Tubb."

"It's no use going on with this, Mama. I tell you I have no friends. Cornell Tubb was never my friend by any stretch of the imagination. The last friend I had on this earth was

Rod Garza, and he was completely dismembered in his Pontiac. They put a bum in his car and blew him up."

"You're not eating. You asked for this jello and now you're just playing with it."

"I wonder if you would do me a favor, Mama."

"I will if I can, Reo."

"I want you to tell Speed here the name of my favorite hymn. He would never guess it in a hundred years."

"I don't remember what it was."

"Yes, you do too."

"No, I don't remember."

" 'Just as I am, without one plea.' How I love that old song. And I'll tell you a secret. It means more to me now than it ever did. The theme of that hymn, Speed, is redemption. 'Just as I am, though tossed about, with many a conflict, many a doubt.' Can you understand the appeal it has for me? Can you see why I always request it, no matter where I am in my travels? I never go to these churches where all their hymns were written in 1956, where they write their own songs, you know. Don't look for me there. I'm not interested in hearing any nine-year-old preachers either."

Mrs. Symes said, "I'll tell you what I do remember, Reo. I remember you standing up there in the choir in Ferriday in your robe, just baying out, 'I'd rather have Jesus than silver or gold!' and all the time you were taking advantage of the deaf people of Concordia Parish. You were taking their money and putting those enormous Filipino hearing aids in their ears that squealed and buzzed when they worked at all, and in some cases, I believe, caused painful electric shock."

Melba said, "It's amazing what people will do. Look at the ancient Egyptians. They were the smartest people the world has ever known—we still don't know all their secrets —and yet they worshiped a tumblebug."

The doctor was still holding the green jello in his spoon, quivering and undelivered. This annoyed Mrs. Symes and she took the spoon from him and began to feed him, thus shutting him up.

She and Melba conferred on their plans for the Tarzan showing. Folding chairs would have to be borrowed to accommodate the crowd. Perhaps Father Jackie would lend them his self-threading and noiseless and yet powerful new projector, in which case standby fuses would be needed.

I asked questions about this Father Jackie and learned that he had been a maverick priest in New Orleans. There he had ministered to the waifs who gather about Jackson Square. One night these young drifters surrounded his small Japanese car, shook it for a while, and then turned it over. They dragged him out into the street and beat him and left him bleeding and unconscious. When he had recovered from the assault, his bishop pondered over the problem and then decided that Belize would be a good place for Father Jackie. Mrs. Symes objected to his breezy manner and his preposterous doctrines and his theatrical attire, but, deep down, she said, he was a genuine Christian. She was well pleased with her Tarzan deal.

I said, "Wait a minute. I've heard of this fellow. I've handled news accounts about this man. This is the well-known 'Vicar of Basin Street.'"

"No, no," she said. "This is another one. Father Jackie has a steel plate in his head. He plays the cornet. He's an amateur magician. He claims he has no fear of the Judgment. I don't know anything about the other fellow."

Dense heat was building up in the house. I helped the doctor back to his bed. Mrs. Symes went to her own room to nap. There was a box fan in the central room, where we had eaten, and I lay down on the floor in front of it to rest for a minute or two. I was heavy and sodden with jello.

Watch out for the florr! When I woke up, it was almost 3:30 in the afternoon. What a piddler! Melba was in her chair looking at me. No slumber for Melba. That is, I thought she was looking at me but when I stood up, her dreamy gaze did not move from some point in the void where it was fixed. The temperature was about 97 degrees in that room and she was still wearing her red sweater. It wasn't for me to instruct Melba in her Christian duties but surely she was wrong to be trafficking with these spirits.

Eight

The post office itself wasn't open but there was a man on duty in the cable office. He leafed through the incoming messages and found nothing for me. I walked back to the hotel. The young men of Belize were shadowboxing on the streets and throwing mock punches at one another. Webster Spooner was in front of the hotel dancing around the tomato plant and jabbing the air with his tiny fists. He too had attended the matinée showing of the Muhammad Ali fight.

"I'm one bad-ass nigger," he said to me.

"No, you're not."

"I'm one bad-ass nigger."

"No, you're not."

He was laughing and laying about with his fists. Biff Spooner! Scipio Africanus! I had to wait until his comic frenzy was spent. He had taken care of the map business all right, but instead of bringing the map to me he had fooled around town all morning and then gone to the movie.

I saw that I could count on Webster to do one thing but not two things in immediate succession. On the other hand I didn't have his five dollars, or his Kennedy coin. I did have a little money that I had diverted into my own pocket from the doctor's wad, though not as much as five dollars. Webster shrugged and made no fuss, being accustomed to small daily betrayals.

In the white margin at the top of the map the policeman had written, "Dupree & Co. Ltd. Bishop Lane. Mile 16.4."

This Bishop Lane was not printed on the map and the policeman had sketched it in, running west and slightly south from Belize. He had marked the Dupree place with a box. Nearby was a Mayan ruin, as I could see from the pyramid symbol. He had marked another place in the south —"Dupere Livestock"—but the spelling was different and this was clearly an afterthought. In the bottom margin he had signed his name: Sgt. Melchoir Wattli.

So at long last I had found them and now I was ready to make my move. Leet had left another leaflet on the windshield of the Buick and I threw it away. I inspected the hood for cat tracks and I had a look underneath. Then I remembered the roll of quarters and I got it from the glove compartment and gave it to Webster, showing him how to conceal it in his fist. It stuck out from one end and made his fingers bulge in a dead giveaway.

The quarter was not a very interesting coin, I conceded, and I said it was true that Washington, whose stern profile was stamped on it, had a frosty manner, and that he was not a glamorous person. But, I went on, warming to this theme, he was a much greater man than Kennedy. *¡Gravitas!* The stuffed shirt, the pill—this sort of person had not always been regarded as a comic figure. I had enormous respect for General Washington, as who doesn't, but I also liked the man, believing as I did that we shared many of the same qualities. Perhaps I should say "some of the same qualities" because in many ways we were not at all alike. He, after all, had read only two books on warfare, Bland's *Exercises* and Sim's *Military Guide*, and I had read a thousand. And of course he was a big man while I am compact of build.

Webster pointed out that Sergeant Wattli had used a pencil instead of a pen so as not to permanently mar the beautiful blue map. I decided that I would make a gift of the map to the officer when I was done with it, though I said

nothing to Webster at the time. That was my way. These
flashy people who make a show of snatching off a new neck-
tie and presenting it to someone on the spot, to someone who
has admired it—that was never my way.

The filthy Buick started on the first shot. Detroit iron!
You can't beat it! Bishop Lane began as a city street and
then at the edge of town it changed abruptly into two sandy
ruts, which comfortably absorbed the tire thump. There
were no suburbs, not even a string of shanties. I drove across
pine flats and I was much surprised at finding this conifer in
the tropics. I had heard or read somewhere that the taproot
of a pine tree plunges as deep into the earth as the tree
grows tall, the identical length, and I didn't see how this was
possible. I thought about the happy and decent life of a
forest ranger. A fresh tan uniform every morning and a
hearty breakfast and a goodbye peck from Norma at the
door of our brown cottage in the woods. It was a field well
worth looking into.

The sand changed to black dirt and mud. I drove
through shallow creeks and the water splashed up on my
feet. I was entering a different kind of forest, dark woods
that pressed in and made a leafy tunnel of the road. There
were scrub trees and giant trees, nothing in between. The
big ones had smooth gray trunks and few branches except at
the very top where they spread into canopies. Roots flared
out at the base for buttressing support. I watched for parrots
and saw none.

I met no traffic and saw no people either until I came to
the Mayan ruin. Two Indian men were there working with
machetes. They were hacking away at brush and swatting at
mosquitoes. Here and there on the ground they had placed
buckets of smoldering woody husks that gave off white
smoke—homemade mosquito bombs.

It wasn't a spectacular ruin, nothing to gape at, just a small clearing and two grassy mounds that were the eroded remains of pyramids. They were about twenty feet high. On one of them a stone stairway had been exposed, which led up to a small square temple on the top. Farther back in the woods I could see another mound, a higher one, with trees still growing from it. I stopped to inquire about the Dupree place.

The Indians spoke no English and they couldn't seem to understand my scraps of Spanish either but they were delighted to see me. They welcomed the break from their hopeless task. They seemed to think I had come to tour the ruin and so I followed them about. I tried to stand in the white smoke and it kept shifting around, away from me. The Indians laughed at this perverse joke of nature, so often on them but this time on me. We looked into a dark stone chamber. There were shiny crystals on the walls where water had been dripping for centuries. The chamber next to it had a canvas curtain across the doorway and there were bedrolls and a radio inside. These birds lived here!

We climbed the stone steps and looked into the temple. I ran my hand over the carvings. The stone was coarse-grained and badly weathered and I couldn't make out the design but I knew it must be a representation of some toothy demon or some vile lizard god. I had read about these Mayans and their impenetrable glyphs and their corbeled arches and their madness for calculating the passage of time. But no wheel! I won't discuss their permutation calendar, though I could. I gave the Indians a dollar apiece. They asked me for cigarettes and I had none. But that was all right too, I was still a good fellow. They laughed and laughed over their hard luck.

I left with no information about the Dupree place. About

two miles farther along I came to a pasture airstrip with a limp windsock, and then a house, an unpainted structure made of broad reddish planks. It stood well off the wet ground so that Webster or Travis might have walked upright beneath it. I would have had to crouch. There was a sorry fence around the house, a sagging wire affair, and a sign, "KEEP OUT THIS MEANS YOU," on the makeshift gate. There was a porch with a rope hammock hanging at one end. In a shed next to the house there was a green tractor.

I parked in a turnout across the road from the house. It was a turning-around place and a garbage dump too, with bottles and cans and eggshells and swollen magazines scattered about. I had no way of measuring 16.4 miles but I thought I must be getting close. These people here would surely know something about the Dupree farm, unless Sergeant Wattli had put me altogether wrong. There was a terrible stink in the air and I thought at first it came from the garbage. Then I saw two dead and bloated cows with their legs flung out stiff.

I got out of the car and started across the road and then stopped when a red dog came from beneath the house. Was this Dupree's chow dog? He yawned and stretched one front leg and then the other one. He looked deformed with his coat trimmed, his big square head now out of proportion to his diminished body. A clear plastic bag was tied around each of his feet.

He walked to the gate and looked at me without recognition. After a while he registered me in his dog brain as a negligible presence and then he sat back on his haunches and snapped at mosquitoes. I couldn't believe this was the same dog I had known in Little Rock, the same red beast I had seen springing from cover to nip the ankles of motorcyclists and to send small children into screaming flight down the sidewalk. He had been unmanned perhaps by the

long journey and the shearing and the plastic bags on his
paws.

The screen door opened and Dupree came out on the
porch. He was shirtless, his skin glistening with oil, and he
was wearing a tall gray cowboy hat. He had grown a beard.
His cowboy boots had pointed toes that curled up like elf
shoes. This was a new, Western Dupree. He had a new walk
too, a rolling, tough-guy walk. He wasn't wearing his glasses
and he squinted at me with one eye. The other one was
black and almost closed. His lips were broken and swollen.
They had already been at him with their fists here. People's
justice! He was holding my .410 shotgun by the barrel in the
position that is called "trail arms" in the drill manuals.

"Popo?" he said.

The weak-eyed monkey couldn't even make out who I
was. He didn't even recognize his own car.

I said, "Well, Dupree, I see you have some little boots on
the dog."

"He doesn't like to get his feet wet. Is that you, Way-
mon?"

He sometimes called me by this countrified version of
"Raymond," not in an affectionate way but with malice.

"You have a lot to answer for, Dupree."

"You'll get your money back. Don't worry about it. Who's
with you?"

"Nobody."

"Who told you where I was?"

"Tell Norma to come on out."

"She's not here."

"Then where is she?"

"Gone. Sick. How did you get here anyway?"

"I don't see my Torino."

"I sold it."

"Where?"

"Everybody will get their money as soon as I can get a crop out. Don't push me. The best thing you can do is leave me alone."

"I'm coming into that house."

"No, you better hold it right there." He raised the shotgun. I didn't think he would shoot but you never know. Here was an unstable person who had threatened the President. It was a pump gun, an old Model 42, and I wasn't sure he even knew how to work it but I certainly didn't want to be killed with a .410.

"This is not much of a place," I said. "I was expecting a big plantation. Where are the people who do the work?"

"They're gone too. The head bozo quit and they all went with him. They tore up the generator and the water pump before they left. They shot some of the cows and ran the others off. About what you could expect. I'm through with those creeps."

"Tell Norma to come out on the porch for a minute."

"She's not here."

"Is she afraid to face me?"

"She's gone, vamoosed."

"I think she's in there looking out at me from somewhere."

"There's no one here but me."

"Does your father know you're here?"

"I'm through with him. His day is over. I'm through with you too. You don't have a clue to what's going on. You never did. Are you driving my Buick Special?"

"Yes."

"How did it do?"

"It did all right but I'm not here to discuss that."

"I thought clods like you were always ready to discuss cars."

"Not this time."

He went over to the hammock and sat down in it with the gun across his knees. I was standing in the road trying to think of what to do and say. I had started with a great moral advantage but it seemed to be slipping away. Was Norma in that house? I couldn't tell. Dupree was a liar but you couldn't even count on him to lie.

I said, "What about the woman who lives behind the Game and Fish Building?"

"What about her?"

"Why didn't you bring her with you?"

"Because I didn't want to."

"Did Norma rub that oil on you?"

"These are my natural body oils. We're short of water. Now leave me alone. Everybody will be paid."

"I'm not leaving until I talk to Norma."

"She doesn't want to talk to you. She said she was tired of living with a little old man."

"She never said that."

"She said she was tired of looking at your freckled shoulders and your dead hair."

"Norma never told you that. She doesn't talk that way."

"She doesn't like your name either."

I knew this was a lie too. From Edge to Midge was at worst a lateral move—no hybrid vigor to be expected from our union—and Norma was never one to make hateful remarks. Leave him alone! Next to me he was the least importuned person in Little Rock—people fled from rooms at the sound of his voice—and he kept saying leave him alone. I took a couple of steps toward the gate. He raised the shotgun.

"Better hold it right there."

"Why can't I come in if Norma is not there?"

"Because all my papers and my graphics are on the table. Does that answer your question?"

"What kind of papers? I didn't know you had any papers."

"There's a lot you don't know."

"Where did you sell my car? How much did you get for it?"

"Everybody will be paid in time. That's if they stop bothering me."

"Did you think I would come all the way down here just to listen to a few of your lies and then go home?"

"You'll get your money. And then you'll be happy. It doesn't take much for people like you."

"What will you do, mail it to me? Should I go home and watch the mail?"

"You'll get it."

"When?"

"As soon as I can get a crop out."

"Get a crop out. I'd like to see that. What kind of crop? You don't know the first thing about farming, Dupree. You don't know how to do anything. Look at that fence."

"You don't have to know much. What you have to know is how to make niggers work. That's the hard part."

"You say that from your hammock. Do you know Webster Spooner?"

"No."

"He's the bellboy at my hotel. He has three jobs, if not four. I'll bet you haven't made one friend in this country."

"You goofball."

"Put that shotgun down, you coward, and meet me out here in this road like a man and we'll see who the goofball is."

Instead of making his blood boil, my straightforward challenge only made him toss his head.

"I'm coming into that house, Dupree."

"Better not try it."

"Then I'll have to come back."

"Better not come at night."

"I have a .44 magnum out here in the glove compartment. It's as big as a flare pistol. You can fire just four more rounds from it and the next day the arch of your hand is so sore and numb you can't pick up a dime. That may give you some idea of its power and range. I'd rather not have to use it."

"What crap."

"I'm going now but I'll be back. Tell Norma I'm staying at the Fair Play Hotel in Belize."

"She's not interested in your accommodations. And I'm through passing along information from lower-middle-class creeps like you. I never did like doing it. Your time is coming, pal, soon. You better just leave me alone. If you people would leave me alone, maybe I could get some work done on my book."

"Your book?"

"My book on horde control."

"I didn't know about this."

"Shaping up the skraelings. Getting them organized. I'll tell them about rights and grievances they haven't even thought of yet in New York City. It's a breakthrough. Nobody has ever been able to get their attention and hold it for any appreciable length of time. I've hit on a way to do it with low-voltage strobe lights and certain audio-visual techniques that I'm not going into at this time. I couldn't expect you to understand it. My outline is almost complete but now I've lost another day's work, thanks to you."

Letters weren't enough for him. This monkey was writing a book! I said, "We are weaker than our fathers, Dupree."

"What did you say?"

"We don't even look like them. Here we are, almost thirty years old, and neither one of us even has a job. We're worse than the hippies."

"Leave it to you to come up with some heavy thinking like that. You find me trapped here in this land of niggers with your water-waster wife and you say we are weaker than our fathers. That's just the kind of crap I'm through passing along."

"I'll be back, Dupree."

"Why do you keep calling me by my name?"

"How do you wish to be addressed now?"

"You're saying my name too much."

"I'll be back."

"Better not come at night."

"I'm leaving this bottle right here in the road. It's Norma's lower-back medicine. Make sure she gets it before a car runs over it."

He went into the house. After a moment I saw the weak glow of a candle or an oil lamp from an inner room. I called out for Norma. There was no answer. I knew it was my duty to walk into that yard and up those steps and into that house but I was afraid to do it. I thought of ramming the two front pilings of the house with the Buick, thereby causing the house to topple forward and spilling forth Dupree through a door or window. Nothing to disconcert a proud man like a sudden tumble from his home. But might not Norma be injured too, flung perhaps from a bathtub? The hammock was still moving and I stood there and counted the diminishing oscillations until the thing came to rest at bottom dead center. I would lay Dupree out in that hammock when I had killed him. I would take a stick and pry his teeth apart—they would be clenched in a rictus—and I would place the candle between them. I would leave him in the hammock with the candle burning in his mouth and let the Belize detectives make of it what they would. I poked idly about in the garbage dump with my foot and turned up nothing of any real interest except for a one-gallon pickle jar. I put it in the car and left.

When I drove by the Mayan ruin, the two brush-cutters were taking another break and this time they had cigarettes. They were talking to a third man who was sitting astride a three-wheel motorcycle rig. Little crosses were painted all over the wooden cargo box and the name "Popo" was spelled out in red plastic reflectors on the back. There were brown-paper sacks in the cargo box. I waved. Then it came to me. Those were probably Dupree's supplies. I turned around and went back.

The Indians thought I wanted to tour the ruin again and so I did. Popo joined us. He was Spanish. We looked into the stone chambers again. Mosquitoes swarmed in our faces. Popo sat on a scooped-out block of stone that must have been a kind of altar. He smirked and crossed his arms and legs and asked me to take his picture. I didn't think he should behave that way on someone's altar but the Indians themselves found his antics funny and in any case I had no camera. Some gringo. No smokes and no camera and no money!

Popo spoke a little English. He said he had seen no woman at the Dupree place, no other person at all since the workers had left, but he had made only one previous delivery and he had not been inside the house. Dupree would not let him go past the gate. I looked through the paper sacks. I found no Pall Mall cigarettes, Norma's brand, or any other kind, and no single item that might have been for her exclusive use, except possibly for a bottle of hand lotion. But maybe Dupree had now taken up the use of Jergen's lotion. It was hard to say what he might or might not be doing in that house, in his strange new life.

I gave Popo a savings bond and told him that Dupree

was flying back to the States in a few hours. An emergency at home. He would no longer need this service. Popo was to keep the food and the beer and the kerosene and the change too, if any. Dupree wanted Popo and his family to have these things.

Popo was baffled. What about his glasses? What about the *remedios*, the *drogas*? He showed me Dupree's eyeglasses, wrapped in a repair order, and a big bottle of St. Joseph aspirins and a smaller bottle of yellow Valium tablets. I hadn't known that Dupree was a pillhead on top of everything else but I can't say I was surprised.

I said yes, Dupree did want the glasses and the drugs and I would see that he got them. Popo was reluctant to go along with all this and I gave him another E bond. The Indians pressed me again for cigarettes and I gave them each a bond too. I asked Popo about these birds. He said they were brothers. They worked for the government and they had been here for years fighting the brush. They could make the clearing no bigger because the stuff grew up behind them so fast. There was a third brother somewhere around, Popo told me, but he was always hiding in the woods and was seldom seen by outsiders.

I made sure that Popo followed me back to town and I drove slow on the sandy part so as not to dust him up.

Nine

The Chinaman's store was still open and I bought some crackers and a thick oval can of Mexican sardines and took them to my room. Karl's radio was playing at moderate volume. I don't think I had even noticed it until I heard the announcer say, "No more calls, please, we have a winner." Then Karl switched it off for the first time since my arrival.

Or maybe tube collapse or power failure or a political coup at the station itself. They always went for the radio station in these places. I wondered if they had ever had a really first-class slaughter of students here. Better watch my step. Dupree had better watch his smart mouth too. Name your cat or dog after the Prime Minister in a place like this and you would be in the jug but pronto.

And there would be no fool here to go his bail, if they had bail. His papers! His book! His social program! It was some sort of nasty Communist claptrap, no doubt, with people who sounded a lot like Dupree as the bosses. He would tell us what to do and when to do it. The chairman! He would reward us and punish us. What a fate! Give me Mr. Dupree any day. The book would never be finished of course. The great outline of history! His slide shows! His skraelings! Pinch their arms and he could get their attention. But was Norma in that house or not? That was the important thing.

I ate my sardine supper and took a bath. I washed the big pickle jar, along with the top, and put them on the

windowsill to dry. Then I called down the stairs for Webster
Spooner. He appeared with his notebook, ready for any as-
signment. I showed him the jar.

"A little surprise for you, Webster."

"Sor?"

"I thought you might have some use for it. It's clean. You
can save pennies in it. Keep a pet fish maybe. You would
have to change the water. If you decide on the fish."

He looked it over but I could see he wasn't interested in
it and I suggested he give it to Ruth, who could make some
household use of it. He took the jar away and a few minutes
later I heard Ruth slam it against something and break it.

I went to bed and reviewed the day's events, a depressing
exercise. I had not handled myself so badly, I thought, and
yet there were no results. I must do better. Tomorrow I
would enter the Dupree house, come what may. I would
watch for an opening and then make a dash across the road.
What I needed was a timetable of things to do. An orderly
schedule. I sat up in bed and ruled off a sheet of paper with
evenly spaced lines and corresponding numbers down to sixteen. It was a neat piece of work, the form itself.

But I suddenly despaired of trying to think of that many
things to do and of getting them in the proper order. I didn't
want to leave any blank spaces and I didn't want to pad it
out with dishonest filler items either, like "tie shoes." What
was wrong with me? I had once been very good at this kind
of thing. I crumpled the paper and dropped it on the floor.

The sardine stink filled the room and overwhelmed the
river stink. Outside on the street I heard the slow grinding
whine of a Mopar starter—a Plymouth or a Dodge or a
Chrysler. The engine caught and idled smoothly and after a
minute or so the car drove away.

Jack Wilkie, perhaps, in his Imperial. He had finally arrived. He had been outside watching my window. But no,

Jack would never lurk. He might break down the door but he wouldn't lurk. That was more in my line. I felt queasy. I took two of the orange pills. I can't say I was really sick, unless you count narcolepsy and mild xenophobia, but I was a little queasy. If there had been a gang of reporters outside clamoring to know my condition, Webster would have had to announce to them that it was satisfactory.

I slept and dreamed fitfully. In one dream I was looking through a Sears catalogue and I came across Mrs. Symes and Melba and the doctor modeling lawn furniture. They were wearing their ordinary clothes, unlike the other models, who were in bright summer togs. The other dream took place in a dark bar. The boy Travis was sitting on a stool with his legs dangling. That is, he looked like Travis, only his name seemed to be Chet this time. He was drinking from a tall frosted glass and he was waiting for five o'clock and victims to chirp at. I took a seat at the other end of the bar. He didn't see me for a while and then when he did see me he shifted around and said, "So how you been, Ray? You never come around anymore." I said I was all right and I asked about his mother. Chet said she was fine. He offered to buy me a drink and I said I had to go to Texarkana.

I woke early and saw that I had been drooling on the pillow. The ear hair couldn't be far behind now. I washed and dressed and ate the rest of the sardines and drove back to the Dupree place.

The hairy monkey was up early too. I had no sooner parked in the turnout than he came to the door with the .410. He said nothing. I opened all the car doors to catch any breeze that might come up and sat in the driver's seat with my feet outside on the garbage. Dupree went back inside. The medicine bottle full of four-dollar capsules was still standing in the road where I had left it.

Now and then I would get out as though to start across

the road and he would instantly appear at the door. He must have been sitting just behind it in the shadow. I called out for Norma. I told her that I had her medicine and her silver and that if she would just come to the fence for a minute I would give it to her. There was no answer.

After the engine had cooled off, I sat on the hood with my heels hooked on the bumper. At the end of each hour, just as the second hand hit twelve, I called out for her. Late in the morning Dupree came out and sat in the hammock with the gun on his lap. He read a magazine, holding it about five inches from his eyes.

He wouldn't answer me when I spoke. His plan, I could see, was to keep silent and not acknowledge my presence, except for the countering moves with the shotgun. When he looked about, he pretended not to see me, in the way of a movie actor whose eyes go professionally blank when tracking across the gaze of the camera. The dog picked up on his mood and he too ignored me. Dupree sat there with his magazine, feigning solitude and peace. He fondled his belly and chest with his fingertips the way some people do when they find themselves in swimming trunks. I got one of the rusty cans of warm beer from the trunk and made a show of opening it and drinking it.

Around noon he stood up and stretched. He strolled out into the yard and peered down the road with his watery eyes. I had been waiting for some such move.

"Popo is not coming today," I said. "He's not coming tomorrow either." I held up his eyeglasses but he wouldn't look at me. "I have your glasses here, Dupree. They're right here. I have your aspirins and your dope too. Look. Here's what I think of your dope." I poured the yellow pills out and crushed them into the garbage with my foot. He couldn't see what I was doing and the effect was thus lost.

He made no reply and went over to the green tractor and

climbed up on it and tried to start it. It was a diesel and by
nature hard to start. Dupree lacked patience. His contempt
for machinery was unpleasant to watch. He slammed and
wrenched things about. A gentler touch and maybe a shot of
ether into the breather and it probably would have cranked
right up, but Dupree, the farmer's son, knew little of these
matters. When he might have been learning how to start a
tractor, he was away at various schools, demonstrating in the
streets and acquiring his curious manners and his curious
notions. The student prince! He even had a place to run to
when things got hot.

He went back to the porch and sat on the hammock. I
drank another can of warm beer. He suddenly made up his
mind to speak, saying, "I suppose you've told everybody
where I am, Burke."

"Not yet, no."

He was calling me Burke! There followed a silent interval of about an hour before he spoke again. He said, "Those
aspirins are for my dog." I had been quietly thinking over
the Burke business and now I had to think about the aspirins
and the dog. I should explain that Burke worked on the copy
desk with us. It is true that Burke and I were only dimly
perceived by the world and that a new acquaintance might
have easily gotten us confused, might have hailed Burke on
the street as "Midge," or introduced me to another person as
"Burke," but Dupree knew us well from long association,
knew the thousand differences between us, and I could only
conclude that he was now so far advanced in his political
thinking that he could no longer tell one person from another. I should say too that Burke was by far the best copy
editor on the desk. Even Dupree was better at the work than
I, who have never had a firm grasp of English grammar, as
may be seen. The flow of civic events that made up the news
in our paper was incomprehensible to me too, but Burke

shone in both these areas. He was always fretting over improper usage, over people saying "hopefully" and "finalized," and he talked knowledgeably about things that went on in the world. That's enough on Burke.

I got the St. Joseph bottle from my pocket and threw it across to the porch. Dupree picked it up and took it back to the hammock and ate four or five aspirins, making a show of relishing them, as I had done with the beer. He said, "My dog never took an aspirin in his life." You couldn't believe a word he said.

That afternoon he tried the tractor again. He got it to chug a few times but the black smoke and the noise of the cold idle knock startled him and he shut it down at once. I stayed there all day. It was a blockade. I was ready to intercept any delivery or visitor, but no one came. There was nothing, it seemed, beyond this place. I watched the windows for Norma, for flitting shadows. I was always good at catching roach movement or mouse movement from the corner of my eye. Small or large, any object in my presence had only to change its position slightly, by no more than a centimeter, and my head would snap about and the thing would be instantly trapped by my gaze. But I saw no sign of life in that house. All this time, of course, I was also watching and waiting for the chance to dash across the road. The circumstances were never quite right and, to put it plainly, I funked it again.

It was still daylight when I got back to Belize and I drove aimlessly about town. Sweat stung my eyes. The heat was such that I couldn't focus my mind. The doctor and Webster Spooner and I had all contrived to get ourselves into the power of women and I could see no clear move for any one of us. It was hard to order my thoughts.

I stopped at the Fort George Hotel for something to drink. The bar was on the second floor and it overlooked a kind of estuary. The water was still and brown and not at all inviting. Out there somewhere, I knew, was a coral reef with clear water and fish of strange shapes and dazzling colors. The bar itself was nice enough. I was up to my old trick of rooming in a cheap place and drinking in a better place. I saw the American woman and the boy sitting on a couch by the windows.

Low tumbling clouds approached from the Caribbean. I drank a bottle of Falcon beer. It had a plain label. There were no boasts about choice hops and the stuff had won no medals at any international exposition but it was cold and tasted like every other beer. Exercise, that was what I needed. That always cleared the brain. I could jog around the entire city and look for my car at the same time. But wouldn't children jeer at me all along such a circuit? Pelting me, perhaps, with bits of filth. And what about the town dogs, all at my heels? It would be much more sensible to install some muscle-building spring devices in the privacy of my room. A stationary bicycle. But Webster would have the devil of a time getting that stuff up the stairs. No, a brisk swim. That would be just the thing. An isolated beach and some vigorous strokes in foamy salt water.

The clouds drew closer and gusts of wind ruffled the surface of the brown water. Drops of rain struck the windows. I left my stool and moved across the room for a better look at things, taking a table next to the American woman. Four pelicans in a column were gliding over the water, almost touching it. Behind them came two more. These two were flapping their heavy wings and they were climbing up to the misty edges of the cloud. A shaft of lightning struck the second bird and he contracted into a ball and fell like a rock. The other one took no notice, missing not a beat with his wings.

I was astonished. I knew I would tell this pelican story

over and over again and that it would be met with widespread disbelief but I thought I might as well get started and so I turned to the woman and the boy and told them what I had seen. I pointed out the floating brown lump.

She said, "It looks like a piece of wood."

"That's a dead pelican."

"I heard the thunder but I didn't see anything."

"I saw the whole thing."

"I love storms."

"I think this is just a convective shower. Afternoon heat."

This woman or girl was about thirty years old and she was wearing blue jeans and one of those grain-sack shirts from Mexico with the faded printing on it. Her sunglasses were parked high on her head. I asked if I might join her. She was indifferent. She had a hoarse voice and both she and the boy had sunburned faces. Her name, I learned, was Christine Walls. She was an artist from Arizona. She had a load of Arizona art in her van and she and the boy had been wandering about in Mexico and Central America. She extended an index finger across the table, for shaking, it finally dawned on me, and I took it and gave it a tentative shake.

I told her that I had recently dreamed of just such a tableau as this—a woman and a small boy and I seated before a low table. She didn't know what to make of me. First the pelican and now this. The details, I should say, didn't correspond exactly. Christine didn't have nice clothes like those of the woman in the dream and Victor didn't appear to be a little smart-ass like Travis, although he was clunking his heels against the seat in a rhythmic way that I found irritating. Still, the overall picture was close enough. Too close!

She asked my date of birth. We exchanged views on the heat. I remarked on her many sparkling rings and said that my wife Norma was also fond of silver and turquoise. She asked me what the prevailing colors were in Little Rock and I couldn't remember, I who am so good on colors. She said her former husband was a Mama's boy. His name was Dean Walls and he wouldn't make a move without first consulting his mother. He was a creepy spider, she said, who repaired watches in a well-lighted cubicle on the first floor of a large department store. We talked about the many different vocations in life and I had to confess that I had none. The boy Victor was being left out of our conversation and so I asked him if he was enjoying his travels. He didn't answer. I asked him how many states he had been in and he said, "More than you." Christine said she planned to return to college one day and study psychology, and that she would eventually make her home in Colorado or San Francisco or maybe Vermont. An earlier plan to marry again had collapsed when her fiancé was killed in a motorcycle accident. His name was Don and he had taught oriental methods of self-defense in a martial arts academy.

"They called it an accident," she said, "but I think the government had him killed because he knew too much about flying saucers."

"What did he know?"

"He knew a lot. He had seen several landings. He was a witness to those landings outside Flagstaff when they were kidnapping dogs."

"What kind of dogs?"

"What kind of dogs were they, Victor?"

"Collies and other work dogs. The aliens stunned them first with electric sticks."

"Yes, and Don had seen all that and so the government had to silence him."

I asked if she and the boy would like to join me in a swim before dark.

"In the pool?"

"No, I'm not a guest here. I was thinking about the beach."

"I love to walk the beach but I can't swim."

"How does it happen that you can't swim, Christine?"

"I don't know. Have you been here long?"

"Just a few days."

"How was your trip down?"

"It was a nightmare."

"A nightmare. I love that. Have you had much trouble with the money?"

"No, I haven't exchanged any yet."

The boy Victor clapped one hand to his forehead and fell back against the seat and said, "Oh brother, is he in for it!"

Christine said, "You're not just a-woofin', buddy boy. This money is really something else. They call it a dollar but it's not the same value as ours. It's worth some odd fraction like sixty-eight cents. Even Victor can't get it straight. Hey, Ray, I want to ask you a question before I forget it. Why are there so darned many hardware stores in Belize?"

"Are there a lot? I hadn't noticed that."

"I've seen two already." She touched my arm and lowered her voice. "Don't stare but wait a second and then look at that fantastic girl."

"Where?"

"That black waitress. The way she holds her head. See. Her regal bearing."

Two hardware stores didn't seem like a lot to me. This was Staci talk. Nerve gas. I would have to stay on my toes to follow this stuff. She suddenly went into a contortion, trying to scratch a place on her back that was hard to reach. She laughed and twisted and said, "What I need is a back scratcher."

I thought she meant just that, a long bronze rod with little claws at one end, and maybe she did, but then I saw what a good chance I had missed for an initial intimacy, always so awkward. The moment had passed, needless to say, the itching abated, by the time I had worked it all out.

Christine wasn't a guest at the Fort George either. She was looking for a place to take a bath. She had tried to rent a room with bath for an hour or so instead of an entire day but the Fort George didn't offer that plan and neither did it accept works of art in payment. I volunteered the use of the communal bath at the Fair Play. She quickly accepted and began to get her things together.

Then I thought about trying to get her past Ruth without paying. I wasn't in the mood for any hotel comedy. I had spoken too soon. The towels were never quite dry at the Fair Play. The bathroom was a foul chamber too, and the door wouldn't lock, the knobs and the brass mechanism being completely gone, the wood all splintered around the hole, where some raging guest had forced an entry or an exit. I knew what would happen. This boy Vic would say, "P.U., Mom!" and make me look bad. So I took them instead to the Unity Tabernacle. They followed me in the van. It was a Volkswagen and it made a four-cylinder micro-clatter. There were decals of leaping green fish and bounding brown deer on both sides of the vehicle, a sporting touch I would not have associated with Christine and Victor—or with Dean, for that matter.

Ten

Mrs. Symes was in front of the church. She was wearing a man's felt hat and she was talking to a gang of boys who were milling about, waiting to see Tarzan. She was upset because Father Jackie had not yet delivered the film for the big showing.

This Christine distraction annoyed her further but she told me to take the girl in and show her the bath. I expected no less, even though I knew that Mrs. Symes's tangled creed must be based more or less on faith rather than works. The doctor himself had told me that she had fed more tramps during the Depression than any other person in Louisiana.

Christine decided to do her laundry too, and I helped her carry it up the stairs, sacks of the stuff. There is always more to these pickup deals than first meets the eye. She proceeded to steam up the place. First she scrubbed Victor down and then she washed her Arizona clothes in the bathtub and hung them about inside on tables and lamps and other fixtures.

Melba didn't like this intrusion. She sat in her chair sulking and chewing on something brittle, or munching rather. Dr. Symes, hearing the stir, peered out from his bedroom. He saw me and he waved a sheet of paper and he came over to join me on the couch.

"Good news, Speed," he said. "Hold on to your hat. Mama has agreed to write a letter for me."

"What kind of letter has she agreed to write?"

"A wonderful letter of authorization. It's a new day."

She still refused to lease him the island but he had per-suaded her to let him use the island in some ill-defined way. Or so he said. In fact, Mrs. Symes had written nothing. The doctor had written a legal-sounding statement on a sheet of Melba's crinkly airmail paper that gave him the right "to dig holes and erect fences and make such other improvements on Jean's Island as he may deem necessary or desirable." It only remained, he said, to get the old lady's signature, and a notary public to witness it and to squeeze the paper with his pliers-like seal.

Notarized or not, the letter didn't impress me much. "What about your financing?" I said. "The banks will want more than this."

"What do you know about it?"

"My father is in the construction business."

He read through the statement. "This would be enough for me. What more could they want?"

"They want to see a lease or a land contract. They want something that will hold up. Your letter doesn't even de-scribe the property."

"It says Jean's Island plain enough."

"Maybe there's another Jean's Island. They want metes and bounds."

"I don't believe you know what you're talking about."

"Maybe not."

"I've never believed it. I don't believe you know your ass from first base. I was closing deals before you were born. Mama owns the land outright and that makes her the prin-cipal. This letter makes me her agent. Will you sit there and tell me that the law of agency has been repealed?"

What he was groping for, I thought, was a letter giving him power of attorney but I didn't want to go on with this and antagonize him further. For all my big talk of finance, it was I who needed a loan, and a quick one. The doctor went to his bedroom and brought back the big pasteboard box. He pawed angrily through the stuff. "I'll give you metes and bounds," he said. "I'll give you section, township, and range."

The plan I had hatched while reclining on the couch was to take Christine to the Fort George for a seafood supper, leaving Victor here at the movie. It was an improper sort of business for a married man who was not legally separated but the idea wouldn't go away. An alternative plan was to get supper here at the church and then take Christine out for drinks alone, which would be much cheaper, unless she went in for expensive novelty drinks. I couldn't tell from the feel of things whether they had eaten supper here yet or not.

I asked the doctor cold if he could let me have another twenty dollars.

Instead of answering my question, he showed me a photograph of his father, the squeamish Otho. It was a brown print on crumbling cardboard. Then he showed me a picture of an intense yokel with a thick shock of hair parted in the middle. The boy was wearing a white medical smock and he was sitting behind a microscope, one hand holding a glass slide and the other poised to make a focal adjustment. It was Dr. Symes himself as a student at Wooten Institute. Young microbe hunter! The microscope had no solid look of machined steel about it, no heaviness, and my guess was that it was a dummy, a photographer's prop.

There were more photographs, of Marvel Clark with Ivo and without Ivo, of an adult Ivo standing by his roofing truck and his hot-tar trailer, of houses, cars, fish, of people on porches, in uniform, of a grim blockhouse medical clinic, of people at a restaurant table, their eyes dazzled by a flash bulb like movie stars caught at play. He showed me a picture of the Wooten Panthers, a scraggly six-man football team. A medical school with a football team! Who did they play? The coach was Dr. Wooten himself, and Dr. Symes, with his bulk, played center. But there seemed to be no picture of the island, the only thing I was curious about.

Suddenly the doctor gave a start and a little yelp of discovery. "Another one! I missed this booger!" It was a window envelope that had not been opened. He wasted no time in ripping the end off and shaking out a check. It was a monthly insurance check for $215 made out to Mrs. Symes. It was almost a year old. "Some of them go back eight and nine years," he said, folding it and sticking it in his shirt pocket. "This makes thirty some-odd I've found so far."

"Why doesn't she cash them?"

"She cashes some and she forgets some. People like Mama, they don't care whether an insurance company can balance its books or not. They never think about things like that. The Aetna books mean less than nothing to her."

"What will you do with them?"

"What do you think?"

"Your mother will have to endorse them."

"They'll be well endorsed, don't worry about it. That's no step for a stepper. And Mama will get it all back a thousand-fold. This is just seed money for the first drilling rig. This is just peanuts. I'm talking big bucks." He looked about for eavesdroppers and then lowered his voice. "There's a billion cubic feet of natural gas under that island, Speed. I plan to have two producing wells down by the first of the year. Do you think that's an unrealistic goal?"

"I don't know. What about The City of Life?"

"The what?"

"The nursing home. The long yellow house."

Waves of confusion passed across his face. "Nursing home?"

"On Jean's Island. The City of Life."

Then he was able to remember, but just barely, and he dismissed it out of hand as though it had been an idea of mine. He resumed his search through the big box and he sang softly the words of "Mockingbird Hill." He passed along odd items of interest to me. I looked at an old diary that Mrs. Symes had kept. It wasn't a very satisfactory one, in that there were only a dozen or so brief entries in it covering a period of five years. The last one had been made on a September day in 1958. "Dry summer," she had written. "Mangoes bitter this year. God's plan unfolding very slowly." I repeated my request to the doctor for a loan and got no answer.

He was studying a brittle newspaper clipping. "I wish you would look at this," he said. "I don't know why in the world Mama keeps all this stuff."

It was an editorial cartoon of a fat man with buttons popping from his shirt. With one hand the chubby figure was clutching a wedge of pie and with the other he was holding out a Band-Aid and saying, "Here, apply this!" to an injured man with his tongue lolling and tire tracks across his head and x's for eyes. The caption underneath said, "Our own Doc Symes."

"What's that about the pie?"

"Newspaper humor. Those boys love to dish it out but did you ever see one who could take it like a man? I weighed about two hundred and ninety-five then. I had to special-order all my suits from Benny's in New Orleans. Fifty-four shorts. I'm just a shadow of that man. The Shreveport *Times* put dark glasses and a fez on me and called me Farouk. This was the original frame-up. I was suspended for six months. They accused me of practicing homeopathy, of all things. Can you imagine that?"

"I've heard of homeopathy but I don't know what it is."

"The hair of the dog. There's a little something to it but not much. There's a little truth in everything. I never practiced it but any stick was good enough to beat a dog like me. Can you see what I'm driving at?"

"Was this the hearing-aid deal?"

"No connection whatsoever. This was my arthritis clinic. The Brewster Method. Massive doses of gold salts and nuxated zinc followed by thirty push-ups and a twelve-minute nap. None of your thermo tubs or hydro baloney. You don't hear much about it anymore but for my money it's never been discredited. I saw marked improvement in those who could actually raise themselves from the floor. The older people found it painful, naturally, but that was the humidity as much as anything. I was to blame for the atmospheric conditions too, you see. Granted, the humidity is around a hundred percent in Ferriday, but everybody can't go to Tucson, can they?

"I worked day and night trying to help those people, trying to give them some relief. I never made so much money in my life and the doctors' gang couldn't stand it. My prosperity just stuck in their craw. 'Get Symes!' they cried, and 'Bust Symes!' and 'Kick him where it hurts!' That was all they could think about for two years. Well, here I am. You will judge of their success. I haven't been a newsmaker for years."

"I don't see how the homeopathy ties in."

"It doesn't tie in. Brewster had once been a homeopath, that's all. He later became a naturopath. So what? He had one or two good ideas. I'll look you square in the eye, Speed, and tell you that I have never practiced anything but orthodox medicine. This was a setup, pure and simple. They were lying in wait. It wasn't my medicine that stirred those boys up, it was my accounts receivable. You can bank on it, that's the only reason any doctor ever turns another one in."

Christine was bustling about in white shorts and a pale

blue work shirt that was knotted in front so as to expose her red abdomen. I could tell she was older than Norma from the fatty dimpling on the backs of her thighs. It was like the patterns you sometimes see in blown sand. She had washed her hair, and her ears stuck through the wet brown strands. I found her very attractive with her sunburn and her hoarse voice and her brisk manner. She was making friends with Melba and I liked that too, a young person deferring and giving her time to an older person. She was showing Melba something, a book or a purse or a stamp album. The old lady had been out of sorts and now she was jiggling her leg up and down, making the floor shake again. Christine was charming Melba!

"A patient named J. D. Brimlett developed osteomyelitis," said the doctor. "That was the claim anyway. I'm convinced he already had it. He had everything else. Emphysema, glaucoma, no adrenal function, you name it. Two little hard dark lungs like a pair of desiccated prunes. He belonged in a carnival instead of an arthritis clinic. The world's sickest living man. No blood pressure to speak of and you couldn't find a vein to save your ass. Renal failure on top of everything else. The Mayo brothers couldn't have pulled that chump through, but no, it was my zinc that killed him. A Class B irritant poison, they said. I should have screened him out. I should have closed my eyes and ears to his suffering and sent him on his way. I didn't do it and I've been paying for that mistake ever since. There's always a son of a bitch like Brimlett hanging around, doing anything to get attention, dying even, and just ruining things for everybody else. Do you want it in a nutshell? I was weak. I was soft."

He raised a hand to repel shouts of protest and then went on, "It wasn't the zinc and they knew it. I took a five-pound bag of the stuff to my hearing and offered to eat it all right there with a spoon but they wouldn't let me do it. Brewster himself admitted that it would give the skin a greenish tint. There was never any secret about that. You get a trivial cosmetic problem in exchange for relief from agonizing pain. Many people considered it a bargain. Talcum powder is cheap enough. It's true, in a very few cases the eyebrows fell out but I've seen cortisone do far worse things. Can you see it now? Do you see what I'm driving at? It was all a smoke screen. The point is, you can't cross the doctors' union. Cross those boys and they'll hand you your lunch. Forget the merits of your case. They kicked Pasteur in the ass. Lister too, and Smitty Wooten. They know everything and Symes is an old clap doctor."

Outside it was dark. I excused myself and went downstairs to get the chest of silverware from the car. When I opened the church door, the milling boys fell back and looked at me in silent terror, fearing another announcement about the movie being delayed. I made my way through them and I saw that Leet or one of his tireless runners had put another leaflet under a windshield wiper.

The silver chest had been knocked around in the trunk. It was greasy and scuffed and the leatheroid skin was peeling and bubbling up in places from glue breakdown. I put the chest under my arm and slammed the trunk lid. I thought I heard someone call my name. I couldn't place the voice, though it was familiar in some way.

I said, "What?"

"This way."

"Where?"

"Over here, Ray."

"Where? Who wants to see me?"

One of the older boys with a cigar said, "Nobody want to see you, mon. The peoples want to see Tarzan." A good laugh all around at my expense.

The forks and spoons and knives were jumbled about in

the chest and I stopped on the stairs to sort them out and stack them in their proper notches and hollows before making my presentation to the doctor. He said nothing when I set it on his lap and opened it, Mrs. Edge's shining array of cutlery under his red eye. I told him that I needed some more money at once and that if I had not settled the entire debt by noon tomorrow the silver service was his to keep. It was all too fast for him, my proposition and the heavy thing on his knees. I said nothing more and waited for him to take it in.

Victor had settled in at my old spot in front of the fan. His mother had spread out the beach towel for him. One side of the towel was a Confederate flag and on the other side there was a kneeling cowgirl in a bikini. Her body was sectioned off and labeled "Round," "Chuck," "Rump," and so on, like a side of beef, and the Western cutie was winking and saying, "What's your cut?" Victor was belly down on the towel reading a Little Lulu comic book. The book was in Spanish but he was still getting a few chuckles from it. "Hoo," he would say, and, "Hoo hoo." There might have been a dove in the room. Dr. Symes looked about for the source of these murmurs.

I said, "That's sterling silver. It's a complete set. All I want is fifty dollars on it until tomorrow."

"Certainly not. Why would I want to tie up my money in spoons? You'd do better to take this to a pawnbroker or a chili joint."

"It's just until noon tomorrow."

"Bill me later. That's your answer for everything. It's no good, Speed. You'll never get anywhere living on short-term credit like this. It's a bad game and I just can't keep carrying you. Who is that little chap on the floor?"

"He's the son of that girl in the bathroom."

"The one who's washing all the clothes?"

"Yes."

"Now who is she?"

I tried to tell him but as he was swinging his big head around Melba swam into his ken and he forgot Christine. He called out, "Melba, can you hear me?"

"I heard that," she said. "I haven't been listening to you, if that's what you mean."

"I want you to get up out of that chair this very minute."

"What for?"

"I want you to get up out of that chair and start walking two miles every day."

"No, Reo."

"Now isn't this a fine thing. She says no to her doctor."

He closed the chest and moved it to one side, away from me, in a proprietary way. I didn't think we had made a deal and I knew I had no money. Mrs. Symes had just made the painful trip up the stairs and she was standing at the top gasping for breath, trying to remember something, what the trip was for. She gave it up as a bad job and went back down the stairs.

The doctor handed me another envelope from the box. "Take a gander at that one, will you? Never opened. I wrote that letter to Mama from San Diego almost three years ago. How in the world can you do business with someone like that?"

"This letter was postmarked in Mexico."

"Old Mexico? Let me see. Yes, it sure was. Tijuana. I was going back and forth to the Caliente track. Notice the thick enclosure. Rod Garza had drawn up a prospectus for me. I wanted Mama to look it over and see if she wouldn't co-sign a note. I wrote this very letter in Rod's law office."

I pointed out that my previous loans were already secured by the bonds, that I had returned his wallet when he thought it was lost, and that this silver set was worth several hundred dollars. He appeared to consider the points and I thought he might even be wavering, but his thoughts were many miles to the northwest.

"Rod had been reprimanded twice by the Ethics Committee of the Tijuana Bar Association," he said, "but he could always work himself out of a corner. All except for that last one. You can't talk your way out of an exploding car, there's not enough time. And they knew he was no leaper. Oh, they had cased him, all right. They knew just how quick he was off the mark. He's gone now and I miss him more every day. Strawberries! Can you imagine that? We were trying to raise strawberries on government land. Rod got some boys out of prison to do the work, if you could call it work. As fast as you got one of those pickpockets on his feet, the one behind you would be squatting down again. And hot? You think this is hot? Those pimps were dropping in their tracks. Rodrigo would park his black Pontiac out there in the desert and then roll the windows up to keep the dust out. When we got back to it, the seat covers would be melting. Open the door and the heat blast would make you faint. An inferno. You could have roasted a duck in the trunk. Precious memories, how they linger. Listen to me, Speed. If your time is worth more than twenty cents an hour, don't ever fool with strawberries. I helped Rod every way I knew how. We were just like David and Jonathan. When he was trying to get his patent, I took him up to Long Beach and introduced him to a good lawyer name of Welch. Rod had an interest in a denture factory in Tijuana and he was trying to get a U.S. patent on their El Tigre model. They were wonderful teeth. They had two extra canines and two extra incisors of tungsten steel. Slap a set of those Tiger plates in your mouth and you can throw your oatmeal out the window. You could shred an elk steak with those boogers. Did I say Everett Welch? I meant Billy. Billy is the lawyer.

He's the young one. I had known his father, Everett, you see, back in Texas when he was a scout there for the Cubs or the White Sox, one of the Chicago teams. He was a great big fine-looking man. He later went to Nevada and became minister of music at the Las Vegas Church of God, introduced tight harmony to those saps out there. He sold water to Jews. Jews are smart but you can put water in a bottle and they'll buy it. He had a high clear voice and when he sang ' 'Tis so sweet to be remembered on a bright or cloudy day,' you could close your eyes and swear you were listening to Bill Monroe him-self. And get this. He's the only man I ever knew who saw Dix in the flesh. He met him once in the public library in Odessa, Texas. Listen to this. Dix was sitting at a table read-ing a newspaper on a stick and Welch recognized him from a magazine picture. It was right after that big article on Dix, right around the time of that famous June 1952 issue of *Motel Life* with the big spread on Dix, pictures of his trunk and his slippers and his mechanical pencil and some of his favorite motel rooms. The whole issue was devoted to Dix. There was a wide red band across the cover that said, 'John Selmer Dix: Genius or Madman?' I didn't have enough sense to stash away a copy of that magazine. I could name my own price for it today. That's the only place where Dix's Fort Worth address was ever published in full."

This was not, as I first thought, a speech or a proclama-tion that Dix had made in Fort Worth, but rather a post office box number and a zip code.

Dr. Symes continued, "This was during the period, you may remember, when Dix was on strike. He had repudiated all his early stuff, said *Wings* was nothing but trash, and didn't write another line, they say, for twelve years. Nobody really knows why. Oh, there were plenty of theories—that he was drunk, that he was crazy, that he was sick, that he was struck dumb before the immensity of his task, that he was just pissed off about something—but nobody really knows. Do you want my thinking on it? I believe he was actually writing all that time, that he was filling up thousands of sheets of paper with his thoughts and then just squirreling the stuff away in his tin trunk. But for some reason that we can't understand yet he wanted to hold it all back from the reading public, let them squeal how they may. Here's my opinion. Find the missing trunk and you've found the key to his so-called silent years. You've found a gold mine is what you've found.

"Anyway, Welch tried to talk to him there in the Odessa library, whisper to him, you know, across the table, but Dix wouldn't say anything. He wouldn't even admit he was Dix. He wanted to read his paper and every time Welch asked him a question Dix would just drum his feet under the table real fast, to show he was annoyed. Welch handled it all wrong. He got mad and grabbed the man by the throat and made him confess he was John Selmer Dix. Then Welch cooled off and apologized and Dix said that was all right but not to ever disturb him again while he was reading the *Star-Telegram*, that his private life was his own and all that. Now the question is, was that stranger really Dix? If it *was* Dix, answer me this. *Where were all his keys*? Everett Welch admitted to me that he saw no jumbo key ring on the man's belt and that he heard no clinking of keys when he was shaking him. Even so, Welch swears it was Dix he talked to that day. Welch is an honest man but I wasn't there and I can't say. I just don't know. The man may have been a very clever faker. There were plenty of fakers going around then, and they're still going around. You've probably heard of the fellow out in Barstow who claims to this day that he is Dix. I've never believed it. He lives out there in the desert in a caboose with his daughter and sells rocks. Can you beat it? Dix in the desert with his delicate skin. Selling ornamental quartz out of an old Southern Pacific caboose. If you believe that, you'll believe anything. Do you know what he says? He says the man who died in Tulsa was just some old retired fart from the oil fields who was trading off a similar name. He makes a lot of the closed coffin and the hasty funeral in Ardmore. He makes a lot of the missing trunk. Good points, you might think, but I've got a trump for him. *Dix never had a daughter!* There's another faker, in Florida, who claims he is Dix's half brother. Go see him out there on the edge of Jacksonville and he'll let you look at the trunk for a fee. A trunk is more like it. He won't dare to open it and you have to stand back about four or five feet behind a rope to even look at it. That little room is dark too, they say. Let me save you a trip to Florida, Speed. I've seen that crook's picture. They ran a picture of him and his little Dix museum in *Trailer Review* and I can tell you he bears no resemblance whatsoever to Dix and is in no way related to him. You can look at a man's ears and tell."

Here the doctor paused, having found the title abstract. He thumbed quickly through the pages until he came to the legal description of the island property. He showed me the authoritative figures, taking delight in the fractions and the "SW" and "NE," and then he left for his room to draft another letter.

I was desperate and shameless and I asked Melba if she could lend me ten dollars. She was willing enough but she couldn't help me because she had cashed a check for Christine and had only a dollar or two left in her purse. She showed me the yellow check. It had been folded so long the creases were fuzzy. It was a two-party check on a bank in Mesa, Arizona. There was nothing left to do but go and see Leet.

Eleven

All that was left of the old ink factory was a tall brick chimney, round and tapering, of the kind that often marks the site of a small college or government hospital. Leet's Motor Ranch, a lesser dream, was a field of weeds that adjoined the factory grounds. It appeared to be more of a salvage yard than a used-car lot, more of a cemetery than a ranch. Two old industrial boilers from the ink factory were standing upright at the entrance to Leet's drive, forming a kind of grand portal. I say "from the ink factory" but that is only a guess because I know next to nothing about the manufacture of ink, whether it is ever boiled or subjected to bursts of steam at any stage, and these boilers may have had an entirely different origin.

I passed between them and drove down the lane and parked in front of Leet's headquarters shed, which was also his dwelling place. It was lighted in front by a yellow bulb. Behind the shed there were three columns of derelict cars, their hoods and trunk lids raised as though for a military inspection. I could hear the steady hum of insects or of advancing rust in the damp field. The only operable vehicle I could see, the only one on wheels, was a Dodge Power Wagon with a winch and a wrecker boom on the back.

Leet was sitting under the yellow light on a disembodied car seat. He had put his picture book aside and he was listening to organ music that came from two disembodied car speakers. They were connected to a disembodied cassette

player which was in turn hooked up to a disembodied car
battery with two alligator clips. He was pink instead of white
and he had the fat pink hands of a child, little star-shaped
hands, remarkably clean for his trade. They were clasped
across his belly and he was stretched out with his ankles
crossed.

I knew he had just polished off a big bowl of porridge or
parsnips or some such dish, I having spotted him at once for
a house pig like me who cherished his room and his kitchen
treats and other solo and in-house indulgences. Beside him
on top of a wooden ammunition box I saw a giant English
chocolate bar, about ten inches by four inches by one inch, a
stack of car magazines, and a three-gallon water cooler with
a tin cup chained to it. Everything was within easy reach of
the pink hands.

He didn't rise to greet me. He put on a pair of round
glasses and said, "That looks like an old V-6 Buick."

"That's what it is."

"Dual-path transmission?"

"It's air-cooled. I don't know the name of it."

"Noisy timing chain?"

"It's a good car."

"No doubt, but it has a very rum transmission. Once it
goes, that's it. You can't find spares."

"That should make it all the more valuable."

"In what way?"

"This car could be a ready source of those hard-to-get
spares, as you call them."

"There's no market, my friend. The demand is zero. Do
please give me credit for knowing my own business."

"I may sell the car if I can get my price."

"Not to me you won't."

I confronted him with one of his leaflets. "You said you
wanted this car."

"No, I don't want that one. What's the true mileage?"

"I don't know. It's a good car. I made it down here all right. That's something, isn't it?"

"Yes, I'll give you that."

He took a flashlight and raised the hood. "What's all that wire around the manifold?"

"Coat-hanger wire. Engine restraint. Broken motor mount."

"Roadside repair?"

"Yes."

"That's interesting." He pulled the dipstick from the transmission and smelled the end of it. Then he started the engine and listened to it through a wooden yardstick, his ear at one end of the stick and the engine block at the other. Then he took a rubber mallet and went around tapping on the body panels. I drank a cup of his cold water.

"Mind the bees," he said. "They can smell fear."

There were white beehives in the shadows beside the shed. Striped bees that looked heavy were going about their deliberate business. I had never known they worked at night. Behind the hives I saw a Ford hulk. It was a long-hooded Torino covered with dried gray mud. The wheels were gone and it was resting flat on the ground amid some coarse flowers.

Leet completed the inspection and returned to his seat, slapping his palm with the yardstick. "You've got bad rust, my friend. I happen to know something about oxidation and what you've got is out of control."

"Where did you get that Torino? That's the first one I've seen down here."

"You don't see many. These niggers like the full-size models. Galaxies and Impalas."

"I have one like that, only mine is blue."

"That one's blue. Fellow burnt up the engine idling it. I

hauled it in for a hundred dollars American and sold the air conditioner the same day for two hundred. I got another hundred for the radio and tape deck, and I got eighty for the tires and the baby moon hubcaps. Everything went but the sheet metal, and went fast too. I wish I had another one."

"How did he burn it up idling it?"

"He was idling it at about fifty-two hundred rpm's. Fell asleep with his foot on the accelerator. Drunk, I suppose, or a nut case. Just sat there dozing away with the engine screaming until the pistons seized. Beautiful 351 Windsor engine. Clean carburetor, clean battery terminals. Clean valve covers until the paint was cooked. No mess or oil seepage. No corrosion. The car had been well cared for."

"That's a shame."

"Yes, it's a great pity. Nice windfall for me, of course."

I already knew the truth but I moved in for a closer look and I saw my Arkansas inspection sticker in the corner of the windshield. This muddy shell was my Torino. I wiped off some of the mud with my hand.

Leet said, "I can give you two hundred for the little Buick. I pay the duty. It's an orphan, as I say, and you won't do any better than that."

"You've already bought my car, Leet. This Torino is my car. I have the title to it."

"Really?"

"Yes."

"It's a bit late to be speaking up."

"Dupree had no right to sell it."

"He had the car."

"Are you going to make it good?"

"Say again?"

"I say, are you going to make it good?"

"Do you mean am I going to reconstruct that car for you? Nothing of the kind. What a hope."

"I mean compensation."

"It's not on, my friend. I bought it in good faith."

"I don't believe you did. You said yourself it was a wind-fall. You spoke of Dupree as a nut case."

Leet flexed his shrimplike fingers. "I would hardly make those admissions again, would I? To a third party."

"Dupree had no papers. You bought it without a title."

"Listen to our little lawyer."

"I'll have to see about this in town."

"See about it all you please. Your word against his. It's nothing to do with me."

"It's more than my word. I have the papers."

"All right, here's some law for you, chum. The car was licensed in Arkansas and the boy had an Arkansas driving license. He had possession of the car. It was not for me to assume he was a thief. I would have been wrong to do so. That's nothing more nor less than good English law."

"Is it English equity?"

"Say again?"

"Equity. Fair play, like the hotel."

"Equity's grandmother. You can't put it all on me. You have a duty to look after your own stuff."

"That's just what I'm doing. I'll have to see about this."

"I thought the car was his to sell. I bought it. That's it. Bob's your uncle. Now you come along and say it's your car. Very well, I pay you too. Now tomorrow a third man comes to the Motor Ranch and makes a similar claim. Do I pay him, and the fourth and fifth man as well? How long could I stay in business, paying for the same car day after day? Not six years."

"Your third man wouldn't have the papers."

"You and your bleeding papers."

As a sign that our business was concluded, he picked up his book, *Flags of the World*, and found his place, Morocco and Mozambique, and fell into a deep study of these banners. It was an English or European book from the looks of the murky colors, or maybe it was the yellow light that made them appear so. I had a fellow-pig feeling for him, and I had the feeling too that he was the last of the Leets, that the House of Leet was winding up here in this tropical junkyard.

I said, "To tell the truth, Leet, I don't care about that car. It's not even mine. My father paid for it like everything else I have. I hate to find it here like this but my quarrel is not with you. I see that now."

These friendly words dispelled the chill somewhat.

He said, "The boy was odd and I suspected something. I'll give you that."

"He has a lot to answer for."

"I knew it was a funny business, I can't say I didn't. But then you get a lot of funny business in this place."

"It wasn't the car at all. I see that now."

"I knew he was a lunatic when I played this. Give a listen. I found this tape under the seat. You'll think it's a comedy recording like I did. I don't know what it is, a dramatic reading or some loony recitation."

He put the cassette into the tape player and the voice of Dr. Buddy Casey rang out across the dark field.

" *'Can you help us, Captain Donahue?' he cried. 'Yes, Major,' came the stout reply, 'my men are fresh and they are just the fellows for that work!'* "

Leet laughed. I snatched the tape from the machine. "That's mine too, Leet." The sudden noise had made the insects stop their racket for a moment but they were soon at it again.

I drove away in the Buick, not deigning to sell it, and I put the whole thing out of my mind, as though Leet had never been cast upon this shore with his fat fingers. I thought instead of Christine and her wet hair. I speculated on squeezing her, and more, being married to her, our life together in Vermont. She was a very good-natured girl. Resourceful too. Would she have to go to the doctor a lot? They all seemed to collapse right after the vows, even the robust ones like Christine. Female disorders. There are one or two points on female plumbing that I have never been clear on. And yet there was Mrs. Symes, in the pink for her age, and Otho in his grave these many years. But what would Christine and I talk about on long drives, or even on short ones? And what about Victor? Turn him over to Dean maybe. Pack all his little shirts and trousers and socks—doll socks!—in a box and send him to Dean. Tag him for Phoenix and put him on an express bus. Then Christine and I could have our own son, little Terry, a polite child, very nimble and fast on his feet.

I passed a sandy turnoff with a sign that said "TO THE BEACH" or something like that, and I fixed the location in my mind. I would take Christine there, to that very spot, for a night swim. It was just the kind of thing that would appeal to her, a moonlight swim. Perhaps Melba would make us some sandwiches. We would go in the van. If that van could talk! I would teach her how to swim in the luminous sea. She probably thought she would die if she put her face under water.

When I drove up to the church, a jeep was pulling away and Christine was in it. She shouted something back to me. The driver was a bearded man in a monk's robe and a planter's straw hat. One of his sandaled feet was cocked up on the floor sill of the jeep in swaggering G.I. Joe fashion. I waved and called after them but they didn't stop, my voice never having arrested anything in flight.

The movie had started. The chapel was packed with excited boys and I could hardly get in the door. I had always liked Tarzan well enough but I didn't see why this white lord of the jungle should be such a favorite with Negroes. Their own people were shown in these films as jabbering and rolling their eyes and dropping their packages and running away at the first sign of trouble. For solid action give me a submarine picture or a picture that opens with a DC-3 having engine trouble over a desert. I pushed my way through to the projector table where Mrs. Symes was leaning on her aluminum cane. The boy Victor was sitting there on her stool, hunched forward and looking like Jack Dempsey. He had been into Mrs. Symes's paper stars and he had stuck one on each of his fingernails.

Sweat was trickling down the poor old lady's powdered cheeks. She was trembling from the heat and intensity in the room. She was wearing a long black dress for the occasion and some pearl devices on her earlobes. The old projector clattered away, Father Jackie not having seen fit to bring along his deluxe machine. The lip movements on the screen were just a beat or so behind the voices.

I told Victor to get up and let Mrs. Symes have the seat. He made a move but she said no, she would rather stand. There was a bright green fly on her veined hand and she didn't seem to feel it. The fly was so still and so cleanly articulated that it didn't look quite real; it looked like something from a jewelry shop or a joke shop.

"Christine wants you to look after Victor," she said to me.

"Look after Victor?"

"She's gone with Father Jackie."

"I don't follow."

"Father Jackie wanted to show her the coconut dolls at the folk art center."

"At night? How long will that take?"

"She wants you to look after Victor till she gets back."

"I can't look after Victor."

"I'm busy, Mr. Midge. It's too hot to talk. I'm trying to watch this, if you don't mind."

"What about Father Jackie's mother? You said she was here. Why can't she look after him?"

"I'm trying to watch this."

It was an old Tarzan picture I had somehow missed on television. He seemed to be in the Coast Guard this time. He was patrolling the bayous of Louisiana in his cutter and he was having trouble with Buster Crabbe, who was some sort of Cajun poacher or crook. They were squabbling over the same sweetheart too, and the girl didn't know what to do. She had the foolish notion that she might be able to reform Buster Crabbe. Everyone was addressing Johnny Weissmuller as "Dave" or "Skipper" instead of Tarzan. A clever wrinkle, this undercover business, but we were all impatient for him to shed his uniform and go into some Tarzan action with vines and big cats and crocodiles. It seemed to me they were putting it off too long.

The boys had settled down by the time Mrs. Symes changed the reel. Some were asleep. I saw Webster Spooner standing against the wall, rocking slowly like a small bank guard, his hands behind his back. It was hot and close in that room and I had no place to sit. I was hungry too. I wanted to flee but I was stuck with Victor. Look after Victor! If the kid broke his arm or got sick or run over by a truck, it would all be my fault! Maybe I could get Webster to act as a companion and relieve me of some of the burden.

The show droned on and the boys began to stir and mutter. Before the second reel was done, one of them stood up in the life-giving radiance from the projector and said, "This don't be Tarzan, Meemaw."

"It is too," she said. "Sit down."

But it wasn't. It was just Johnny Weissmuller in the Coast Guard and not even at war. We could watch this thing all night and he wasn't going to stop being Dave. Father Jackie had a full bag of tricks!

The boys began to drift out in twos and threes and the door monitor made no effort to stop them. I asked Victor if he didn't want to leave too. He seemed to be drugged, stupefied. I caught Webster as he was making his way to the door.

"How are you tonight, Webster?"

"Meemaw is vexed."

"I know. Here, I want you to meet Victor Walls. Victor, give me your attention for a minute. This is Webster Spooner, a friend of mine. He's the bell captain at my hotel. I have a job to do and I want you boys to help me."

"What kind of job?"

"An important job. We're going for a drive."

Both of them rode in the front seat. I stopped at the Fair Play and told them to wait in the car while I went to my room and put on my boots. Ruth was gone. I went behind the desk and poked around to see if anything had come in for me. I opened the shoebox and found the message to my father, with the money still pinned to it. Ruth had never sent it to the cable office. All my letters were there too, the British Honduras covers I had addressed to myself in Little Rock. What a hotel!

I unpinned the money and took it with me upstairs and searched my room for boots. They were not in the suitcase and they were not under the bed. Where could they be? There was no other place in this bare cube of a room where black engineer's boots might be concealed. A dog, I said to myself. Some town dog has nosed open the door here and carried off my boots in his mouth. But both boots? Could a dog manage that? Two trips maybe. Or two dogs. But had I in fact ever seen a dog in the hotel? No. Not counting the foyer where they sometimes gamboled and fought around

Webster's box. I had never seen a dog on the stairs or in the hallway. Then it came to me with a swelling rush that I didn't own a pair of black engineer's boots either, or any other kind of boots.

Next door I could hear a heavy person walking back and forth on the creaking boards. Karl, perhaps, pondering his next move, whetting his knife and pacing, trying to decide whether to buy a new radio or get the old one repaired, the old tube set that had served him so well in so many different rooms. I felt a visceral twinge of pain, lungs maybe, and I sat down on the bed to wait for it to pass. The pain was concentrated in one burning spot about the size of a dime. I wondered if I might have been hit by a small stray bullet sometime during the afternoon. I had handled news accounts of men who had been shot and then walked about for hours, days, a lifetime, unaware of such wounds. Maybe the heart itself. I took the last of the orange pills, first blowing off the pocket lint. Downstairs the boys were honking the horn.

Twelve

I drove with care on Bishop Lane. The shadows were deceptive under the headlights and it was hard to tell the big holes from the little holes. I soon became fatigued from making so many judgments, half of them wrong, and so I gave up making them, or rather, acting on them, and I hit the holes as they came, without regard to width or depth.

Victor had shaken off his grogginess in the night air. After each violent jolt he would shout, "Good deal, Lucille!" and Webster would laugh. Victor fiddled with all the knobs too, and he wanted to know why things didn't work, the dash lights and the radio.

He said, "How much will this thing do, hey? What kind of old car is this anyway? I hate it. You need to get you a Volkswagen where you can sit up high. My mom says Volkswagens are the most powerful cars in the world." There was a sharp edge to his voice. The little Yankee had never been taught to say "sir."

"It'll do plenty," I said, and I stepped on the gas and we hit the creeks at high speed. Water shot up through the floor and the boys began to squeal and jump about. Now I was driving recklessly.

A catlike animal sprang into the road and then stopped. I saw his face in the glare and it looked almost human in that brief moment of indecision. He decided against chancing it, the full crossing, and scrambled back to his starting place.

"A fox!" said Victor.

"No," I said. "That was a coati, or coatimundi. He's related to another animal that we know well. A very clever
fellow who washes his food. He has a ringed tail and a black
burglar's mask. Can anyone tell me the name of that animal?"

They weren't listening to me. We came up out of a creek
bottom and topped a low rise and there in the middle of the
road was a dead cow. I swung the car to the left, catching
the bloated corpse with the right headlights. It was only a
glancing blow and I didn't stop. Both headlights on the right
side were smashed and the steering was further affected so
that there was now almost a half-turn of slack in the steering
wheel. The position of the crossbar on the wheel was altered
too, from horizontal to vertical, and with this new alignment
I couldn't seem to get my hands placed right.

"Webster?"

"Sor?"

"Who is responsible for removing dead animals from
your roads?"

"I don't know."

"One of those rib bones could go right through a tire at
today's high speeds."

It was more than I could do to keep the car in the narrow
lane, what with the steering and the lighting problems. We
swung from one side to the other, our progress describing a
sine curve. Bushes slapped against the undercarriage each
time we left the road. It didn't occur to me to slow down. On
one of these swoops we hurtled through the Mayan clearing
where the Indian brothers had retired for the night to their
stone chamber. That is, I could see the glow of a candle
behind the doorway curtain as we passed within inches of it,
but we were in and out of the place before they could do
much more than exchange apprehensive glances.

The end came a few minutes later. Webster and Victor were wrestling and crawling back and forth over the seat and one of them kicked the shift lever down into reverse, which, on this singular car, was on the far right side of the shifting arc. The transmission shuddered and screeched and quit before I could make a move, my hands being occupied with the wheel. The car coasted to a stop in a marshy place.

"Now see what you've done!"

We got out and stood around in the mud. The boys were quiet for a change. I would have cut a limb and gladly beaten them both but you always have to weigh one thing against another and I didn't want to listen to their bawling. They might have run too, the second one anyway. I could hear transmission fluid dripping and I could smell the odor of burnt sugar. There was another sound that I couldn't place immediately. Something unpleasant was disturbing the air. Then I figured out that it was rock-and-roll music and that it must be coming from the Indians' transistor radio.

I said, "All right then, we'll walk. It's not far now. There better not be any more monkeyshines, I can tell you that."

"Where are we going?"

"We're going to see Guy Dupree."

"You don't have no electric torch?"

"We don't need one. I can see at night. I can see stars down to the seventh magnitude. Just stay behind me and step where I step."

Above the trees in the narrow cut of the road there was a dazzling band of stars. My eye went directly to the Clouds of Magellan, although I had never seen them before. I knew then that I would not be able to see the Southern Cross, not at this time of year. I had only a rough picture in my mind of the southern celestial sphere but I did know that the Southern Cross was very far away from those clouds, perhaps as much as 180 degrees. I pointed out the two galaxies to Webster and Victor, or tried to. They found the large cloud easily enough but I couldn't make them see the pattern, the luminous smudge of the small cloud, low in the south.

I said, "Can anyone tell me what a galaxy is? A little knowledge about these things can greatly increase our enjoyment of them."

There was no answer, as before, with the much easier raccoon question. Webster asked me about a red star, not Betelgeuse or Antares, directly overhead. I couldn't identify it. "These are poor horizons," I said, "and I'm not really familiar with these skies. Now here's something interesting. Victor and I can't see all those stars where we live. We have different stars, you see, depending on how far north or south we live."

Victor spoke up. "My mom says this is the age of Aquarius."

I set off down the road at a brisk marching pace. Victor continually disobeyed my orders. He ran ahead and stirred up some small hopping birds, shooing them before him with his hands.

"Stop chasing those birds, Victor. You can't catch a bird. I want you both to stay behind me. I'm supposed to be in front at all times."

"What kind of birds are they?"

"They're just road birds."

"Can they talk?"

"No."

"Do they lay their tiny eggs in the road?"

"I don't know. Get behind me and stay there. I won't tell you again."

"I hate this road and I hate all these trees."

"You boys must do just as I say. I want us to stay together. If you mind me and don't give me any more trouble, I'm going to buy you each a nice gift when we get back to town. But you must do just what I say."

Webster said, "I already know what I want. I want a tack hammer and a rubber stamp with my name on it and a walkie-talkie radio."

"The tack hammer and the rubber stamp are all right. I'm not buying any walkie-talkie."

Victor said, "I don't get this. What are we doing out here anyway?"

"I told you we're going to see Guy Dupree. He has my wife in his house out here and I mean to go in there after her. I'm through fooling around with him. It's a long story and I don't want to go into it any further than that."

"What was his name again?"

"Guy Dupree."

"You mean you're going to fight this Guy Dupree?"

"Yes."

"Oh boy, this will be good. I'm glad I came now. Will you have to kill him?"

"No more chatter."

"Oh boy, this will really be good. What we ought to do is cut off Guy Dupree's head with a knife and see what his eyes look like then."

"What I want you to do is hush."

"If somebody got my mom, I'd cut off his head and see if it could talk and then I would watch his eyes to see if they moved any."

"Webster is minding me and you're not. Do you know what that means, Victor? That means he'll get a nice gift and you'll get nothing."

No sooner had I commended Webster for his silence and

put him forward as an example than he pinched my arm and asked a question. "Does Guy Dupree be in the hands of the devil?"

"Guy Dupree is sorry. We'll leave it at that. I can't answer any of your questions about the devil. That's out of my field."

"Meemaw say the devil he have a scaly body and a long tongue that run in and out of his mouf like a snake."

"That's a traditional representation, yes. And goat feet."

"She say he have a gold pocket watch a million years old that don't never run down."

"I've never heard anything about the watch."

"He always know what time it is."

"My mom says there's no such thing as the devil."

"Your mom is misinformed about many things, Victor. She may well be wrong about that too."

"How do the devil be everywhere at one time?"

"I don't know, Webster. I tell you I can't answer questions like that. You see me as a can-do guy from the States, but I don't have all the answers. I'm white and I don't dance but that doesn't mean I have all the answers. Now I want you both to listen up. From here on in we're playing the quiet game. I don't want to hear another peep out of anybody until I give the all-clear signal, which will be my open hand rotating rapidly above my head, like this."

Victor said, "I want a pellet gun for my present. I want one you can pump up about thirty times."

"I'm not buying any pellet gun. Forget it. That's out."

"Why can't we have what we want?"

"I'm not buying any expensive junk. The pellet gun and the walkie-talkie are both out."

"I hate these mosquitoes."

As for the gifts, I had already given some thought to setting Webster up in the snow-cone business. No one seemed to be selling snow cones in this steaming land. A small cart and an ice scraper and some flavored syrups and conical paper cups and he would be ready to roll. Mr. Wu knew a good thing when he saw it. He was making a fortune off soft ice cream and spending it on God knows what Oriental cravings, or more likely, stashing it away in a white Chinese sock with a toe pouch. Webster would have the advantage of being mobile. He could take his refreshing ices directly to the chicken fights and harvest festivals. One thousand grape snow cones at the summer corn dance! I had not yet mentioned the idea because I didn't want it to get out. Something cheap would do for Victor. I had seen a little book called *Fun with Magnets* in the window of a variety store in Belize. The book was faded and shopworn and I could probably get it for less than a dollar.

He was walking along behind me chanting, "Guy Dupree, Guy Dupree, Guy Dupree," and Webster picked it up, this chant. I made them stop it. Victor asked me if they could walk backward.

"You can walk any way you please as long as you keep up and don't make a lot of noise."

"Can we hold our knees together and just take little short steps?"

"No, I don't want you to do that."

"You said—"

"I don't want you to walk like that. And if you don't shut up I'm going to put a rubber stopper in your mouth."

"A stopper? I don't get that."

"One of those things that babies suck on. With a flange and a ring on the outside. If you behave like a baby, I'll have to treat you like a baby."

He was quiet for a while and then he began to pester me with questions about the Buick. How would we get back to town? What if a crook stole it? What would I do if it was full of animals when we got back?

"I may just leave it there," I said. "A man told me today that there are no spare parts here for that particular transmission. I'm no longer interested in that car and I'm not answering any more questions about it. Do you hear me?"

"You can't just leave your car out in the woods."

"The subject is closed. I don't want to hear another word. I haven't had anything to eat since this morning and I can't answer any more questions."

"If you leave it there, how will you get back to Texas?"

"I'm not *from* Texas."

"You can't ride in our van."

"Have you heard me say at any time that I wanted to ride in your van?"

"We just have two bucket seats. One is mine and one is my mom's."

"For your information, Victor, I plan to fly home with my wife."

"Yeah, but what if the plane goes into a tailspin and you don't have a parachute to bail out in?"

"The plane is not going into a tailspin for the very simple reason that these commercial pilots know what they're doing. All those planes get regular maintenance too. So many flying hours and that's it, they're back in the shop."

There was no light in the Dupree house and I wondered if he had heard us coming. All this chatter. He was very likely posted at one of the darkened windows and cooking up a plan. I felt sure he couldn't see us in any detail with his feeble eyes. He wouldn't be able to make out that Webster and Victor were children. For all he knew, they could be short hired thugs or two boy detectives. I had a plan of my own. I didn't intend to expose the boys to any real danger but I thought they could serve well enough and safely enough as a base of fire. I knew that the attacking force should always be at least three times the size of the defending force.

I marked off a place beside the garbage dump and told the boys, whispering, to gather rocks and place them in a pile there.

"What kind of rocks?"

"Rocks like this, for throwing. Not too big and not too little."

We set about our task without speaking. The quality of the rocks was poor, running mostly to thin limestone shards, and even these were hard to find. Victor appeared to be doing a fine job. He scurried about and made two and sometimes three trips to the pile for every one that Webster and I made. Then I saw that he was just picking up whatever came to hand, sticks and cans and clods of dirt, and was making the rock pile ridiculous with these things. He soon stopped work altogether and said he was tired.

"All right," I said. "We'll rest for a minute."

Webster said, "What do these rocks be for?"

"We're going to throw them at that house."

"At Guy Dupree's house?"

"Yes."

"I don't like to do that, sor."

"Dupree has my wife in that house and she may be sick. People get sick down here."

Webster was shamed into silence.

"How would you like it if a gang of howling raiders came over here from Guatemala and stole your women? You would strike back, wouldn't you? And very properly so. We'll make Dupree keep his head down with these rocks and then I'll dash across the road. I'll be in the house before he knows it."

We lined up three abreast and flung a volley across the road. I was disappointed by the puny effect, by the soft thunks of the rocks striking wood. I had the boys lie down, against the possibility of a shotgun blast, but there was no answer of any kind, not even a bark.

I stepped up the attack. With each salvo our aim improved and before long we were breaking windows. Webster and Victor quickly got into the spirit of the thing, so much so that I had to restrain them. Still there was no response. I mixed things up so that Dupree could not count on a recurring pattern. One volley might follow another instantly, or there might be an interval of several minutes. Once, instead of loosing the expected flurry of small rocks, I heaved one big rock the size of a cantaloupe onto the porch. Watch out for the florr! Dupree would soon be whimpering for his pills.

But he was clever and after a while I could see that his plan was to sit out the barrage. He hoped to discourage us and wear us down. Two could play that game. I stopped all activity.

"We'll wait one hour exactly," I said. "If we keep perfectly quiet, he'll think we've left and then we'll let him have it again harder than ever. That's the thing that will break him."

"When will you make your dash, sor?"

"I'll make my dash when I'm ready. Put that in your notebook."

The minutes dragged. I anticipated a problem keeping the boys still and I wished I had brought something with which they could pass the time, perhaps a little ball they could roll back and forth. But they were exhausted and they fell asleep at once despite the mosquitoes.

I lay down too, behind a low rock parapet. It was very quiet out there for a jungle, or more accurately, a marginal rain forest with a few deciduous trees. I strained to see and hear things, always a mistake, the reconnaissance manuals say, leading one to see animated bushes. Once I thought I could make out two small, dim, ratlike figures walking upright, holding hands and prancing in the road. I even imagined I could hear rat coughs. Curious illusion. I checked the time again and again. My watch crystal was fogged on the inside. I lost interest in the wheeling stars. It occurred to me that if I had brought along the doctor's flashlight I could move about giving fake signals.

I crawled forward a few feet and fashioned myself a new watching place, recalling that Pancho Villa had been a great night mover. The troops would be sitting around the campfire and he would yawn and say, "Well, boys, I think I'll turn in," or something to that effect in Spanish, and then he would lie down and roll up in a blanket in full view of everyone. But he wouldn't stay in that place! He would move three or four times during the night and not even the most trusted of his Dorados could say where General Villa might finally turn up the next morning. I crawled forward again. And perhaps once more.

I dozed and woke. I thought I could see the Southern Cross, the broken cross pattern of stars, just brushing the southeast horizon. But was that possible? I dozed and woke again. Baby frogs with a golden sheen were capering about at my feet. They were identical in size and appearance, brothers and sisters hatched from the same jellied mass, and they all moved as one like a school of fish when I wiggled a foot. I looked at them and they looked at me and I wondered how it was that I could see them so clearly, their placid frog faces. Then I realized it was dawn. The frogs only looked golden. I was lying in the middle of the road and I had slept for hours. The world's number one piddler had taken to his bed again.

Webster and Victor slept on. There was an odd stillness as though some familiar background machinery had stopped. I could see on the porch scattered evidence of the rock storm. I got up and entered the yard through the flimsy gate. The dog was nowhere about.

At the foot of the steps I called out for Norma, although I knew there was no one in the place. I could sense this was an empty house. I went about inside from room to squalid room. There were containers of water everywhere, buckets and cans and jugs. On the back porch there was a washtub filled with water. A drowned gray bat was floating in it, his fine wet fur slightly darker than the galvanized tub. There were no Dupree papers to be seen on the kitchen table, only some orange peelings and a slender bottle of red sauce and a small photograph. It was a picture of Dupree and his dog that had been taken in one of those coin-operated photo booths. There they were, their heads together, Gog and Magog, looking dully at me. I came across nothing of Norma's, no golden hair on a pillow, but I didn't look closely at things and I didn't stay long.

Thirteen

The Buick was sunk to the bumpers in black mud. A D-9 Caterpillar couldn't have pulled it out of that muck, von Guericke's vacuum principle being what it is, implacable, and in another day or so the car would be swallowed whole by the earth. Leet's scouts had not yet found it and the windshield was clear of leaflets. I could see inside that a disgusting mound of living mud had forced its way up through the floor hole.

We walked on to the Mayan ruin, our trouser legs wet with dew and picking up grass seeds along the way. We were sore from sleeping on the ground and our faces and hands were blotchy with mosquito bites. I led the way. We kept our early-morning thoughts to ourselves. Victor carried a rock that was coated with dark green moss on one side. He wouldn't answer any questions about it, wouldn't say what his plans were for the rock. He just kept shifting it from hand to hand as his clenching fingers grew tired.

Our approach to the ruin was in no way noisy or alarming but neither was it stealthy enough to permit us a glimpse of the third brother. He had already flown to his hiding place. The other two were as merry as ever at the prospect of another full day in the brush. They greeted us with shouts of laughter and they gave us some coffee and tortillas and canned white lard from their meager stores. We spread the lard on the tortillas.

After breakfast we toured the ruin. They pulled a stone

from the pyramid and showed me their hidden cache of figurines and other artifacts, but they wouldn't let me handle the objects. Then they pointed to the tire ruts in the soft earth and they acted out a car blasting through the clearing, each in his own way, in a kind of motor dance. A drunken Popo, I suggested, but they indicated that Popo's rig was much smaller and slower than the phantom machine. They asked me for cigarettes again and I gave them some of the money I had taken from Ruth's shoe box. They got out their E bonds and I thought at first they were trying to give them back to me. They went to the cache and brought back an incised monkey skull to add to the bonds. Finally I got the drift. They wanted to exchange these things for a little nine-volt radio battery. Of course I had no battery and I gave them the rest of my money and accepted the skull. We shook hands all around.

Victor and Webster were dozing in the grass. I got them on their feet and we walked another two miles or so before we caught a ride in a pickup truck. The driver was an American, a hippie-looking fellow but rugged too at the same time, a pioneer. We rode in the back with the milk cans, our rigid limbs splayed out in all directions to provide support.

We got out at the market in Belize. The air was moist and very still. Webster treated us to some Pepsi-Colas at the Chinaman's store and I was a little surprised at this because most children are close with their money. Mr. Wu himself was indisposed, or maybe around the corner making a deposit at Barclays Bank, under that heraldic black eagle sign, or maybe he was just sleeping in. His mother or wife or sister was running the store. The firemen were at their table and I said to myself, Things are happening all over and they go on drinking their coffee. As long as it isn't a fire, they don't care.

Webster left for his hotel duties. Victor and I walked on

to the tabernacle. Christine's van was parked in front of the place and so was Father Jackie's jeep. I knew Christine would have some sharp words for me when she saw her son's swollen face.

The door was open but no one seemed to be about. The chapel was in disarray. Some of the borrowed chairs were overturned and the floor was littered with flat scraps of paper that would be hard to sweep up. The movie projector was still on the table uncased, the lenses unprotected from drifting bits of lint that would take on a hairy, jerky life when magnified and illuminated.

We went upstairs. Christine had moved her bags in and there by the door to the doctor's room was his pebbly grip, all packed. More suitcase facts. The breakfast or supper dishes were still on the table. I couldn't understand the sudden housekeeping decline. I stood there and thoughtfully ate some cold black beans from a bowl. I was eating at every opportunity. Victor curled up in Melba's chair. His chin glistened with lard. Christine probably wasn't much of a cook. The lard tortillas had been perfectly acceptable to him.

I roused him and we went back downstairs and then we heard voices from behind the movie screen. There was a door in the rear wall that opened into a yard and it was there we found them—Dr. Symes and Melba and Christine and Father Jackie. But where was Mrs. Symes?

This back yard was a nook I had not known about, a small fenced area with crushed white shells on the ground. Roses grew along the board fence and there were chairs made from rough sticks and leather straps, although there was none for me. Under the roof drain there was a rain barrel, to catch soft water for hair-washing. The place was no doubt intended as a meditation spot, a private retreat, but on this occasion everyone was eating watermelon. Dr. Symes used salt. He couldn't see the fine white grains as they dribbled from the shaker and he bounced them off the back of his hand so as to gain some idea of the rate of flow. The flesh of the watermelon was orange instead of red.

Victor went at once to Christine's lap. The rock was a gift for her. She said, "Hey, a super mossy!" and she looked it over and then put it aside and began to pick bits of dirt and gravel from Victor's hair. She had no words at all for me and no one was curious about our adventures because of a grave development that overshadowed such things. Far from being a luau, this was a wake!

Mrs. Symes had suffered a stroke and, I gathered, had died during the night. Dr. Symes and Christine had taken her to the hospital in the van, and had stayed there with her until they were told there was no hope. I couldn't believe it. A person I knew. Here one day and gone the next. An old enough story but it never fails to knock me for a loop. Then I get over it about as fast as anyone else and very soon I am able to carry on again. Melba cut me a section of watermelon and I sat on the rough shells and ate it with my fingers.

Father Jackie, who had a strong nasal voice, was doing most of the talking. He said, "She drank far too much ice wanter but you couldn't tell her anything."

Dr. Symes shifted his weight about on the sagging leather straps. He was fully dressed, even to the hat and bow tie and flashlight. On the ground beside his chair there was an old-fashioned steel lockbox, of a dark green color. He wiped his sticky hands on his white trousers. I could see he was impatient with Father Jackie's lay opinion, with the notion that cold water could cause death or even serious illness. He had been holding his mother's aluminum cane between his knees and now he began to rotate it rapidly back and forth between his open hands, like a scout trying to make fire. All this in preparation for an important statement.

Before he could get it out, Father Jackie said, "I know one thing. There was nothing on this earth that Meemaw was afraid of."

"She was afraid of hurricanes," said Melba. "Waterspouts. Any strong wind or black rain from the south. That little cloud right up there would make her uneasy. She was afraid that bits of flying glass would cut her neck."

Father Jackie told a story about a trip he had taken with Mrs. Symes to a place called Orange Walk. They had gone in his jeep to attend a sale or an auction of some kind at a bankrupt ranch. Throughout that day he had played various good-natured tricks on her, some of which she turned back on him to good effect. It was an interesting story, if a little long, full of lively incident illustrating different aspects of the old lady's character.

What part of the U.S.A. did Father Jackie hail from? I wrestled with this problem and couldn't work it out. He talked on and on. A theory formed in my head on the origin of his nasal tones. It was this. When he was a small child, his prankster father—a bitter man, jealous of the boy's promise —had taught him to speak in this fashion, taught him to honk, to recite, "The three lintle kintons they lost their mintons and they began to cry," thus fixing the habit early and assuring his failure in the world, the boot from every job, even street attacks. But was that really probable? Wasn't it more likely that this was just a kind of pulpit whine that was taught in his particular seminary?

The Orange Walk story was a pretty good one, as I say, and when it was over, Christine laughed and squeezed his knee in an intimate way and said, "You stinker you!" One of his knees showed through the parting of the brown robe. He reached over and plucked a shiny coin from Victor's ear and said, "My goonness, what's this?" But the boy was in a stupor again, his mouth ajar, and the illusion did not delight him.

Dr. Symes saw his chance and got his statement out. He said, "I don't know what the poets of Belize are doing this morning but I can tell you what they should be doing. They should all be in their little rooms composing memorials to that grand lady."

A large speckled insect flew slowly about before our faces, going in turn from one speaker to the next as though listening. Melba slapped at it ineffectually. She asked me if I had a camera. I said no and then she asked Dr. Symes. "I sure don't," he said. "Marvel used to have a little box camera but I myself have never owned one. I have never personally photographed anything in my life. Why do you ask such a question?"

"I thought it would be nice to have our picture taken out here with the roses and then later we could look at it and say, Yes, I remember that day."

Dr. Symes said the last time he had his picture made was in California. It was for his driver's license and they wouldn't let him wear his hat. "Don't ask me why. It's just some rule they have. No hats and no caps. They've got a million rules in California and that just happens to be one of them." He shook his head and laughed at the memory of the bizarre place.

Melba said, "If it's your own hat, I don't see why you couldn't wear it if you wanted to."

"I don't either, Melba, but you can't. I've seen plenty of good pictures of people wearing hats. Some of the finest pictures I've ever seen have been of people with their hats on. All I'm saying is that it's forbidden in California."

Father Jackie said he had a 35-millimeter camera at his cottage. But this was just by way of information and he made no move to go and get it. Christine said that her former husband, Dean, had a number of expensive cameras and that his favorite subject was his watch-repair tools. He would arrange the tiny instruments on a green cloth and photograph them from atop a stepladder, the challenge being to capture all the tools with a minimum of distortion. She was not allowed in the room while he was doing this but afterward he would show her the finished prints and ask her which one she liked best. After she had left Dean and moved to Mesa, she said, he annoyed her by prowling outside her apartment at night and shining different kinds of lights through her windows. I don't know whether she meant lights of different intensities or lights of different colors because all she said was "different kinds of lights."

Father Jackie asked Melba if she wanted him to arrange for death notices in the local papers and the New Orleans papers.

"Let's hold up on that," said the doctor. "We don't want to rush into this thing."

"I'll be glad to type up a full obituary if you'll give me the information. I'll tell you right now, these newspapers will just throw your stuff in the wastebasket if it's not wrinten up on a typewriner. I found that out from wrining lenners to the ennitor."

The doctor said, "Just hold up on that, if you will, my friend. You can do what you please at this end, but I have already told Melba that I will handle the Louisiana end. I will make all the notifications that need to be made. Do you understand what I'm telling you?"

"It's no trouble, I assure you."

"I appreciate that and I appreciate your concern but I want you to leave that part of it alone."

"Whatever you say."

"Fine, fine. That's what I say."

Dr. Symes then told Melba that he didn't like the idea of his mother being buried here in this Honduras mud, so far from her real home in Louisiana where Otho lay. Melba said it was a question of a person's wishes. Mrs. Symes had insisted on burial in the Belize cemetery with the pirates and drowned children and nameless wanderers, and a person's last wishes, when reasonable, had to be respected. She had not insisted on one of those simple funerals that cause everybody so much trouble, but there were one or two special requests. Her age, for instance. She was sensitive about her age and didn't want a date of birth inscribed on her tombstone. So be it. Melba intended to see that all of Nell's reasonable wishes were carried out.

The doctor made no strong protest. "Very well," he said. "I leave it in your hands, Melba. I know you'll do the right thing. Whatever you decide to do will just tickle me to death."

"I don't see why you can't stay for the funeral."

"You know I would if I could. We can't always do what we'd like to do, Melba. I'm needed in Ferriday now and it's a trip I can't put off. It's imperative that I be on the ground there personally. I won't be missed here anyway. There'll be so many mourners at the service that you'll have to put up loudspeakers outside the chapel. And all around the altar, just beaucooz of beautiful flowers. I'd give anything if I could see that lovely floral display, or just one glistening tear in the eye of some small child whose heart Mama had touched."

They had already been over this ground, I could tell. Melba sent me to the market for a second watermelon and when I came back they were discussing very frankly the disposal of Mrs. Symes's property. Melba had been a witness to the will and she knew the terms. It was clear that she and the doctor had already chewed over this matter too, and were returning to it now for mere secondary comment. Even so, I was able to get the picture and it was a bleak one for Dr. Symes. His mother had left him nothing. Nothing, that is, except for the green lockbox, which contained a poem she had written about a hurricane, of some three hundred-odd verses. The tabernacle went to Melba, and certain sums of money to the girl Elizabeth and to a cabdriver and handyman named Rex. The rest of the estate went to Mrs. Symes's great-granddaughter, Rae Lynn Symes, who was Ivo's daughter. It was a handsome settlement and was to be used to further the girl's music education.

Wasn't this a sensational disclosure? A bombshell? The doctor's hopes all dashed? And yet he showed little concern. He was subdued, all right, but there was also a kind of monstrous jauntiness in his manner.

I said, "What about Jean's Island?"

"She gets the island too," he said. "There's not a thin dime for me but there's hundreds of thousands of dollars for Rae Lynn and her piano lessons. You can see where that puts Marvel. Right in the driver's seat. Mama has now brought about the very situation she so hoped to avoid."

"Then there's nothing to be done."

"I wouldn't say nothing."

"What then?"

"Let me tell you how it is, Speed. I need to be on the ground in Louisiana. All right? Nuff said?"

It wasn't quite enough but it was all I was ever going to get.

Victor was asleep. Christine held him with one arm and she was sketching something with her free hand. She said, "How old was Meemaw anyhow?"

I said, "Melba just got through saying that her age was a secret, Christine. Didn't you hear that about the tombstone?"

"I didn't hear that. What was it?"

It wasn't that Christine's question was improper in itself but I thought she should have been paying closer attention to what people were saying. I had been thinking about the tombstone business all along, even during the more important will discussion, wondering at this posthumous vanity. What were Mrs. Symes's fears? That cemetery strollers would pause before her stone and compute the age? *Here, look at this one. No wonder she's dead.*

Christine tore the sketch from her pad and passed it around. It was a portrait of Melba with her hands clasped together on her lap in resignation. Christine may have been an artist, who can say, but she was no draftsman. The only thing she got right was Melba's hair, the wisps. The face was misshapen and dead, a flat, identikit likeness with one Mongoloid eye lower than the other. But Melba herself was pleased, if not with the portrait, at least with the attention. She said, "You're a fine girl, Christine."

Dr. Symes came to his feet and stretched. He asked Melba if he could keep the aluminum cane and she said he could take what he pleased from his mother's personal things.

"No, no, the stick is all. I have my lockbox and I'll just take this stick along for support and protection. It will also serve as a memento, what is it, mori."

"We ought to be ashamed of ourselves, talking like this, and poor Nell down there in the hospital struggling for her life."

"She's beyond the struggle, Melba. You can take my word for it as a physician."

"I don't know, Reo. You remember way back there when she had the incurable bone disease. The doctors just gave up on her. You remember they said she had to die. They said she would never rise from her bed. Five doctors said she had to die in three days. They wanted to give her a shot and just put her to sleep like an animal. And that was thirty-six years ago. I expect every one of those doctors is dead today."

"Pneumonia, Melba. Aspiration. Pulmonary fluids. The infection is setting in at this moment and she'll never be able to throw it off. I've seen way too much of it with these old people. You can take my word for it, church is out this time."

He gathered up his lockbox and said, "And now if you good people will excuse me I'm going to the hospital and kiss my old mother goodbye." He tapped my shoe with the cane and said, "Speed, behave yourself," and he went away.

I had rebuked Christine for not listening and all the time it was I who had been asleep at the switch. Mrs. Symes had not yet expired!

A few drops of rain fell on us, big ones. Melba said the big drops meant that we could expect a downpour, along with violent electrical discharges from the sky. She caught a silver drop in her hand and closed her fingers on it and said it reminded her of something we might find interesting. It was a recent vision. She had seen Dr. Symes being struck down by a big truck on a busy American highway. It was night and sleet was falling on the expressway and she could only see him off and on by the headlights of the giant trucks as they hit him over and over again, tossing him about like a bullfighter.

As she spoke, the speckled insect hovered in front of her eyes in an annoying way. She slapped at it again and said, "Get out of here, you naughty bug!" She asked us not to divulge the grim vision to Dr. Symes if we saw him again, and she went inside.

There followed an awkward silence, as with strangers being suddenly thrown together. Then Father Jackie leaned toward me and said that Mrs. Symes was a good woman but she had no business baptizing little children, or anyone else. She had no authority. And she had no business filling their heads with a lot of Calvinist nonsense. As for Melba, he said, tapping one finger to the steel plate in his own reconstructed skull, she was a little cracked. She laughed at inappropriate times. She had once given a little girl a toasted mouse for her cat. I didn't say anything because I didn't want to invite further confidences from this fellow.

Christine asked me who John Selmer Dix was and I told her he was a famous writer. Father Jackie said he had read a number of Dix's books and had found them excellent. He said he had always been fond of English detective stories, though he objected to the English practice of naming all the American characters Hiram or Phineas or Homer, and of making them talk in an odd way. I couldn't follow that, and then I saw that he must have Dix mixed up with some other bird, with the vain grunts of some other writer. He asked Christine if she would like to join him for lunch at his cottage.

"Some of the guys and chicks from the Peace Corps are dropping in for a rap session," he said. "I know you'll like them. They're really neat dudes. It's a regular thing we have. Nothing fancy, I assure you. We just have red wine and cheese and crackers and other munchies and we kick around a few ideas. But don't say I didn't warn you! It can get pretty heated at times!"

Christine said she thought she would stay at the tabernacle and relax and visit with Melba and listen to the rain on the tin roof.

He said, "How about you, Brad?"

He thought my name was Brad! I recognized the polite afterthought for what it was and I suspected too that those Peace Corps people might have guitars and so I too declined.

Fourteen

Melba was right about the downpour. There wasn't a great deal of lightning but the rain fell and the wind blew. Wooden shutters were battened down all across town. Broken palm fronds and power lines had fallen to the streets. The electricity was knocked out early and all the stores were dark inside, though it wasn't yet noon. I sloshed through the foyer of the Fair Play Hotel where an inch or so of water had already accumulated. Ruth was gone. Webster's sleeping box had begun to float and I put it up on the counter.

I ran up the stairs and found a skinny stranger sitting on my bed. He was wearing heavy boots of a European design, with laces running from one end to the other. He was sitting there in the gloom writing in a spiral notebook. He jumped when I opened the door and he closed the notebook and shoved it under a pillow. This bird has been composing something! I had caught him in the very act of putting pen to paper and his shame was painful to see.

"What do you want?" he said.

"This is my room."

"This is the one they gave me."

"Where's my suitcase?"

"I don't know. This is the room they showed me. There was nothing in here. Are you checking out?"

"I didn't think so, no."

He was tall and yellow and fleshy around the middle, an ectomorph with a paunch. He looked to be an intelligent person. His stuff was packed in a rubberized cloth bag that was choked off tight at the top with a drawstring. He pulled it closer to him and rested one hand on it in a protective way. He saw me as a threat not only to his notebook but to his bag too.

I questioned him. He said he was booked on a Nicaraguan Airlines flight to New Orleans but it had been canceled because of the weather. For the past few months he had been back in the hills prospecting for immaculite and jade and tail feathers from the rare quetzal bird. He was now going home to see his brother ride in a prison rodeo, and, if it could be worked out, he also wanted to attend the state fair. Then he would return here to his immaculite diggings and to certain jade-bearing stream beds.

"What is immaculite?" I said. "And why is it mined?"

"It's a fine crystal that is used in precision optical instruments."

"Is that it?"

"That's it. That's the story of immaculite."

"It's funny I've never heard of it. I wouldn't mind seeing some of that stuff."

"I don't have any with me. I don't have any jadeite or quetzal feathers either."

The way he said it made me think he was lying. My clothes were soaked and I was dripping water on the floor. We had to speak with raised voices because of the rain drumming on the tin roof. The din was terrible and I thought of Christine, who was not often treated to a tattoo like this in Phoenix.

"I'm wondering about my things," I said. "Did the boy or the woman take my suitcase out of here?"

"I don't know anything about it. This is the room they gave me. I've already paid for it but if there's been a mistake I'll be glad to move to another room."

"Look here, why should there be a problem about going to the state fair?"

"There's not any problem that I know of."

"I got the idea that there was some problem. It's no great trick to go to the fair, is it?"

"The rodeo is in Huntsville and the fair is in Dallas."

"Two widely separated towns then. That's all you meant to say."

"Yes."

He was still uncomfortable from having been caught red-handed at his vice—writing songs or what?—and I could see too that our loud, expository conversation was distasteful to him, he just having come in from the solitude of the bush. The wind peeled back a sheet of tin above his head. The thing flapped up and down a few times and then blew away. It will be understood when I say "tin" that I am using the popular term for galvanized and corrugated sheet iron. A cascade of water came down on the bed and we pushed it to an inside corner of the room. Now we had to talk even louder because of the wind shrieking through the hole in the roof. But that hole, I told myself, will act as a safety vent and will keep the house from exploding or imploding under a sudden pressure differential. The floor heaved and the walls creaked. The frame structure was ill-suited for withstanding these violent stresses.

"I think this is a hurricane," he said. "What do you think?"

"It's certainly a severe depression of some kind."

"Maybe we should go to another place."

"All the other houses are just like this one."

"The Fort George Hotel is fairly solid."

"But don't they say stay inside? Where you are?"

"I think we should try for the Fort George."

"You may be right."

He took his own sweet time in opening the bag and packing the notebook and tying it up again, in a special way. It was all something of an act, this cool manner we were at such pains to display to one another, but in fairness I must say that I was not unnerved by this convulsion of nature. The storm made a change from the enervating heat and it is not going too far to say I found it bracing—or much too far. I should say too that it provided a welcome distraction from my personal problems.

The Texas fellow carried his bag under one arm. His running gait was badly coordinated and funny, mine deliberate. He ran like a duck. Water was running in the streets, which made it hard to lift our feet. We moved in a darting fashion from the lee of one house to that of another. The black creek was backed up and out of its banks, whether from the heavy rains upstream or from the driven sea blocking its discharge, I couldn't say, perhaps both. There seemed to be no pattern in the way the wind was blowing. It came from all points of the compass. The velocity was irregular too, and it was the gusts that did most of the damage. My concern was for the twisted sheets of tin that were banging about. One of those things could take your head off. Some of the roofs had been completely stripped, leaving only exposed beams and stringers. I saw a gum tree with its limbs more or less intact but every leaf blown away. It had a wintry look.

We didn't make it to the Fort George. A policeman hustled us off the street into a fenced compound and put us to work in a sandbag brigade. The wire fence enclosed a motor-pool area behind the police station, and this was a scene of wild activity. Men were running about and Bedford trucks and Land-Rovers were coming and going through the gate. Most of the workers seemed to be prisoners. They had been turned out of jail to fill small sisal bags with sand and broken oyster shells. The stuff was piled up in mounds at a construction site near the garage bays.

There weren't nearly enough shovels. The Texas fellow and I were assigned to the loading detail. We carried sandbags, one in each hand, and slung them up into the truck beds. They were then hauled away to build dikes and to weigh down the flimsy roofs—much too late, it seemed. A big black officer with a riding crop and a bullhorn was directing things. I couldn't understand a word he said. They called him Captain Grace. He had a Webley revolver in a canvas holster on his hip. As befitted his rank, he was the calmest man in the yard.

Everyone had his job. Webster was there and he and some other boys held the bags open while the prisoners filled them. A third gang tied the tops with string and the rest of us were loaders. The rain swept across us in blinding sheets, and the sand, wet though it was, swirled about in eddies, stinging our arms and faces. We were working in the open but the chainlike fence provided some protection from flying objects. I had no opportunity to ask Webster about my things.

There were two white Americans among the jailbirds—a young doper and an older, heavier man. He was barefooted, this older fellow, as were all the prisoners, and he wore a knit shirt that was split on both sides from his exertions. He appeared to be the boss of the shovelers. They were hard put to keep up, there being so few of them, and he was trying to prod them on to heroic efforts with a lot of infield chatter. His team! He was digging like a madman and yelling at the boys for being slow and for not holding the bags fully open. I had noticed him early but he was little more than a noisy wet blur to me.

I soon made a pickup at his station and he said, "Wrong

way! Wrong way! Get your bags on this side and go out the other way!" I had been holding my head down to protect my eyes against all the blowing stuff and when I raised it to get a look at this loud person I was knocked for a loop. It was Jack Wilkie! I spoke to him. He recognized me and waved me off. We were meeting under strange circumstances in a faraway place and there were many questions to be answered—but this was no time for a visit! That was what I understood him to be saying with his urgent gestures. He hadn't shaved for several days and there were clumps of sand stuck to his copper-wire whiskers. He had to keep hitching up his trousers because he had no belt.

I went back to work and considered the new development. Someone called out to me. It was the skinny fellow from Texas, hanging on the back of a truck and holding to one end of a long wooden ladder. He had been shanghaied into a new gang, a ladder gang. His bag was stowed in one of the garage bays and he wanted me to keep an eye on it while he was gone. I nodded and waved, indicating that I would do so, message understood. The truck pulled away and that was the last time I saw that mysterious bird alive. His name was Spann or Spang, more likely Spann.

Three army trucks came through the gate and wheeled about together in a nice maneuver. British soldiers jumped to the ground with new shovels at the ready. Now we had plenty of shovels but there was no more sand. The army officer and Captain Grace conferred. A decision was quickly reached. All the small boys were left behind and the rest of us were herded into the trucks and taken to some grassy beach dunes north of town. The captain led the convoy in his blue Land-Rover. Jack and I were together and there were about twenty other men in the back of our truck. We had to stand. The tarpaulin top was gone and we clung to the bentwood frame members. I could see that I was taller than at least one of these Coldstream Guards, if indeed that's who they were. We were flung from side to side. Jack punched out angrily at people when they stepped on his bare toes.

Captain Grace had made an excellent choice. This new place was the Comstock Lode of sand and I could hardly wait to get at it. The dunes were thirty feet high in places and were situated about three hundred yards from the normal shoreline, so we were fairly well protected from the sea. Even so, an occasional monster wave swept all the way across the beach and broke over the top of the dunes, spraying us and leaving behind long green garlands of aquatic vegetation. The sand had drifted up here between an outcropping of rock and a grove of palm trees. The slender trunks of the palms were all bent in picturesque curves and the fronds at the top stood hysterically on end like sprung umbrellas. None of the trees, however, had been uprooted, and I decided then that this blow, already falling off somewhat, was probably not a major hurricane.

It was a good place for sand, as I say. The only catch was that the trucks had to cross a strip of backwater on the inland side of the dunes. The water wasn't very deep but the ground underneath was soft and the trucks wallowed and strained to get through it with a full load of sandbags. We were now filling them and loading them at a much faster rate. Jack took charge once again and whipped us up into frenzies of production. No one seemed to mind. The prisoners and the soldiers thought he was funny and the officers stood back and let him do his stuff.

The truck drivers followed one another, taking the same route across the water each time, such was their training or their instincts or their orders, and they soon churned the fording place into a quagmire. As might have been foreseen, one of the trucks bogged down and we, the loaders, had to stand in the water and remove every last bag from the bed.

Thus lightened, the truck moved forward about eight inches before settling down again.

The officious Jack stepped in and began to direct this operation too. He took the wheel from a soldier. It was a matter of feel, he said. The trick was to go to a higher gear and start off gently and then shift down one notch and pour on the steam at the precise moment you felt the tires take hold. Jack did this. The truck made a lurch, and then another one, and things looked good for a moment, before all ten wheels burrowed down another foot or so, beyond hope. Jack said the gear ratios were too widely spaced in that truck. The young British officer, none too sure of himself before, pulled Jack bodily from the cab and told him to stay away from his vehicles "in future"—rather than "in *the* future."

The second truck went down trying to pull the first one out and the third one made a run to town and never came back, for a reason that was not made known to us. We had a mountain of undelivered bags and no more empties to fill. Shovels were downed and we lay back against the bags, our first rest break in four or five hours. By that time there was very little fury left in the storm, though the rain still came. An army sergeant walked back and forth in front of us to show that he himself wasn't tired.

"Good way to get piles," he said to us. "Best way I know. Sitting on wet earth like that." But no one got up, just as no one heeded him when he warned us against drinking a lot of water in our exhausted state.

Jack was breathing noisily through his mouth. He was the oldest and he had worked the hardest. The palms of his hands were a ragged mess of broken blisters. I watched my own fingers, curled in repose, as they gave little involuntary twitches.

It was our first chance for a talk. Jack said he had had his

Chrysler towed into Monterrey, where he arranged to have the drive shaft straightened and two new universal joints installed. There had been no difficulty in tracking me from San Miguel. The juiceheads at the Cucaracha bar had put him on to the farm in British Honduras. He couldn't locate me immediately in Belize. He went to the American consul and learned of the two Dupree farms in the country. I had missed a bet there, going to the consul, but Jack missed one too. He went to the wrong place, the Dupere farm, the one south of town.

The ranch manager there was an old man, he said, a Dutchman, who claimed he knew nothing of any Guy Dupree from Arkansas. Jack wasn't satisfied with his answers and he insisted on searching the premises. The old man reluctantly allowed him to do so and before it was over they had an altercation, something about an ape. It must have been a pet monkey, only Jack called it an ape.

"That nasty ape followed me around everywhere I went," he said. "He stayed about two steps behind me. The old man told him to do that. I had seen him talking to the ape. Whenever I opened a door or looked into a building, that nasty beast would stick his head in and look around too. Then he would bare his nasty teeth at me, the way they do. The old man had told him to follow me around and mock me and spit on me. I told that old Dutchman he better call him off but he wouldn't do it. I said all right then, I'll have to shoot him, and then he called him off. That was all. It didn't amount to anything. I wouldn't have shot the ape even if I had had a gun. But when I got back to town they arrested me. That old guy had radioed ahead to the police and said I pulled a gun on him. I didn't even have a gun but they took my belt and shoes and locked me up."

The black prisoners had begun to stir. They had come to their feet and were muttering angrily among themselves.

The young American doper said they wanted cigarettes. Their tobacco and their papers were wet and they wanted something to smoke. It was a cigarette mutiny! Captain Grace whacked the ringleader across the neck with his leather crop and that broke it up. He ordered everyone to be seated and he addressed us through his bullhorn.

I couldn't make out what he was saying. Jack couldn't make it out. I asked a red-faced corporal and I couldn't understand him either. The young doper had acquired an ear for this speech and he explained it all to us. The emergency was now over. The prisoners and the soldiers were to wait here for transport. Those of us who had been roped in off the streets were free to go, to walk back to town if we liked, or we too could wait for the trucks.

Captain Grace got into his Land-Rover and signaled the driver to be off. Then he countermanded the order with a raised hand and the driver stopped so short that the tires made a little chirp in the wet sand. The captain got out and came over to Jack and said, "You. You can go too."

"Thanks," said Jack. "Are you going to town now in that jeep?"

"Yes, I am."

"How about a lift?"

"Lift?"

"A ride. I need a ride to town."

"With me? Certainly not."

"You've got my shoes at the station. I can't walk all the way in like this."

Captain Grace was caught up short for a moment by Jack's impudence. He said, "Then you can wait for the lorries like everyone else."

We walked all the way back to Belize, my second long hike of the day. Since Jack was handicapped, I let him set the pace. We soon pulled ahead of the others. Jack was barefooted but he was not one to dawdle or step gingerly on that account. He stopped once to rest, hands on knees, head low, in the dramatic posture of the exhausted athlete. The sun came out. We rounded a bend in the road and a cloud of pale blue butterflies appeared before us, blown in perhaps from another part of the world. I say that because they hovered in one place as though confused. We walked through them.

Jack talked about how good the fried eggs were in Mexico and how he couldn't get enough of them. They were always fresh, with stand-up yolks, unlike the watery cold-storage eggs in our own country. He talked about eggs and he talked about life. There was altogether too much meanness in the world, he said, and the source of it all was negative thinking. He said I must avoid negative thoughts and all negative things if I wanted my brief stay on earth to be a happy one. Guy Dupree's head was full of negative things, and so to a lesser extent was mine. That was our central problem. We must purge our heads, and our rancorous hearts too.

For all I knew he was right, about Dupree anyway, but this stuff didn't sound like Jack. This didn't sound like the Jack Wilkie I knew in Little Rock who had a prism-shaped thing on his desk that said, "Money Talks and Bullshit Walks." It was my guess that he had been reading something in his cell. Two or three days in jail and he was a big thinker! The ideas that are hatched in those places! I told him that Dupree's malaise, whatever it might be, was his own, and that to lump the two of us together was to do me a disservice.

"Food for thought," he said. "That's all. I won't say any more."

The waters had receded from town. We were greeted by a spectacular rainbow that arched from one end of the estuary to the other. I watched for it to shift about or partially disappear as our angle of approach changed but it remained fixed. The color bands were bright and distinct—blue, yellow, and pink—with no fuzzy shimmering. It was the most substantial rainbow I've ever seen. There were mud deposits in the streets and a jumble of grounded boats along the creek banks. They lay awkwardly on their sides. Their white hulls had fouled bottoms of a corrupt brown hue not meant to be seen. Everyone seemed to be outside. Women and children were salvaging soggy objects from the debris. The men were drunk.

Jack went into the police station to claim his things. I stayed outside in the motor pool and looked around for Spann's bag. It was gone. I had told him I would keep an eye on his bag and then I didn't do it. Someone had made off with it. Someone was at this very moment pawing over his songs and his jade and his feathers, which, I suppose, Spann himself must have stolen, in a manner of speaking. I found out later about his death. He was hanging sandbags over the crest of a tin roof—one bag tied to each end of a length of rope—when he slipped and fell and was impaled on a rusty pipe that was waiting for him below in the grass.

Jack came out on the porch fully shod in his U.S. Navy surplus black oxfords. His socks, I guessed, had been mislaid by the property clerk, or perhaps burned. He stood there chatting in a friendly way with a black officer, Sergeant Wattli maybe, two comrades now in law enforcement. All was forgiven. Jack saw me and waved his car keys.

The yellow Chrysler was parked in one of the garage bays. We looked it over and Jack pointed to some blood spatters on the license plate and the rear bumper. He laughed over the success of his trap, which was a razor blade taped to the top of the gas-filler cap. An unauthorized person had grabbed it and sliced his fingers. For a person whose own hands were bloody, Jack showed amazing lack of sympathy. No such security measures had been taken at the front of the car. The battery was gone. The two cable heads hung stiffly in space above the empty battery pan. Jack was angry. He said he was going to demand restitution. He was going to demand of Captain Grace that the city of Belize buy him a new battery.

"I'll be right back and then we'll go get us some bacon and eggs."

He went into the station again but this time he didn't come out. I grew tired of waiting and left a note in the car saying I would be at the Fair Play Hotel taking a nap.

Fifteen

I made my way through a sea of boisterous drunks. It was sundown. There would be no twilight at this latitude. The air was sultry and vapors were rising from the ground. The drunks were good-natured for the most part but I didn't like being jostled, and there was this too, the ancient fear of being overwhelmed and devoured by a tide of dark people. Their ancient dream! Floating trees and steel drums were piled up beneath the arched bridge. Through a tangle of branches I saw a dead mule.

A man pinched my arm and offered me a drink from a bottle—clear rum, I think. A few translucent fish scales were stuck to the bottle. He watched me closely for signs of gratitude. I took a drink and sighed and thanked him and wiped my mouth with the back of my hand in an exaggerated gesture. At the edge of the stream some children were taunting a coiled black snake with an inflated inner tube. They were trying to make him strike at it. He would bump it with his snout but he had already sensed that the fat red thing wasn't living flesh, only a simulacrum, and he refused to bring his hinged fangs into play.

I asked about Webster. The children hadn't seen him. I wondered how he and other people had fared during the storm, thinking of them one by one, even to Father Jackie's mother, on whose yellow flesh I had never laid eyes. Had Dr. Symes made it safely out of town? And if so, how? He wouldn't ride a bus and he wouldn't fly and he was certainly no sailor. What did that leave?

Cars and trucks were moving once again in the streets. There was a lot of honking, at drunks who blocked the way, and in celebration too of life spared for another day. I picked out the distinctive beep of a Volkswagen and almost at the same instant I saw Christine in her van. She was caught in the traffic jam. She was beeping away and slapping her left hand against the door. Victor was in his seat blowing a plastic whistle.

I went to her and said, "You shouldn't be out in this."

"I'm all right. It's Melba."

The glass louvers on the driver's side were open and I saw Melba lying down in the back, nestled in amid all the art and green coconuts.

"What's wrong with her?"

"I don't know. I'm trying to get her to the hospital."

"This is an emergency then."

"You bet your boots it is."

I walked point, flapping my arms in front of the van and clearing the way like a locomotive fireman shooing cattle from the tracks. "Gangway!" I shouted. "Make a hole! ¡Andale! Coming through! ¡Cuidado! Stand back, please! Hospital run!" I can put up a fairly bold show when representing some larger cause than myself.

All the rolling tables were in use at the hospital and I had to carry Melba inside the place and down a long corridor jammed with beds. She weighed hardly anything. She was all clothes. Her eyes were open but she wasn't speaking. There was standing room only in the emergency room and not much of that. Victor found a folded wheelchair in a closet and Christine pulled it open and I set Melba down into it. We couldn't find anything in the way of restraining straps and so I put a big Clorox carton on her lap to keep her from pitching forward.

Christine waylaid a nurse or a female doctor and this

person looked into Melba's eyes with the aid of a penlight and then went away, doctor-fashion, without telling us anything. I rested Melba's chin on top of the empty brown box to make her more comfortable. A male doctor, an older man, began to shout. He brandished a stainless-steel vessel and ordered everyone out of the room who wasn't a bona-fide patient. He had to repeat the order several times before anyone made a move. Others took up the cry, various underlings. Christine told me that proper identification was very important in a hospital. We looked about for admittance forms and name tags. But now the crazed physician was shouting directly at us. He wouldn't allow us to explain things and we had to go. I wrote "MELBA" on top of the box in front of her chin and we left her there. I couldn't remember her last name, if I had ever known it.

Scarcely was I out of the room when I was pressed into service again. This time it was helping orderlies push bedridden patients back to their rooms. These people, beds and all, had been moved into the central hallways during the storm, away from the windows.

Christine went off on her own to look for Mrs. Symes and to buck up sick people. She made a cheery progress from bed to bed, in the confident manner of a draft-dodger athlete signing autographs for mutilated soldiers. Some were noticeably brightened by her visits. Others responded not at all and still others were baffled. Those capable of craning their necks stole second and third glances as she and Victor passed along.

I worked with a fellow named Cecil, who knew little more about the layout of the hospital than I did. He was out of sorts because it was his supper hour. He looked sick himself and I took him at first for an ambulatory patient, but he said he had worked there almost two years. Once he led us blundering into a room where seven or eight dead people were laid out on the floor, the tops of their heads all lined up flush as though by a string. Spann must have been among them but I didn't see him that time, having quickly averted my gaze from their faces.

Our job was not as easy as it might seem. The displaced beds were not always immediately outside the rooms whence they came, and there were complicated crossovers to be worked out. The patients were a nuisance too. They clamored for fruit juice and dope and they wanted their dressings seen to and they complained when we left them in the wrong rooms or when we failed to position their beds in precisely the same spots as before. Cecil, old hand at this, feigned deafness to their pleas.

I was dead on my feet, a zombie, and not at all prepared for the second great surprise of that day. I found Norma. It was there in that place of concentrated misery that I found her at last, and my senses were so dull that I took it as a matter of course. Cecil and I were pushing her into an empty room, a thin girl, half asleep and very pale, when I recognized her from the pulsing vein on her forehead. Her hair was cut short and there was a red scarf or handkerchief tied around her neck, just long enough to tie and leave two little pointed ends. Some thoughtful nurse has provided this spot of color, I said to myself, though it was no part of her job to do so. My heart went out to those dedicated ladies in white.

I spoke to Norma and she looked at me. There were dainty globules of sweat on her upper lip. She had trouble focusing. I had a weak impulse to take her in my arms, and then I caught myself, realizing how unseemly that would be, with Cecil standing there. I drew closer but not rudely close. I didn't want to thrust my bird face directly into hers as Melba had done so often to me.

"Midge?" she said.

"Yes, it's me. I'm right here. Did you think it was a dream?"

"No."

She couldn't believe her eyes! I explained things to Cecil, babbling a little, and I searched my pockets for money or some valuable object to give him, to mark the occasion, but I had nothing and I just kept patting him on the back, longer than is usually done. I told him that I would now take charge of her and that he could go on about his business. Cecil was turning all this over in his brain and I could see he didn't believe she was my wife, even though she had called my name. I could see in his eyes that he thought I was a perverted swine who would bear watching. And it is to his credit, I suppose, that he refused to leave me alone with her. He stood in the doorway and watched for his supper and kept an eye on me.

I questioned Norma at some length. Her answers were slow in coming and not always to the point. I was patient with her and made every allowance for her condition. She said she had been in the hospital about a week or ten days. Her appendix had been removed. A week ago? Yes, or maybe longer. Then why was she not yet on her feet? She didn't know. How had she happened to get appendicitis? She couldn't say. Had she been in a private room all along, or a ward? She couldn't remember. Couldn't remember whether there was anyone else in her room or not? No. Did she not know there was a great difference in the cost of the two arrangements? No.

She turned away from me to face the wall. The maneuver made her wince. She stopped answering my questions. I had been careful to avoid mention of Dupree and other indelicate matters but I had somehow managed to give offense. I smoothed out her sheet and pulled it tight here and there.

She didn't shrink from my touch. She had turned away from me but my touch wasn't loathsome to her.

"I have a little surprise for you," I said. "I brought your back pills all the way from Little Rock."

She extended a cupped hand behind her.

"I don't have them now but I did have them. What is your doctor's name?"

No reply.

"I want to have a talk with that bird. What is he giving you? Do you know?"

No reply.

"Do you realize you're just skin and bones?"

"I don't feel like talking, Midge. I'm trying to be polite but I don't feel good."

"Do you want to go home?"

"Yes."

"With me?"

"I guess so."

"What's wrong with me?"

"You just want to stay in the house all the time."

"I'm not in the house now. I could hardly be further out of the house."

"You don't want me back."

"Yes, I do. I'm hard to please too. You know that."

"I don't feel like talking right now."

"We don't have to talk. I'll get a chair and just sit here."

"Yes, but I'll know you're there."

I found a folding chair and settled in for a vigil. An elderly fat woman passed by in the hall and Cecil grunted and directed her into the room. It was his mother. She had his supper in a plastic bucket. He glared at her for being late, a hurricane was no excuse, and he picked over the food and rejected outright some of the things in the bucket. I was surprised she didn't know what he liked after all these years. Maybe it was impossible to anticipate his whims. They exchanged not a word. Cecil had no thanks for her and she was content to stand there and hold the bucket in silence and watch him eat, a slow, grinding business.

An unconscious old man was wheeled into the room and then a girl came by with trays of food on a cart. Norma drank some tea but I couldn't get her to eat anything. The sick man in the other bed was snoring. I ate his supper. A nurse stopped in to take temperatures. She ordered Cecil to the nursery, where he was needed to clean up a mess. He said he was off duty now and was going home, addressing the nurse as "Sister," though she wasn't a nun. He and his mother left.

The nurse told me that Norma was slow in recovering because she would eat nothing but ice. She was dehydrated too, from a long siege of diarrhea. But there was no fever to speak of and no other signs of peritonitis. Weren't intravenous fluids indicated, I asked, in cases of dehydration? At this implied reproach the nurse became snippy. As for the current plan of treatment, she said, I would have to take that up "with doctor"—not "with *the* doctor."

I crumbled some bread into a glass of milk and every half-hour I woke Norma and forced her to swallow a spoonful or two. Later, another nurse came around with some candles and asked that the lights and the fan be turned off so as to allow more electricity for areas of greater need. It didn't matter to me about the light because the emergency generator was producing just enough wattage to heat the bulb filament a dull red. I missed the fan for its companionable hum. After the first candle burned out, I didn't light another one. A small gray coil of anti-mosquito incense smoldered on the windowsill. The smoke curled about the room in a long tendril that kept its integrity for quite some time. I fanned

Norma with a magazine when I thought about it. She asked me to stop waking her. I told her it wouldn't be necessary if she would only finish eating the bread and milk and the little cup of yellow custard with the nutmeg on top. She grudgingly did so and then we both slept, I in my chair.

She woke me before daylight and asked for a glass of crushed ice. Ice at five in the morning! I got some ice cubes at the nursing station and chopped them up with a pair of scissors. Now she was fully awake and ready to talk. I suppose it came more easily to her in the dark. She crunched on the ice and told me about her travels with Dupree. I was fascinated. Her voice was little more than a whisper but I hung on every word. She could have been one of Melba's psychic heroines, with eyes "preternaturally bright."

What a story! What a trip! They had first gone to Dallas, where Dupree was to meet with the well-known radical photographers, Hilda Monod and Jay Bomarr. I say "well known," although Norma had never heard of these people. Dupree had been in touch with them through a third party in Massachusetts, a fellow who had vouched for him, telling Hilda and Jay that Dupree had threatened to kill the President and was okay. He also told them, or maybe it was Dupree himself, that Dupree owned a shopping center in Memphis which produced a vast income that was now available to the radical movement. Hilda and Jay were eager to confer with him, or so they said.

But they didn't show in Dallas, telephoning instead from Florida to say they would be delayed, that they were conducting a workshop at a home for old radicals in Coral Gables. Dupree was to continue on to San Angelo and wait. There was another hitch and he was told to proceed to Wormington and see a fellow named Bates. Bates was to put them up in his house. But Bates had not been informed about the arrangement and he refused to talk to Dupree.

Bates owned a cave near Wormington in which the temperature remained constant at 59 degrees Fahrenheit. How this grotto figured in the overall plans of the radicals, or if it figured at all, Norma couldn't say, and it must remain a matter for speculation. She and Dupree checked in at the motel. He paced the room and became impatient and called Hilda and Jay with an ultimatum. Either they stopped giving him the runaround or he would take his money and ideas elsewhere.

A meeting in Mexico was agreed upon, at San Miguel de Allende. Hilda and Jay were to take part in a seminar there with a visiting radical from Denmark. It would be a safe and quiet place to talk business. But they needed a car. Could Dupree furnish them with a car? Not at that time, he said, but once in San Miguel, on completion of a satisfactory personal interview, he would give them the keys to a Ford Torino.

So off they went to Mexico. Norma drove most of the way because Dupree wanted to polish up the presentation he was preparing for the two infamous radicals. He shuffled his papers and muttered to himself and ate candy bars and drank pink Pepto-Bismol from a bottle. He was very excited, she said, but he wouldn't discuss his ideas on the new social order with her, saying she was too dumb to understand his work.

Why, at that point, did she not slap his face and come home?

"I don't know," she said.

She didn't know! She knew he had threatened the President of the United States and that he was now involved in some other devilish political enterprise and on top of that he was making rude personal remarks, and still she hung around for more! Then I saw the answer. I'm slow but sure. I had read things and heard many songs about people being poleaxed by love and brought quivering to their knees and I thought it was just something people said. And now here it was, true love. She was in love with that monkey! I was amazed but I couldn't really hold it against her. I knew she was puzzled by life and marriage, thinking the entire range of men ran only from Dupree to me and back again, and I couldn't really be angry with her, in her pitiable condition. She told me later that Dupree had promised her they would be remarried "in a forest," where they would exchange heart-shaped rings and some sort of on-the-spot vows. He had no shame.

Jay and Hilda limped into San Miguel a week late. They had been held up for a few days in Beaumont, Texas, after a tailgater had rammed their Saab sedan from behind, and there had been many subsequent breakdowns along the way. Neither of them drove, of course, and they traveled with three flunkies who handled all such chores. Five stinking radicals in a three-cylinder Saab! Norma couldn't remember the names of the flunkies. She said they wore small caps and moved about quickly like squirrels and smiled in a knowing way when they looked a person in the face. Jay and Hilda were polite to her but the flunkies made fun of her accent.

The conference was a failure. Jay and Hilda were upset to learn that Dupree owned no shopping center and had no money of his own and no intention whatever of giving them a car. Not only that, but he talked to them in a familiar way, as an equal or a superior, as one having authority, saying he wanted them to revise their entire program from top to bottom, incorporating, among other things, a new racial doctrine. He showed them some provocative slogans he had written, for shouting. He even lectured them on photography. They couldn't believe their ears! Norma said Jay Bomarr was particularly indignant. Since the Beaumont crash he had been wearing a rigid and uncomfortable plastic collar around his neck and he couldn't easily turn aside as Dupree ticked off important points on his fingertips.

The meeting ended with recriminations and with Dupree's papers scattered on the floor of the Bugambilia Café. There followed several empty days. Dupree walked about town with his dog. Norma had already begun to suffer from internal disorders and she didn't range far from the hotel. I forced her to describe every bite she had eaten since leaving Little Rock, so far as she could remember. She became peeved and irritable as I hammered away at her but it was worth it in the end because in this way I was able to put my finger on the rancid peanuts that had started her trouble. Once the point was cleared up, I permitted her to go on with her story.

She said the radicals passed most of their time in a snack bar just off the square. Long-distance calls could be made there and Jay was a great one for the telephone. There they sat at a table all day, holding court before young admirers and taking their skimpy meals and conspiring lazily and placing and receiving numerous phone calls. One flunky was posted in the crumpled Saab at all times to watch the camera gear. The other two called themselves the Ground Observer Corps, and they moved around town and eavesdropped on conversations and then reported back to Hilda and Jay on what people were saying, the topics of the day in that particular place. Hilda, who had little to say, appeared to be the real boss of the gang.

Dupree stopped in once and tried to stare them down from the doorway of the snack bar. They turned their chairs around. He came back the next day and walked slowly through the place with his dog. He went out the back door and reappeared almost instantly at the front door again. The chow dog was now in on the trick! If the radicals were

knocked for a loop, they didn't let on and they continued to
regard Dupree with a contemptuous silence.

The Dane never showed up but they had the "seminar"
anyway, under some shade trees in a place called the French
Park. Jay Bomarr opened it with his famous speech, "Come
Dream Along with Me." I had heard it myself, at Ole Miss of
all places, back in the days when Jay was drawing big
crowds. It was a dream of blood and smashed faces, with a
lot of talk about "the people," whose historic duty it was to
become a nameless herd and submit their lives to the abso-
lute control of a small pack of wily and vicious intellectuals.
Norma said it went over fairly well with the young Americans and Canadians, judging from the applause. No Mexicans came except for the professor who was chairman of the
thing. Dupree was there, standing at the front, and he
heckled Jay for a while. He had a New Year's Eve noise-
maker, a ratchet device that he swung around. The flunkies
took it away from him and carried him off in the woods and
beat him up.

Hilda followed Jay at the speaker's stand, to discuss her
prize-winning photographs of "hermits." That is the word
Norma understood Hilda to say, though it may have been
something else. Varmints? Linnets? Spinets? Harlots?
Norma couldn't be sure because Hilda was interrupted early
by Jay, who had a disturbing announcement. Their thermos
jug had been stolen. He said no questions would be asked if
the person who had taken the jug would return same without delay. The appeal failed. Hilda tried threats. She said
she was going to stop talking if the jug was not returned at
once. There were groans of consternation from the crowd of
young shutterbugs. The three flunkies made a lightning
search through the park and turned up various objects but
nothing in the way of a thermos jug. Someone offered Hilda

a replacement jug of comparable size and quality. She said that wouldn't do at all and she put away her lecture materials and declared the seminar suspended until further notice. Jay and the professor tried to persuade her to continue, promising a full investigation. She said it was out of the question. The radicals packed their visual aids and returned to the snack bar, there to await the collapse of the conscience-stricken thief.

All that is fairly clear. Norma told it to me in a straightforward way and I have made it even clearer in my summary. But she could give me no satisfactory account of the rest of the journey, nothing but tantalizing scraps. She couldn't even remember when the idea first came up of going on to British Honduras. Dupree had told her it was an idyllic spot. She looked forward to her forest wedding there.

Then, she said, he began to behave "strangely," and for her to make such an acknowledgment I expected to hear next that Dupree had been seized by nothing short of barking fits. But it wasn't quite that. After leaving San Miguel he spoke to her through a small megaphone. She had asked him to repeat some remark—on just one occasion—and after that he pretended to believe she was deaf. He rolled a piece of cardboard into a cone and taped the ends, and he pretended to believe she couldn't hear him unless he spoke through it, directly into her ear from a foot or so away. The memory of the farmhouse made her shudder. She was there for about four days and sick the whole time. Terrible things went on outside. The workers shot the cows and beat up Dupree and destroyed the water pump. From that point on he was impossible. He went into a rage when he caught her bathing in the washtub, using scarce water. He accused her, through the megaphone, of malingering, and he accused her of introducing worm pills into his food. He had some deworming medicine for his dog and he couldn't find it. By that time the pain in Norma's side was hardly bearable and even Dupree could see that she was seriously ill. He drove her into town at night and left her at the hospital, and that must have been the night he got drunk and burned up my Torino.

What a story! Denmark! Coral Gables! But I was beginning to fade and I could no longer follow the details. Norma asked me to get her some more ice and I told her what we both needed now was not ice but a little more shut-eye.

The old man in the other bed woke at dawn. He woke suddenly and raised his head about an inch, gravity overtaking him there, and said, "What the devil is going on anyway?"

"I don't know," I truthfully replied.

He had one boggling, red-rimmed eye like Mr. Proctor. He wanted coffee and I went to see if I could find some.

Sixteen

Ruth had bounced me from the Fair Play without a hearing and Webster had taken my bag to a cheaper hotel called the Delgado, and told the manager there, another woman, that I was a model roomer in every way except for that of payment. She took a chance on me. There was no difficulty. I went personally to the cable office and wired my father for money and got it the next morning. The Delgado wasn't as conveniently located as the Fair Play and had fewer amenities. The rates, however, were very reasonable.

I took Norma from the hospital in a taxicab and put her to bed in my room. The woman boss at the Delgado made a kind of fish soup or stew that was pretty good and I fed this to Norma, along with boiled rice. The English doctor had told me she could eat whatever she liked but I thought it best to be on the safe side and I allowed her no fried foods. I had to turn down her request for fresh pineapple too, it being so coarse and fibrous. After two days of forcing soup down her gullet I had her on her feet again, taking little compulsory hikes about the room. She tottered and complained. I bought her a shark's-tooth bracelet. I read to her from old magazines until she asked me to stop doing it.

Mrs. Symes had slept through the hurricane. She herself was released from the hospital that same week, though she continued to be more or less bedridden. Christine and the girl Elizabeth attended to her. The stroke had left a slight paralysis in her left arm and a slight speech impediment. Still, she didn't appear to be severely disabled.

"Another blast from Almighty God," she said to me. I nodded, not knowing whether she meant the storm or the stroke. Christine was flexing the old lady's arm and fingers so that the muscles would not become atrophied.

"Do you know why these things are sent?"

I said, "No, ma'am, I don't."

"They are sent to try us. Tell me this. Are the doors sticking too?"

"Yes, they are."

"I thought as much. It makes it hard for us when the doors stick."

"I was wondering if you would do me a favor, Meemaw."

"I will if I can, hon. You see the sorry shape I'm in."

"I was wondering if you would write a note to Captain Grace on behalf of a friend of mine. He's in jail and needs some help."

She had forgotten my first name and she asked me what it was. I told her and she told me once again that there was no one named Ray in the Bible. But that was all right, she said, Ray would do as well as any other name here on earth. Only God knew our true names.

Everyone was either sick or in jail. Melba was laid up in the bedroom with the brown picture on the wall. There had been nothing really wrong with her at the hospital but when she came out of her trance in the emergency room she got up and walked home and it was this unaccustomed trek across town that had put her under. So she was in bed too, for the first time in years, and Christine had her hands full, what with all the cooking and nursing. Brave Christine! The girl Elizabeth was a good worker too, and Victor was a useless whiner. I asked him why he didn't go outside and play and get out of Christine's hair and he said a chicken had pecked him on the street.

I did what I could, at the urging of Mrs. Symes, to find

out what had happened to the doctor. I inquired at the bus station and the airport and the consular office. I took another look at the dead bodies in the hospital, where I saw poor Spann, his busy pen stilled forever. I inquired at the Shell station and the Texaco station. I talked to fishermen. When I visited Jack in jail, I looked over all the prisoners. Of course I had my eye out for Dupree too. I thought there was an excellent chance he might have been arrested again, for one thing or another. I found no trace of either of them. Mrs. Symes said she had a strong feeling that Reo was dead, cut off abruptly in his sins. Melba said no, he was still very much alive and she knew it in her bones. I found Melba's hunch the more convincing of the two.

I had dropped in at the tabernacle to report my investigation a failure, and to pick up the silver set, having in mind a nice surprise. I was going to take one of those round spoons from the silver chest and feed Norma her soup with it, and then, with a flourish and a roguish smile, reveal to her the familiar floral pattern on the handle. This, I thought, an unexpected touch of home, would trigger happy domestic memories, by way of the well-known principle of association.

But first I had to go by the newspaper office. Mrs. Symes wanted me to call there and have the doctor's name added to the published list of missing persons. Webster and some other boys were in front of the place dividing up a stack of *Bugles*. On an impulse, and this was very unlike me, I gave him Mrs. Edge's silver. I called him over and said, "Here, do you want this? I'm tired of fooling with it." The chest was wrapped in an old towel and he was suspicious. "It's not a jar this time," I said. "That's sterling silver." I advised him to take it to Father Jackie or some other trustworthy adult for safekeeping or for sale.

"My point is this. I don't want you to let Ruth take it

away from you." I told him to cultivate good study habits and I left him there holding the heavy chest and went to the Delgado and told Norma what I had done, apologizing for my rash action. She said she didn't care. She wanted to go home.

Finally I was able to get Jack released from jail, no thanks to the American consul. That bird said it was none of his business and he wouldn't interfere even if he could. The testimonial note from Mrs. Symes did the trick, combined with an irregular payment and a promise that Jack would leave the country immediately. He was glad to be free again. We got a used battery at the Texaco station and I suggested a quick run out on Bishop Lane. I would show him the Dupree place and he could look around and maybe pick up some leads, see some things that had escaped my untrained eye. But Jack was no longer concerned with Dupree. He said, "You can do what you want to, Ray. I'm going home."

Norma and I rode home with him in the Chrysler. He drove all the way with his sore hands, not trusting other people at the wheel. What a trip! What a glum crew! Norma snapped at me, and Jack, who had been reading things in his cell again, talked about economic cycles and the fall of the Roman Empire and the many striking parallels that might be drawn between that society and our own. Norma called me "Guy" a couple of times. My own wife couldn't even remember my name.

I told them about the pelican that was struck by lightning. They didn't believe it. I tried to tell them about Dr. Symes and Webster and Spann and Karl and their attention wandered. I saw then that I would have to write it down, present it all in an orderly fashion, and this I have done. But I can see that I have given far too much preliminary matter and that I have considerably overshot the mark. So be it. It's done now. I have left out a few things, not least my own laundry problems, but I haven't left out much, and in the further interests of truth I have spared no one, not even myself.

Our journey home was a leisurely one. Jack drove only during daylight hours. We stayed in nice motels. Norma perked up a little after I began to let her order her own meals. We stopped at a beach south of Tampico for a swim in the Gulf. Norma wore her dress in the water like an old woman because she'd didn't want Jack to see the raw scar on her abdomen. A man came along with a brazier made from a bucket and he broiled some shrimp for us right there on the beach. The food and beer made us sleepy and we stayed the night. Jack slept in the car.

Norma and I lay on the warm sand all night under a piece of stiff canvas that Jack carried in his trunk. We listened to the surf and watched the incandescent streaks of meteors. I pointed out to her the very faint earthshine on the darker, gibbous part of the new moon. She admitted that her escapade with Dupree had been very foolish and I said we must now consider the matter closed. We reaffirmed our affection for one another.

The next day we were all in good spirits and we sang "Goodnight, Irene" and other old songs as we approached the border at Matamoros. The euphoria in turn passed as we drew closer to home and when we reached Texarkana we were pretty much ourselves again. Jack became solemn and he began to pose rhetorical questions. "What is everybody looking for?" he said. Norma didn't hesitate; she said everybody was looking for love. I gave the question some thought and then declared that everybody was looking for a good job of work to do. Jack said no, that many people were looking for those things, but that everybody was looking for a place where he could get food cheap—on a regular basis. The qualification was important because when I mentioned the cheap and tasty shrimps we had eaten on the beach, Jack said yes, but you couldn't count on that Mexican bird coming by every afternoon with his cooking can and his bulging wet sack.

Much later we learned that Dupree had gone overland— walked! in cowboy boots! bumping into trees!—down into Honduras, the genuine Honduras. He went first to a place on the coast called La Ceiba and then caught a ride on an oil-survey plane to the capital city of Tegucigalpa. I looked for him to come dragging in after a few months. A lot of people leave Arkansas and most of them come back sooner or later. They can't quite achieve escape velocity. I expect it's much the same everywhere. But that monkey is still down there, as far as I know.

I never said anything to Mr. Dupree about my Torino. I do know he paid off the bail forfeiture and I suspect he used his political influence to have the charge against Guy shelved, if not dropped altogether. Dupree's whereabouts are certainly no secret but nothing has been done toward having him picked up and extradited.

His mother has flown down there twice to see him, the second time to take him a pit bulldog. That was the kind of dog he wanted and he couldn't find one in Honduras. She must have had no end of trouble introducing that dog into another country by air, particularly a grotesque animal like the pit bull, but she managed to do it. I don't know what happened to the chow dog. She tells everyone Guy is "thinking and writing" and is doing fine. I have heard from other people that he walks around Tegucigalpa all day in a narcotic haze, nodding at Hondurans and taking long strides in his runover boots. He keeps his left hand in his pocket, they say, with the right hand swinging free in an enormous military arc. I assume she sends him money. You can cadge drinks but I think you have to have money for dope.

At Christmas I mailed Mrs. Symes a Sears catalogue and I enclosed my own copy of Southey's *Life of Nelson* for Webster. I heard nothing from Belize and I suspect the parcel was lost or stolen.

Norma regained her health and we got on better than ever before. We went to football games and parties. We had a fine Christmas. We went to the Cancer Ball with Mrs. Edge and one of her florid escorts and I even danced a little, which isn't to say I became overheated. In January I got my B.A. degree and I decided to stay in school and try engineering again, with an eye toward graduate work in geology and eventual entry into the very exciting and challenging field of plate tectonics. Then in April, after the last frost, Norma became restless again. She went to Memphis to visit a friend named Marge. "Goodbye, goodbye," she said to me, and the next thing I knew she had her own apartment over there, and a job doing something at a television station. She said she might come back but she didn't do it and I let her go that time. It's only about 130 miles to Memphis but I didn't go after her again.